D1139916

'I know whi**** are, sir,' the young woman interrupted. 'That's why I sought you out. I have a proposition for you. So to speak,' she added, her cheeks pinkening.

Max blinked at her, sure he could not have heard her properly. 'A *proposition*?' he repeated.

'Yes. I'm Caroline Denby, by the way. My father was the late Sir Martin Denby of Denby Stables.'

Thinking this bizarre meeting was getting even more bizarre, Max bowed. 'Miss Denby. Yes, I've heard of your father's excellent horses. My condolences on your loss. However, whatever it is you wish to say, perhaps Mrs Ransleigh could arrange a meeting later. Truly, it's most imperative that you quit my presence immediately, lest you put your reputation at risk.'

'But that's exactly what I wish to do. Not just risk it, but ruin it. Irretrievably.'

THE RANSLEIGH ROGUES

Where these notorious rakes go, scandal always follows…

Max, Will, Alastair and Dominic Ransleigh—cousins, friends…and the most wickedly attractive men in Regency London. Between war, betrayal and scandal, love has never featured in the Ransleighs' destinies—until now!

Don't miss this enthralling new quartet from Julia Justiss, starting with Max's story

THE RAKE TO RUIN HER

Look for Will Ransleigh's story

Available April 2013

THE RAKE
TO RUIN HER

Julia Justiss

MILLS &
BOON

First published in Great Britain 2013
by Mills & Boon, an imprint of Harlequin (UK) Limited.
Harlequin (UK) Limited, Eton House, 18-24 Paradise Road,
Richmond, Surrey TW9 1SR

ISBN: 978 0 263 89812 5

Printed and bound in Spain
by Blackprint CPI, Barcelona

Julia Justiss wrote her first plot ideas for a Nancy Drew novel in the back of her third-grade notebook, and has been writing ever since. After such journalistic adventures as publishing poetry and editing an American Embassy newsletter she returned to her first love: writing fiction. Her Regency historical novels have been winners or finalists in the Romance Writers of America's Golden Heart™, *RT Book Reviews* magazine's Best First Historical, Golden Quill, National Readers' Choice and Daphne Du Maurier contests. She lives with her husband, three children and two dogs in rural east Texas, where she also teaches high school French. For current news and contests, please visit her website at www.juliajustiss.com

Novels by the same author:

AUTHOR NOTE

The 2012 London summer games are unfolding as I write this note, and as the athletes tell their stories I'm repeatedly reminded of how many years of hard work and single-minded dedication are necessary to earn them a place among the best of the best. Yet sometimes, after devoting all one's energies to achieving an aim, some totally unexpected catastrophe destroys in an instant the possibility of reaching that goal. Standing shocked and disbelieving amid the wreckage of that dream, the survivor is forced to find a different path.

Such is the case with 'Magnificent Max' Ransleigh, the earl's son and charismatic leader of a group of cousins known as *The Ransleigh Rogues*. With his father a force in the House of Lords, Max has prepared all his life for a high diplomatic position, and seems well on his way when he's chosen as one of the Duke of Wellington's aides at the Congress of Vienna. But when an assassination attempt on the Duke is perpetrated by relatives of a Frenchwoman Max has befriended, even his valour at Waterloo can't resurrect the tatters of his career.

Returning after the battle, with none of his former associates—including his father—willing to see him, he turns to the Rogues. He stops at Alastair's country home, unaware that his aunt, Alastair's mother, is hostessing a house party to acquaint her youngest daughter, soon to make her London debut, with other young ladies of the Ton.

While Max mourns the loss of a conventional future, Caroline Denby schemes to destroy her own. Sole heiress of a wealthy baron, she has good reasons for avoiding wedlock, and is actively resisting her stepmother's attempts to marry her off—what future is there for a woman but marriage? Lady Denby argues—so she may return to Kent and run the horse-breeding farm she established with her father.

When Caro discovers the infamous Max Ransleigh has dropped in on her hostess's house party, she decides he is just the rogue to ruin her. With her reputation in tatters, her suitors will depart, her stepmother will refocus her matrimonial schemes on her own daughter, and Caro will be left in peace to tend her horses.

But sometimes the goal we yearn for turns out *not* to be the path for which we're destined. And a love we never expected to find becomes the most precious blessing of our life.

I hope you'll enjoy Max and Caro's journey.

Soon to follow in 2013 and 2014 will be the stories of the other Rogues: 'Wagering Will', illegitimate son of the earl's brother, who never met a game of chance he couldn't win, 'Ingenious Alastair', philosopher and poet who thinks to best Byron until a humiliating betrayal turns him into the worst rake in England, and 'Dandy Dominic', handsomest man in the Regiment, who returns from Waterloo maimed, scarred, and searching for meaning in the ruins of his life.

I love to hear from readers! Find me at my website, www.juliajustiss.com, for excepts, updates and background bits about my books, on Facebook at www.facebook.com/juliajustiss and on Twitter @juliajustiss.

Prologue

Vienna—January 1815

The distant sound of waltz music and a murmur of voices met his ear as Max Ransleigh exited the anteroom. Quickly he paced toward the dark-haired woman standing in the shadowy alcove at the far end of the hallway.

Hoping he wouldn't find on her more marks of her cousin's abuse, he said, 'What is it? He hasn't struck you again, has he? I fear I cannot stay; Lord Wellington should arrive in the Green Salon at any moment and he despises tardiness. I would not have come at all, had your note not sounded most urgent.'

'Yes, you'd told me you were to rendezvous there; that's how I knew where to find you,' she replied. The soft, slightly French lilt of her words was charming, as always. Lovely dark eyes, whose

hint of sadness had aroused his protective instincts
from the first, searched his face.

'You've been so kind. I appreciate it more than I
can say. It's just that Thierry told me to obtain new
clasps for his uniform coat for the reception tomorrow and I haven't any idea where to find them.
And if I fail to satisfy my cousin's demands…' Her
voice trailed off and she shivered. 'Forgive me for
disturbing you with my little problem.'

Disgust and a cold anger coiled within him at
the idea of a man—nay, a *diplomat*—who would
vent his pique on the slight, gentle woman beside
him. He must find some excuse to challenge Thierry St Arnaud to a boxing match and show him
what it was like to be pummelled.

Glancing over his shoulder toward the door of
the Green Salon, the urgent need to leave an itch
in his shoulder blades, he tried not to let impatience creep into his voice. 'You mustn't worry.
I won't be able to escort you until morning, but
there's a suitable shop not far. Now, I regret to be
so unchivalrous, but I must get back.'

As he bowed and turned away, she caught at
his sleeve. 'Please, just a moment longer! Simply
being near you makes me feel braver.'

Max felt a swell of satisfaction at her confidence, along with the pity that always rose in him
at her predicament. All his life, as the privileged
younger son of an earl, others had begged favours
of him; this poor widow asked for so little.

He bent to kiss her hand. 'I'm only glad to help.

But Wellington will have my hide if I keep him waiting, especially with the meeting of plenipotentiary officials about to convene.'

'No, it wouldn't do for an aspiring diplomat to fall afoul of the great Wellington.' She opened her lips as if to add something else, then closed them. Tears welled in her eyes. 'I'm so sorry.'

Puzzled, he was about to ask her why when a pistol blast shattered the quiet.

Thrusting her behind him, Max pivoted toward the sound. His soldier's ear told him it had come from within the Green Salon.

Where Wellington should now be.

Assassins?

'Stay here in the shadows until I return!' he ordered over his shoulder as he set off at a run, dread chilling his heart.

Within the Green Salon, he found chairs overturned, a case of papers scattered about and the room overhung by the smell of black powder and a haze of smoke.

'Wellington! Where is he?' he barked at a corporal, who with two other soldiers was attempting to right the disorder.

'Whisked out of the back door by an aide,' the soldier answered.

'Is he unharmed?'

'Yes, I think so. Old Hookey was by the fireplace, snapping at the staff about where you'd got to. If he had not looked up when the door was flung open, expecting you, and dodged left, the ball would have caught him in the chest.'

I knew where to find you...

Those French-accented words, the tears, her apologetic sadness slammed into Max's gut. Surely the two events couldn't be related?

But when he ran back into hallway, the dark-haired lady had disappeared.

Chapter One

Devon—Autumn 1815

'Why don't we just leave?' Max Ransleigh suggested to his cousin Alastair as the two stood on the balcony overlooking the grand marble entry of Barton Abbey.

'Dammit, we only just arrived,' Alastair replied, exasperation in his tones. 'Poor bastards.' He waved towards the servants below them, who were struggling to heft in the baggage of several arriving guests. 'Trunks are probably stuffed to the lids with gowns, shoes, bonnets and other fripperies, the better for the wearers to parade themselves before the prospective bidders. Makes me thirsty for a deep glass of brandy.'

'If you'd bothered to write that you were coming home, we might have altered the date of the house party,' a feminine voice behind them said reproachfully.

Max turned to find Mrs Grace Ransleigh, mistress of Barton Abbey and Alastair's mother, standing behind them. 'Sorry, Mama,' Alastair said, leaning down to give the petite, dark-haired lady a hug. When he straightened, a flush coloured his handsome face; probably chagrin, Max thought, that Mrs Ransleigh had overhead his uncharitable remark. 'You know I'm a terrible correspondent.'

'A fact I find astonishing,' his mother replied, retaining Alastair's hands in a light grip, 'when I recall that as a boy, you were seldom without a pen, jotting down some observation or other.'

A flash of something that looked like pain passed across his cousin's face, so quickly Max wasn't sure he'd actually seen it. 'That was a long time ago, Mama.'

Sorrow softened her features. 'Perhaps. But a mother never forgets. In any event, after all those years in the army, always throwing yourself into the most dangerous part of the action, I'm too delighted to have you safely home to quibble about the lack of notice—though I fear you will have to suffer through the house party. With the guests already arriving, I can hardly call it off now.'

Releasing her son's hands with obvious reluctance, she turned to Max. 'It's good to see you, too, my dear Max.'

'If I'd known you were entertaining innocents, Aunt Grace, I wouldn't have agreed to meet Alastair here,' Max assured her as he leaned down to kiss her cheek.

'Nonsense,' she said stoutly. 'All you Ransleigh lads have run wild at Barton Abbey since you were scrubby schoolboys. You'll always be welcome in my home, Max, no matter how... circumstances change.'

'Then you are kinder than Papa,' Max replied, trying for a light tone while his chest tightened with the familiar wash of anger, resentment and regret. Still, the cousins' unexpected appearance must have been an unpleasant shock to a hostess about to convene a gathering of eligible young maidens and their prospective suitors—an event of which they'd been unaware until the butler warned them about it upon their arrival half an hour ago.

As he'd just assured his aunt, had Max known Barton Abbey would be sheltering unmarried young ladies on the prowl for husbands, he would have taken care to stay far away.

He'd best talk with his cousin and decide what to do. 'Alastair, shall we get that glass of wine?'

'There's a full decanter in the library,' Mrs Ransleigh said. 'I'll send Wendell up with some cold ham, cheese and biscuits. One thing that never changes—I'm sure you boys are famished.'

'Bless you, Mama,' Alastair told her with a grin, while Max added his thanks. As they bowed and turned to go, Mrs Ransleigh said hesitantly, 'I don't suppose you care to dine with the party?'

'Amongst that virginal lot? Most assuredly not!' Alastair retorted. 'Even if we'd suddenly developed a taste for petticoat affairs, my respectable married sister would probably poison our wine were we to intrude our scandalous presence in the midst of her aspiring innocents. Come along, Max, before the smell of perfumed garments from those damned chests overcomes us.'

Thumping Max on the shoulder to set him in motion, Alastair paused to kiss his mother's hand. 'Tell the girls to visit us later, once their virginal guests are safely abed behind locked doors.'

Max followed his cousin down the hallway and into a large library comfortably furnished with well-worn leather chairs and a massive desk. 'Are you sure you don't want to leave?' he asked again as he drew out a decanter and filled two glasses.

'Devil's teeth,' Alastair growled, 'this is *my* house. I'll come and go when I wish, and my friends, too. Besides, you'll enjoy seeing Mama and Jane and Felicity—for whom the ever-managing Jane arranged this gathering, Wendell told me. Jane thinks Lissa should have some experience with eligible men before she's cast into the Marriage Mart next spring. Though she's not angling to get Lissa riveted now, some of the attendees did bring offspring they're trying to marry off, bless Wendell for warning us!'

Sighing, Alastair accepted a brimming glass. 'You'd think my highly-publicized liaisons with actresses and dancers, combined with an utter lack of interest in respectable virgins, would be enough to put off matchmaking mamas. But as you well know, wealth and ancient lineage appear to trump notoriety and lack of inclination. However, with my equally notorious cousin to entertain,' he inclined his head toward Max, 'I have a perfect excuse to avoid the ladies. So, let's drink to you,' Alastair hoisted his glass, 'for rescuing me not only from boredom, but from having to play the host at Jane's hen party.'

'To evading your duty as host,' Max replied, raising his own glass. 'Nice to know my ruined career is good for *something*,' he added, bitterness in his tone.

'A temporary setback only,' Alastair said. 'Sooner or later, the Foreign Office will sort out that business in Vienna.'

'Maybe,' Max said dubiously. He, too, had thought the matter might be resolved quickly... until he spoke with Papa. 'There's still the threat of a court-martial.'

'After Hougoumont?' Alastair snorted derisively. 'Maybe if you'd defied orders and *abandoned* your unit before Waterloo, but no military jury is going to convict you for throwing yourself *into* the battle, instead of sitting back in England as instructed. Some of the Foot Guards who survived the fighting owe their lives to you and headquarters knows it. No,' he concluded, 'even Horse Guards, who are often ridiculously stiff-rumped about disciplinary affairs, know better than to bring such a case to trial.'

'I hope you're right. As my father noted on the one occasion he deigned to speak with me, I've already sufficiently tarnished the family name.'

It wasn't the worst of what the earl had said, Max thought, the memory of that recent interview still raw and stinging. He saw himself again, standing silent, offering no defence as the earl railed at him for embarrassing the family and complicating his job in the Lords, where he was struggling to sustain a coalition. Pronouncing Max a sore disappointment and a political liability, he'd banished him for the indefinite future from Ransleigh House in London and the family seat in Hampshire.

Max had left without even seeing his mother.

'The earl still hasn't come round?' Alastair's soft-voiced question brought him back to the present. After a glance at Max's face, he sighed. 'Almost as stubborn and rule-bound as Horse Guards, is my dear uncle. Are you positive you won't allow me to speak to him on your behalf?'

'You know arguing with Papa only hardens his views—and might induce him to extend his banishment to you, which would grieve both our mothers. No, it wouldn't serve…though I appreciate your loyalty more than I can say—' Max broke off and swallowed hard.

'No need to say anything,' Alastair replied, briskly refilling their glasses. '"Ransleigh Rogues together, for ever,"' he quoted, holding his glass aloft.

"'Ransleigh Rogues,"' Max returned the salute, his heart lightening as he tried to recall exactly when Alastair had coined that motto. Probably over an illicit glass of smuggled brandy some time in their second Eton term after a disapproving master, having caned all four cousins for some now-forgotten infraction, first denounced them as the 'Ransleigh Rogues.'

The name, quickly whispered around the college, had stuck to them, and they to each other, Max thought, smiling faintly. Through the fagging at Eton, the hazing at Oxford, then into the army to watch over Alastair when, after the girl he loved terminated their engagement in the most public and humiliating fashion imaginable, he'd joined the first cavalry unit that would take him, vowing to die gloriously in battle.

They'd stood by Max, too, after the failed assassination attempt at the Congress of Vienna. When he returned to London in disgrace, he'd found that, of all the government set that since his youth had encouraged and flattered the handsome, charming younger son of an earl, only his fellow Rogues still welcomed his company.

His life had turned literally overnight from the hectic busyness of an embassy post to a purposeless void, with only a succession of idle amusements to occupy his days. With the glorious diplomatic career he'd planned in ruins and his future uncertain, he didn't want to think what rash acts he might have committed, had he not had the support of Alastair, Dom and Will.

'I'm sure Aunt Grace would never say so, but having us turn up now must be rather awkward. Since we're not in the market to buy the wares on display, why not go elsewhere? Your hunting box, perhaps?'

After taking another deep sip, Alastair shook his head. 'Too early for that; ground's not frozen yet. And I'd bet Mama's more worried about the morals of her darlings than embarrassed by our presence. Turned out of your government post or not, you're still an earl's son—'

'—currently exiled by his family—'

'—who possesses enough charm to lure any one of Jane's innocents out of her virtue, should you choose to.'

'Why would I? I'd thought Lady Mary would make me a fine diplomat's wife, but without a career, *she* no longer has any interest in me and *I* no longer have any interest in marriage.' Max tried for a light tone, not wanting Alastair to guess how much the august Lady Mary's defection, coming on the heels of his father's dismissal, had wounded him.

'I wish I could think of another place to go, at least until this damned house party concludes.' With a frustrated jab, Alastair stoppered the brandy. 'But I need to take care of some estate business and I don't want to nip back to London just now, with the autumn theatre season in full swing. I wouldn't put it past Desirée to track me down and create another scene, which would be entirely too much of a bore.'

'Not satisfied with the emeralds you brought when you gave her her *congé*?'

Alastair sighed. 'Perhaps it wasn't wise to recommend that she save her histrionics for the stage. In any event, the longer I knew her, the more obvious her true, grasping nature became. She was good enough in the bedchamber and possessed of a mildly amusing wit, but, ultimately, she grew as tiresome as all the others.'

Alastair paused, his eyes losing focus as a hard expression settled over his face. Max knew that look; he'd seen it on Alastair's countenance whenever women were mentioned ever since the end of his ill-fated engagement. Silently damning once again the woman who'd caused his cousin such pain, Max knew better than to try to take him to task for his contemptuous dismissal of women.

He felt a wave of bitterness himself, recalling how easily *he*'d been lured in by a sad story convincingly recited by a pretty face.

If only he'd been content to save his heroics for the battlefield, instead of attempting to play knight errant! Max reflected with a wry grimace. Indeed, given what had transpired in Vienna, he was more than half-inclined to agree with his cousin that no woman, other than one who offered her talents for temporary purchase, was worth the trouble she inevitably caused.

'I've no desire to return to London either,' he said. 'I'd have to avoid Papa and the government set, which means most of my former friends. Having spent a good deal of time and tact disentangling myself from the beauteous Mrs Harris, I'd prefer not to return to town until she's entangled with someone else.'

'Why don't we hop over to Belgium and see how Dom's progressing? Last I heard, Will was still there, looking after him.' Alastair laughed. 'Leave it to Will to find a way to stay on the Continent after the rest of us were shipped home! Though he claimed he only loitered in Brussels for the fat pickings to be made among all the diplomats and army men with more money than gaming sense.'

'I don't know that Dom would appreciate a visit. He was still pretty groggy with laudanum and pain from the amputation when I saw him last. After he came round enough to abuse me for fussing over him like a hen with one chick, he ordered me home to placate my father and the army board.'

'Yes, he tried to send me away too, though I wasn't about to budge until I was sure he wasn't going to stick his spoon in the wall.' Setting his jaw, Alastair looked away. 'I was the one who dragged the rest of you into the army. I don't think I could have borne it if you hadn't all made it through.'

'You hardly "dragged" us,' Max objected. 'Just about all our friends from Oxford ended up in the war, in one capacity or another.'

'Still, I won't feel completely at ease until Dom makes it home and…adjusts to life again.' With one arm missing and half his face ruined by a sabre slash, both knew the cousin who'd always been known as 'Dandy Dominick', the handsomest man in the regiment, would face a daunting recovery. 'We could go and cheer him up.'

'To be frank, I think it would be best to leave him alone for a while. When life as you've always known it shatters before your eyes, it requires some contemplation to figure out how to rearrange the shards.' Max gave a short laugh. 'Though *I*'ve had months and am still at loose ends. You have your land to manage, but for me—' Max waved his hand in a gesture of frustration. 'The delightful Mrs Harris was charming enough, but I wish I might find some new career that didn't depend on my father's good will. Unfortunately, all I ever aspired to was the diplomatic corps, a field now closed to me. I rather doubt, with my sullied reputation, they'd have me in the church, even if I claimed to have received a sudden calling.'

'Father Max, the darling of every actress from Drury Lane to the Theatre Royal?' Alastair grinned and shook his head. 'No, I can't see that!'

'Perhaps I'll join John Company and set out for India to make my fortune. Become a clerk. Get eaten by tigers.'

'I'd feel sorry for any tiger who attempted it,' Alastair retorted. 'If the Far East don't appeal, why not stay with the army—and thumb your nose at your father?'

'A satisfying notion, that,' Max replied drily, 'though the plan has a few flaws. Such as the fact that, despite my service at Waterloo, Lord Wellington hasn't forgotten he was waiting for *me* when he was almost shot in Vienna.' The continuing coldness of the man he'd once served and still revered cut even deeper than his father's disapproval.

'Well, you're a natural leader and the smartest of the Rogues; something will come to you,' Alastair said. 'In the interim, while we remain at Barton Abbey, best watch your step. Mrs Harris was one thing, but you don't want to get *entangled* with any of Jane's eligible virgins.'

'Certainly not! The one benefit of the débâcle in Vienna is that, with my brother to carry on the family name, I'm not compelled to marry. Heaven forbid I should get cornered by some devious matchmaker.' And trapped into a marriage as cold as his parents' arranged union, he thought with an inward shudder.

Picking up the decanter, Alastair poured them each another glass. 'Here's to confounding Uncle and living independently!'

'As long as living independently doesn't involve wedlock, I can drink to that,' Max said and raised his glass.

Chapter Two

'No, no, you foolish creature, shake out the folds before you hang it!'

Caroline Denby looked up from her comfortable seat on the sofa in one of Barton Abbey's elegant guest bedchambers to see her stepmother snatch a spangled evening gown from the hapless maid and give it a practised shake.

'Like this,' Lady Denby said, handing the garment back before turning to her stepdaughter. 'Caroline, dear, won't you put that book away and supervise Dulcie with that trunk while I make sure this girl doesn't get our evening dresses hopelessly wrinkled?'

'Yes, ma'am,' Caroline replied, setting down her book with regret. Already she was counting the hours until the end of this dreary house party so she might return to Denby Lodge and her horses. She hated to lose almost ten days' training with the winter sales approaching. The Denby line her father had bred had earned a peerless reputation among the racing and army set, and she wasn't about to let her stepmama's single-minded efforts to marry her off get in the way of maintaining her father's high standards.

Besides, while working in the fields and stables in a daily regimen as comfortable and familiar as her father's old riding boots, she could still feel the late Sir Martin's kindly presence, watching over her and the horses that had been his life. How she still missed him!

Sighing, she closed her book and dutifully cast her gaze over at Dulcie, who was currently lifting a layer of chemises, stays and stockings out of a silken rustle of tissue paper. She should be thankful she'd been delegated to supervise the undergarments and leave the gowns to her stepmother. At least she wouldn't have to cast her eyes on them again until she was forced to wear one.

Better to appear in some hideously over-trimmed confection of unflattering colour, she reminded herself, than to end up engaged.

'I'll help with the unpacking, but afterwards, I intend to ride Sultan before the light fades.' As her stepmother opened her lips, probably to argue, Caroline added, 'Remember, you agreed that if I consented to come to Mrs Ransleigh's cattle auction, I'd be allowed to ride every day.'

'Caroline, please!' Lady Denby protested, her face flushing. Leaning closer and lowering her voice, she said, 'You mustn't refer to the gathering in such terms! Especially…' She angled her head toward the maids.

Caroline shrugged. 'But that's what it is. A few gentlemen in search of rich wives gathering to look over the candidates, evaluate their appearance and pedigree, and try to strike a bargain. Just as they do at cattle fairs, or when they come to buy Papa's horses, though I suppose the females here will be spared an inspection of their teeth and limbs.'

'Really, Caroline,' her stepmother said reprovingly, 'I must deplore your using such a vulgar analogy. Just as the ladies wish to ascertain the character of prospective suitors, gentlemen want to assure themselves that any lady to whom they offer matrimony possesses suitable background and breeding.'

'And dowry,' Caroline added.

Ignoring that comment, Lady Denby said, 'Couldn't you, for once, allow yourself to enjoy the attentions of some handsome young men? I know you don't want to spend another Season in London!'

'You also know I'm not interested in getting married,' Caroline said with the weariness of long repetition. 'Why don't you forget about trying to lure me into wedlock and concentrate on making a match for Eugenia? My stepsister is beautiful and wealthy enough to snare any suitor she fancies, and she's eager enough for both of us. Only think how much blunt you'd save, if you didn't have to take her to town in the spring!'

'Unlike you, Eugenia is eagerly anticipating *her* London Season. Besides which, though I don't wish to be indelicate, you are…getting on in years. If you don't marry soon, you will be considered quite on the shelf.'

'Which would be quite all right with me,' Caroline retorted. 'Harry won't care a fig for that, when he comes back.'

'But, Caroline, India is such an unhealthy, heathenish place! Marauding maharajas and fevers and all manner of dangers. Difficult as it is to consider, you must acknowledge the possibility that Lieutenant Tremaine might not return.' Lady Denby's eyes widened, as if the notion had only just occurred to her. 'Surely he wasn't so heedless of propriety as to ask you to wait for him!'

'No,' Caroline admitted. 'We have no formal understanding.'

'I should think not! It would have been most improper, with him leaving for Calcutta while everything was still in such an uproar after your papa's…demise. Now, I understand you've known Harry Tremaine for ever and are comfortable with him, but if you would but give the notion a chance, I'm sure you could find some other gentleman equally…accommodating.'

Of her odd preferences for horses and hounds rather than gowns and needlework, Caroline silently filled in the unstated words. With Harry she'd had no need to conceal her unconventional and mannish interests, nor did she have to pretend a maidenly deference to his masculine opinions and decisions.

For her dearest childhood friend she might consider marrying and braving the Curse—though just thinking about the prospect sent an involuntary shudder through her. But she certainly wasn't willing to risk her life for some lisping dandy who had his eyes on her dowry...or the Denby stud.

Unfortunately, she was wealthy enough that, despite her unconventional ways, there'd been no lack of aspirants to her hand during her aborted Season, before news of her father's sudden illness had called them home. Caroline remained sceptical of how 'accommodating' any prospective husband might be, however, once he gained legal control over her person, property—and beloved horses. With the example of her now much-wiser and much-poorer widowed cousin Elizabeth to caution her, she had no intention of letting herself become dazzled by some rogue with designs on her wealth and property.

If she must marry, she'd wait to wed Harry, who knew her down to the ground and for whom she felt the same sort of deep, companionable love she'd felt for her father. Another pang of loss reverberated through her.

Gritting her teeth against it, she said, 'In the five years since Harry joined the army, I've not found anyone I like as well.'

'Well, you certainly can't claim to have seriously looked! Not when you managed to talk your dear father, God rest his soul, out of taking you to London, or even attending the local assemblies, until I managed to convince him of the necessity last year. It's just not…natural for a young lady to have no interest in marriage!' Lady Denby burst out, not for the first time.

Before Caro could argue that point, her stepmother's expression turned cajoling. 'Come now, my dear, why not allow Mrs Ransleigh's guests to become acquainted with you? It's always possible you might meet a gentleman you could like well enough to marry. You know I have only your best interests at heart!'

The devil of it was Caroline knew the tenderhearted Lady Denby did want only the best for her, though what her stepmother considered 'best' bore little resemblance to what Caroline wanted for herself.

Her resolve weakening in the face of that lady's genuine concern, Caroline gave her a hug. 'I know you want me to be happy. But can you truly see me mistress of some *ton* gentleman's town house or nursery? Striding about in breeches and boots rather than gowns and dancing slippers, stable straw in my braids and barn muck on my shoes? Nor do I possess your sweetness of character, which allows you to listen with every appearance of interest even to the most idiotic of gentlemen.

I'm more likely to pronounce him a lackwit to his face, right in the middle of the drawing room.'

'Fiddle,' her stepmother replied, returning the hug. 'You're often a trifle…impatient with those who don't possess your quickness of wit, but you've a kind heart for all that and would never be so rag-mannered. Besides, it was your papa's dying wish that I see you married.'

When Caroline raised her eyebrows sceptically, Lady Denby said, 'Truly, it was! Though I suppose it's only natural of you to doubt it, since he made so little effort to push you towards matrimony while he was still with us. But I promise you, as he breathed his last, he urged me to help you find a good man who'd make you happy.'

Caroline smiled at her stepmother. 'You brightened what turned out to be his last two years. Knowing how much you did, I suppose I shouldn't be surprised that, at the end, he urged you to cajole me into wedlock.'

Lady Denby sighed. 'We were very happy. I've always appreciated, by the way, how unselfish you were in not resenting me for marrying him, after it had been just the two of you for so long.'

Caroline laughed. 'Oh, I resented you fiercely! I *wished* to be sullen and distant and spiteful, but your sweet nature and obvious concern for us both quite overwhelmed my ill humour.'

'You're not still concerned about that silly notion you call 'the Curse'?' Lady Denby enquired. 'I grant you, childbirth poses a danger to every woman. But when one holds one's first child in one's arms, one knows the risk was well worth it! I want you to experience that joy, Caroline.'

'I appreciate that,' Caro said, refraining from pointing out again just how many of her female relations, including her own mama, had died trying to taste that bliss. Her stepmother, ever optimistic, chose to see their deaths as unfortunate chance. Caro did not believe it to be mere coincidence, but there was no point continuing to argue the matter with Lady Denby.

Her stepmother's genuine concern for her future usually kept Caroline from resenting—too much—Lady Denby's increasingly determined efforts to push her towards matrimony...as long as the discussion didn't drag on too long. Time to end this now, before her patience, always in rather short supply when discussing this disagreeable topic, ran out altogether.

'Enough, then. I promise I will view the company with an open mind. Now, I must change if I am to get that ride in before dinner.' She gave Lady Denby an impish grin. 'At least I'll don a habit, instead of my usual breeches and boots.'

Caroline was chuckling at her stepmother's shudder when suddenly the chamber door was thrown open. Caro's stepsister, Eugenia, rushed in, her cheeks flushed a rosy pink and her golden curls tumbled.

'Mama, I've heard the most alarming news!

Indeed, I fear we may have to repack the trunks and depart immediately!'

'Depart?' Lady Denby echoed. With a warning look at Eugenia, she turned to the maids. 'Thank you, girls; you may go now.'

After the servants filed out, she faced her daughter. 'What calamity has befallen that would require us to leave when we've only just arrived? Has Mrs Ransleigh fallen ill?'

'Oh, nothing of that sort! It seems that her son, Mr Alastair Ransleigh, just arrived here unexpectedly. Oh, Mama, he has the most dreadful reputation! Miss Claringdon says he always has an actress or high-flyer in keeping, or is carrying on a highly publicised affair with some scandalous matron! Sometimes both at once!'

'And what would you know of high-flyers and scandalous matrons, Eugenia?' Caro asked with a grin.

'Well, nothing, of course,' her stepsister replied, flushing. 'Except what I learned from the gossip at school. I'm just relating what Miss Claringdon said. Her family is very well connected and she spent the entire Season in town last spring.'

'Poor Mrs Ransleigh!' Lady Denby said. 'What an embarrassing development! She can hardly forbid her son to enter his own home.'

'Yes, it's quite a dilemma! *She* cannot send him away, but if any of us should encounter him…why, Miss Claringdon said merely being seen conversing with him is enough for a girl to be declared

fast. How enormously vexing! I was so looking
forward to becoming acquainted with some of the
ladies and gentlemen that I shall meet again next
Season in London. But I don't want to remain
and have my reputation tarnished before I've even
begun.' She sighed, a frown marring her perfect
brow. 'And that's not all!'

'Goodness, more bad news?' Lady Denby
asked.

'I'm afraid so. Accompanying Mr Ransleigh
is his cousin, the Honourable Mr Maximillian
Ransleigh.'

'Why is that a problem?' Caro asked, dredging out of memory some of the details about the
ton Lady Denby had drummed into her head during her short stay in London. 'Isn't he the Earl
of Swynford's younger son? Handsome, wealthy,
destined for a great career in government?'

'He *was*, but his circumstances now are sadly
changed. Miss Claringdon told me all about it.'
Eugenia gave Caroline a sympathetic look. 'It's no
wonder you didn't hear about the scandal, Caro,
with Sir Martin falling ill and you having to rush
back home. Such a dreadful time for you both!'

'What happened to Mr Ransleigh?' Lady
Denby asked.

'"Magnificent Max", they used to call him,'
Miss Claringdon said. 'Society's favourite, able
to persuade any man and charm any lady. He'd
served with distinction in the army and was sent
to assist General Lord Wellington during the

Congress of Vienna—the perfect assignment, everyone believed, for someone poised to begin a brilliant diplomatic career. But then came the affair with the mysterious woman and the attack on Lord Wellington, and Mr Ransleigh was sent home in disgrace.'

Caroline frowned, remembering now that Harry had told her before leaving for Calcutta how the English commander, then in charge of all the Allied occupation troops in Paris after Napoleon's first abdication, had been forced to station a personal guard because of assassination threats. 'How did it happen?'

'Miss Claringdon didn't know the details, only that he returned to London under a cloud. Then, if that wasn't bad enough, when Napoleon escaped from Elba and headed to Paris, gathering an army as he marched, Mr Ransleigh disobeyed a direct order to remain in London until the Vienna matter was investigated and sailed to Belgium to rejoin his regiment.'

'Did he fight at Waterloo?' Caroline asked.

'I suppose so. There's still talk of a court-martial, though. In any event, Miss Claringdon says his father, the Earl of Swynford, was so incensed, he ordered his son out of the house! Lady Mary Langton, whom everyone thought he would marry, refused to see him, which ought to have been a vast good fortune for some other lucky female. Except that it's now said that he has vowed never to marry and has been going about London with his cousin Alastair, always in the company of some actress or…or lady of easy virtue!'

A glimmer of a memory stirred in Caroline's mind…Harry, talking about the 'Ransleigh Rogues', four cousins who'd been at school with him before they all joined the army and served in assorted regiments on the Peninsula. Brave, strapping lads who could always be found in the thick of the fight, Harry had described them approvingly.

'Miss Claringdon was nearly in tears as she told me the story,' Eugenia continued. 'She'd quite thought to set her cap at him before he began making up to Lady Mary…but now, with him dead set against marriage and keeping such scandalous company, no well-bred maiden would dare associate with him.'

'An earl's son, too.' Lady Denby sighed. 'How vexing.'

'Well, Mama, must we leave? Or do you think we can remain and avoid the Ransleigh gentlemen?'

For a moment, Lady Denby stared thoughtfully into the distance. 'Mrs Ransleigh and her elder daughter, Lady Gilford, are both eminently respectable,' she said at length. 'In fact, Lady Gilford is the most influential young hostess in the *ton*. I'm sure they will talk privately with the gentlemen who, once the situation has been explained, will either take themselves off, or remain apart, so as not to compromise any of Mrs Ransleigh's guests.'

'So they don't inadvertently ruin some young innocent before she even begins her Season?' Caro asked, winking at Eugenia.

'Exactly.' Lady Denby nodded. 'Though I'm convinced it will be handled thus, just to make certain, I shall go at once in search of Mrs Ransleigh and make enquiries.'

Caroline laughed. 'Goodness, Stepmama, how are you to phrase such a question? "Excuse me, Mrs Ransleigh, I just wished to make sure your reprobate son and disgraceful nephew aren't going to hang about, endangering the reputation of my innocent girls!"'

Eugenia gasped, while Lady Denby chuckled and batted Caroline on the arm. 'To be sure, it will be more than a little awkward, but I'll word my question a good deal more discreetly than that!'

'Perhaps she will lock the gentlemen in the attic—or the wine cellar, so none of the young ladies are at risk of irretrievable ruin,' Caroline said.

'Caro, you jest, but it is a serious matter,' Eugenia insisted, a worried frown on her face. 'A girl's whole future depends upon her character being thought above reproach! A ruined reputation *is* irretrievable, and I, for one, don't find the discussion of so appalling a calamity amusing in the least...especially after Miss Claringdon told me Lady Melross arrived this afternoon.'

Lady Denby groaned. 'The worst gossip-monger in the *ton*! What wretched luck! Well, you must both be extremely careful. Lady Melross can winkle out a scandal faster than a prize hound scents a fox. She'd like nothing better than to uncover some misdeed she can report back to her acquaintances in town.'

'Very well,' Caroline said, sobering at the sight of her stepmother's agitation. 'I shall behave myself.'

'And I shall go and make discreet enquiries of our hostess,' Lady Denby said. 'Eugenia, let me escort you to your room, where you should remain until dinner, while I…acquaint myself with the arrangements.'

'Please do, Mama. I shan't stir a foot from my chamber until you tell me it is *safe*!'

'You'd best make haste,' Caroline said, anxious to see them out of the door before her stepmother recalled her intention to ride and forbade *her* to leave her room. She didn't intend to let adherence to some silly society convention get in the way of riding the best horse she'd ever trained.

The two ladies safely dispatched, Caroline tugged the bell pull to summon Dulcie to help her into her habit. Extracting the garment from the wardrobe, she sighed as she thought of the much more comfortable breeches and boots she'd sneaked into her portmanteau. Though she was sensible enough not to don them when her hostess or the guests might be about, she did intend to wear them on her daily dawn rides.

Might she encounter one of the scandalous

Ransleigh men this afternoon? If Mrs Ransleigh was going to banish them from the house, the stables were a likely place for them to retreat.

Despite Eugenia's alarm, Caroline felt no apprehension about encountering either Alastair or Max Ransleigh. She doubted either would be so overcome by her charms that they'd try to ravish her in the hayloft. As for having her reputation ruined merely by chatting with them, Harry would consider that nonsense, and his was the only opinion besides her own that mattered to her.

A knock at the door heralded Dulcie's arrival. Caroline hurried into her habit, anxious to be changed and gone before her stepmother finished her errand and returned, possibly to ban her from riding for the duration.

She didn't slow her pace until she'd escaped the house and made it safely down the lane leading to the stables. Curious now, she looked about the grounds as she walked and peered around the paddock, but saw no sign of anyone besides the groom who had saddled Sultan for her.

She had enjoyed the ride tremendously, thrilled as always to order Sultan through his paces and receive his swift and obliging responses. As she turned him back towards the stables, she had to admit she was a bit disappointed she hadn't caught so much as a glimpse of the infamous Ransleigh men.

It would be interesting to come face to face

with a real rogue. Her stepmother, however, would
be aghast if she were to converse with either of
them, given their terrible reputations and the fact
that Lady Melross was now in residence. Were
that woman to observe her exchanging innocu-
ous comments about the weather with either Mr
Ransleigh, she'd probably find herself branded a
loose woman by nightfall.

Although, Caroline thought with a grin as she
guided Sultan back into the stable yard, being
pronounced 'ruined' in the eyes of society might
be positively advantageous, if it relieved her of
having to suffer through another Season and
made her unacceptable as a bride to anyone save
Harry.

The idea struck her then, so audacious that her
heart skipped a beat and her hands jerked on the
reins, causing Sultan to toss his head. Soothing
him with a murmur, she took a deep breath, her
pulse accelerating. But outrageous as it was, the
idea caught and would not be dislodged.

For the rest of the way back to the stables and
from there to her chamber, she examined the
idea from every angle. Stepmother would probably be appalled at first, but soon enough, she and
Eugenia would be off to London, where Caro's
small scandal would be swiftly forgotten in the
excitement and bustle of Eugenia's first Season.

By the time she'd summoned Dulcie to help

her change out of her habit into one of the unattractive dinner gowns, she'd made up her mind.

Now all she needed to do was track down one of the Ransleigh Rogues and convince him to ruin her.

Chapter Three

In the late afternoon three days later, Max Ransleigh lounged, book in hand, on a bench in the greenhouse, shaded from the setting sun by a bank of large potted palms, his nose tickled by the exotic scents of jasmine and citrus. Alastair had gone off to see about purchasing cows or hens or some such for the farms; armed with an agenda prepared by his aunt that detailed the daily activities of her guests, he'd chosen to spend his afternoon here, out of the way.

A now-familiar restlessness filled him. Not that he wished to participate in this petticoat assembly, but Max missed, and missed acutely, being involved in the active business of government. His entire life, he'd been bred to take part in and take charge at a busy round of political dinners, discussions and house parties. To move easily among the guests, soliciting the opinions of the gentlemen about topics of current interest, drawing out the ladies, setting the shy at ease, skilfully managing the garrulous. Leaving men and women, young or old, eloquent or tongue-tied, believing he'd found their conversation engrossing and believing him intelligent, attentive, masterful and charming.

Skills he might never need to exercise again.

Anguish and anger stirred again in his gut. Oblivious to the amber beauties of the sunset, he stared at the narrow iron framework of the glass-house. Somehow, somewhere, he had to find a new and worthwhile endeavour to which he could devote his energy.

So abstracted was he, it was several minutes before he noticed the muffled pad of approaching footsteps. Expecting to see Alastair, he pasted on a smile and turned towards the sound.

The vision confronting him made the jocular words of greeting die on his lips.

Instead of his cousin, a young woman halted before him, garbed in a puce evening gown dec-orated with an eruption of lace ruffles, irides-cent spangles and large knots of pink-silk roses wrapped in more lace and garnished with pearls. So over-trimmed and vulgar was the dress, it was some minutes before his affronted senses recov-ered enough for him to meet the female's eyes, which were regarding him earnestly.

'Mr Ransleigh?' the lady enquired, dipping him a slight curtsy.

Only then did he remember, being young and

female, she must be one of Aunt Grace's guests
and therefore should not be here with him. Especially unchaperoned, which a quick glance towards the door of the glasshouse revealed her to
be.

'Have you lost your way, miss?' he asked, giving her the practised Max smile. 'Take the left-
most path to the terrace; the French doors will lead
you into the drawing room. Hurry, now; I'm sure
your chaperon must be missing you.'

He made a little waving motion towards the
door, wishing her on her way quickly before anyone could see them. But instead of turning around,
she stepped closer.

'No, I'm not looking for her, I'm looking for
you and very elusive you've proven to be! It's
taken me three days to run you to ground.'

Max stirred uneasily. Normally, when attending a gathering such as this, he'd have taken
care never to wander off alone to a location that
screamed 'illicit assignation' as loudly as this se-
cluded conservatory. He couldn't imagine that he
and Alastair had not been the topic of a good deal
of gossip among the attendees—hadn't the girl
in the atrocious gown been warned to stay away
from them?

Or perhaps she was looking for Alastair?
Though he couldn't imagine why a respectable
maiden would agree to a clandestine rendezvous
with as practised a rogue as his cousin—or why
his cousin, whose tastes ran to sensual and so-

phisticated ladies well skilled in the game, would trouble himself to lead astray one of his mother's virginal guests.

'I'm sorry, miss, but I'm not who you are seeking. I'm Max Ransleigh and it would be thought highly inappropriate if anyone should discover you'd spoken alone with me. For your own good, I must insist that you depart imm—'

'I know which Ransleigh you are, sir,' the young woman interrupted. 'That's why I sought you out. I have a proposition for you. So to speak,' she added, her cheeks pinking.

Max blinked at her, sure he could not have heard her properly. 'A *"proposition"*?' he repeated.

'Yes. I'm Caroline Denby, by the way; my father was the late Sir Martin Denby, of Denby Stables.'

Thinking this bizarre meeting was getting even more bizarre, Max bowed. 'Miss Denby. Yes, I've heard of your father's excellent horses; my condolences on your loss. However, whatever it is you wish to say, perhaps Mrs Ransleigh could arrange a meeting later. Truly, it's most imperative that you quit my presence immediately, lest you put your reputation at risk.'

'But that's exactly what I wish to do. Not just risk it, but ruin it. Irretrievably.'

Of all the things the lady might have said, that was perhaps the most unexpected. The glib, never-at-a-loss Max found himself speechless.

While he goggled at her, jaw dropped, she rushed on, 'You see, the situation is rather complicated, but I don't wish to marry. However, I have a large dowry, so any number of gentlemen want to marry *me*, and my stepmother believes, like most of the known world—' her tone turned a bit aggrieved at this '—that marriage is the only natural state for a woman. But if I were to be found in a compromising situation with a man who then refused to marry me, I would be irretrievably ruined. My stepmother could no longer drag me about, trying to introduce me to prospective suitors, because no gentleman of honour would consider marrying me.'

Suddenly, in a blinding flash of comprehension, he understood her intentions in seeking him out. Chagrin and outrage held him momentarily motionless. Then, with a curt nod, he spat out, 'Good day, Miss Denby', turned on his heel and headed for the door.

She scurried after him and snagged his sleeve, halting his advance. 'Please, Mr Ransleigh, won't you hear me out? I know it's outlandish, and perhaps insulting, but—'

'Miss Denby, it is without doubt the most appalling, outlandish, insulting and crack-brained idea I've ever heard! Naturally, I shall say nothing of this, but if your doubtless long-suffering stepmother—who has my deepest sympathies, by the way—should ever learn of it, you'd be locked up on bread and water for a month!'

The incorrigible female merely grinned at him. 'She is long suffering, the poor dear. Not that it would do her any good to lock me up, for I'd simply climb out of a window. You've already been outraged and insulted. Could you not allow me a few more moments to explain?'

He ought to refuse her unconditionally and beat a hasty exit. But the whole encounter was so unexpected and preposterous, he found himself as intrigued as he was affronted. For a moment, curiosity arm-wrestled prudence…and won.

'Very well, Miss Denby, explain. But be brief about it.'

'I realise it's an…unusual request. As I said, I possess a substantial dowry and I'm already past the age when most well-dowered girls are married off. It wasn't a problem while my father lived—' sorrow briefly shadowed her brow '—for he never pressed me to marry. Indeed, we've worked together closely these last ten years, building the reputation of the Denby Stables. My only desire is to continue that work. But since Papa's death, my stepmother has grown more and more insistent about getting me wed. Because of my dowry, she has no trouble coming up with candidates, even though I possess almost none of the attributes most gentleman expect in a wife. If I were ruined, the suitors would disappear, my stepmother would be forced to give up her efforts and I could remain where I wish to be, at Denby Lodge with my horses.'

'Do you never want to marry?' he asked, curious in spite of himself.

'I do have a…particular friend, but he is in India with the army, and won't return for some time.'

'Wouldn't this "particular friend" be incensed if he were to discover you'd been ruined?'

She waved a hand. 'Harry wouldn't mind. He says most society conventions are contrived and ridiculous.'

'He might feel differently about something that sullied the honour of the woman he wished to marry,' Max pointed out.

'Oh, I'd have to explain, of course. But Harry and I have been the closest of friends since we were children. He'd understand that I only meant to…to save myself for him,' she finished.

'Let me see if I understand you correctly. You wish to be found in a compromising situation with *me*, then have me refuse to marry you, so you would be ruined, which would prevent any honourable gentleman but your friend Harry from ever seeking your hand in wedlock?'

She nodded approvingly, as if he'd just worked out a particularly difficult proof in geometry. 'Exactly.'

'First, Miss Denby, let me assure you that though the world may call me a rogue, I am still a gentleman. I do not ruin innocents. Besides, even if I were obliging enough to agree to this scheme, how could I be sure that in the ensuing uproar—

and there would be considerable uproar, I promise you—that you would not change your mind and decide you had better wed me after all? Because— no offence meant to present company—I have no wish at all to marry.'

'Nor do I—no offence meant either—wish to marry you. But no one can *force* us to marry.'

Leaving aside that dubious claim, he said, 'If it's ruination you seek, why did you not approach my cousin Alastair? His reputation is even more scandalous than mine.'

'I considered him, but thought he wouldn't suit. For one, it's his mother's house party and he wouldn't wish to embarrass her. Second, I understand that since being disappointed in love, he's held females in aversion, whereas you are said to genuinely like women. And finally, since your plans for your career were recently shattered, I thought perhaps you would understand what it is like to have your future dictated by the decisions of others, with little control over your own destiny.'

His eyes widened, for the observation struck home. Despite the impossible nature of her request, he felt a rush of sympathy for this young woman who'd lost the only advocate who could guarantee her the life she wanted, while everyone else was trying to force her into a role not of her choosing.

She must have seen the realisation in his eyes, for she said, 'You do understand, don't you? Despite the setback in your choice of career, you are a man; you can make new plans. But when a woman marries, everything she owns, even power over her very body, becomes the possession of her husband, who can sell it, game it away, or ruin it, as he pleases. You must admit, few gentlemen would permit their wives to run a horse-breeding farm. I don't want to see Papa's lifetime of work pass into the hands of a man who would forbid me to manage it, who might neglect, ruin—or even sell it! *My* horses! There's no one I trust with Papa's legacy, except for Harry. So…won't you help me?'

The whole idea was outlandish, as she herself had admitted. He ought to refuse categorically and send her on her way…before someone discovered them and she was compromised in truth. But he hadn't been so intrigued and amused for a very long time. 'You're in love with this Harry, I suppose?'

'He's my best friend,' she said simply, her gaze resting on the glass panes behind them. 'We're comfortable together and we understand each other.'

'What, no passionate declarations, or sighs, or sonnets to your eyebrows? I thought all females dreamt of that.'

She shrugged. 'It might be lovely, I suppose. Or at least my stepsister, who always has her nose in a Minerva Press novel, says so. But I'm not a beauty like Eugenia, the sort of delicate, clinging female who inspires gentlemen to poetry. Harry will marry me when he gets back from India, but that's no help now.'

'Why don't you just contact him about entering into an engagement?'

She sighed. 'If I'd been thinking rationally at the time, I would have asked him to announce we were affianced before he left for India. But Papa had just died unexpectedly and I...' her voice trembled for a moment '...I wasn't myself. Not until weeks later, when my stepmother, fearing Harry might never return, began pressing me to marry, did I realise what Papa's demise would mean to my work and my future. Meanwhile, Stepmama keeps trying to thrust me into society, hoping I will meet another gentleman I might be persuaded to marry. I shall not.'

'I sympathise—' and he truly did '—with your predicament, Miss Denby. But what of your family, your stepmother and stepsister? Do you not realise that if I were to agree to ruin you, the scandal would devastate them as well? Surely you wouldn't wish to subject them to that.'

'If we were discovered embracing in the garden at a London ball during the height of the Season and refused to marry, it might embarrass Stepmother and Eugenia,' she allowed. 'But I can't believe anything that happens here would even be remembered by the time next Season begins. In any event, Eugenia's a Whitman, not a Denby, so there'll be no contagion of blood and her dowry is handsome enough to make gentlemen overlook her unfortunate connection of a stepsister. By next Season, any stain on your honour for not marrying a girl you were thought to have compromised would have faded also.'

Max shook his head. 'I'm afraid you don't know society at all. So, though I am, ah, honoured that you considered me for your...unusual proposal—'

She chuckled, that unexpected reaction throwing him off the polite farewell he'd been about to utter.

'It's rather obvious you were not *"honoured"*,' she retorted. 'But speaking of honour, did you serve with the Foot Guards at Waterloo?'

'Yes, in a Light Guard unit,' he replied, wondering where she meant to go now with the conversation.

'Then you were at Hougoumont,' she said, nodding. 'The courage and valour of the warriors who survived that engagement will have earned you many admirers. Once most of the army returns home, you will have supporters aplenty to champion your cause. If you cannot be a diplomat, why not rejoin the service? But while you are lounging about, being naught but a rogue, why not do something useful and rescue me?'

'Rescue you by ruining you?' he summarised wryly, shaking his head. 'What an extraordinary notion.' But even as the words left his lips, he recalled how he'd told Alastair earlier that he'd be glad if his aborted career were good for *something*.

Despite the dreadful dress, Miss Denby was an

appealing chit, perhaps the most unusual female he'd ever encountered. Spirited and resourceful, too, both factors that tempted him to grant her request, no matter how imprudent. Because despite what she seemed to believe, compromising her *would* cause an uproar and he *would* be honourbound to marry her.

A realisation that should speed him into giving her a firm refusal and sending her away. But as his thoughtful gaze travelled from her hopeful face downwards, he suddenly discovered the hideous dress's one redeeming feature.

Miss Denby might be a most unusual young woman, but the full, finely rounded bosom revealed by the low-cut bodice of her evening gown was lushly female.

His senses sprang to the alert, flooding his body with sensation and filling his mind with images of ruining her…the scent of orange trees and jasmine washing over them as he tasted her lips… caressing the full breasts straining at her bodice, rubbing his thumb over the pebbled nipples while she moaned with pleasure…

He jerked his thoughts to a halt and his gaze back to her face. She might be startlingly plainspoken, but she was unquestionably an innocent. Did she have any idea what she was asking, wanting him to compromise her?

Instead of bidding her goodbye, he found himself saying, 'Miss Denby, do you know what you must do to be ruined?'

Confirming his assessment of her inexperience, she blushed. 'Being found alone in a compromising position should be enough. You being a gentleman of the world, I thought you would know how to manage that part. As long as you don't go far enough to get me with child.'

For an instant, he was again speechless. 'Have you no maidenly sensibility?' he asked at last.

'None,' she replied cheerfully. 'Mama died giving birth to me. I was my father's only child and he treated me like the son he never had. I'm more at home in breeches and topboots than in gowns.' Catching a glimpse of herself reflected in the glass wall, she shuddered. 'Especially gowns like this.'

He couldn't help it; his gaze wandered back to that firm, rounded bosom. Despite the better judgement urging him to dismiss her before someone discovered them and the parson's mousetrap snapped around him, a pesky thought started buzzing around in his mind like a persistent horsefly, telling him that compromising the voluptuous Miss Denby might almost be worth the trouble. 'Some parts of the gown are quite attractive,' he murmured.

He hadn't really meant to say the words out loud, but she glanced over, her eyes following the direction of his gaze. Sighing, she clapped a hand over the exposed bosom. 'Fiddle—I shall have to add a fichu to the neckline. As if the garment were not over-trimmed enough!'

The shadowed valley of décolletage just visible beneath her sheltering fingers was even more arousing than the unimpeded view, he thought, his heartrate notching upwards. Adding a fichu to mask that delectable view would be positively criminal.

Shaking his head to try to rid himself of temptation, he said, 'Your speech is so forthright, I would have expected your dress to be...simpler. Did Lady Denby press the style upon you?'

She laughed again, a delightful, infectious sound that made him want to share her mirth. 'Oh, no, Stepmama has excellent taste; she thinks the gown atrocious. But I put up such a fuss about being forced to waste time shopping, she let me purchase pretty much whatever I selected. Although I couldn't manage to talk her into the yellow-green silk that made my skin look so sallow.'

The realisation struck with sudden clarity. 'You are deliberately dressing to try to make yourself unattractive?' he asked incredulously.

She gave him a look that said she thought his comment rather dim-witted. 'Naturally. I told you I was trying to avoid matrimony, didn't I? The dress is bad enough, but the spectacles are truly the crowning touch.' Slanting him a mischievous glance, from her reticule she extracted a pair of spectacles, perched them on her nose and peered up at him.

Huge dark eyes stared at him, so enormously magnified he took an involuntary step backwards.

At his retreat, she burst out laughing. 'They make me look like an insect under glass, don't you think? Of course, Stepmama knows I don't wear spectacles, so I can't get away with them when she's around, which is a shame, because they are wondrous effective. All but the most determined fortune hunters quail at the sight of a girl in a hideously over-trimmed dress wearing enormous spectacles. I shall have to remember about the fichu, however. The spectacles can't do their job properly if gentlemen are staring at my bosom.'

Especially when the bosom was as tempting as hers, Max thought. Still, the whole idea was so ridiculous he had to laugh, too. 'Do you really need to *frighten* away the gentlemen?'

Probably hearing the scepticism in his tone, she coloured a bit. 'Yes,' she said bluntly, 'although I assure you, I realise it has nothing at all to do with the attractions of my person. Papa's baronetcy is old, the whole family is excessively well-connected and my dowry is handsome. As an earl's son, do you not need stratagems to protect yourself from matchmaking mamas and their scheming daughters?'

She had him there. 'I do,' he acknowledged.

'So you understand.'

'Yes. None the less,' he continued with genuine regret, 'I'm afraid I can't reconcile it with my conscience to ruin you.'

'Are you certain? It would mean everything to me and I'd be in your debt for ever.'

Her appeal touched his chivalrous instincts—the same ones that had got him into trouble in Vienna. Surely that experience had cured him for ever of offering gallantry to barely known females?

Despite his wariness, he found himself liking her. The sheer outrageousness of her proposal, her frank speech, disarming candour and devious mind all appealed to him.

Still, he had no intention of getting himself leg-shackled to some chit with whom he had nothing in common but a shared sympathy for their inability to pursue their preferred paths in life. 'I'm sorry, Miss Denby. But I can't.'

As if she hadn't heard—or couldn't accept—his refusal, she continued to stare at him with that ardent, hopeful expression. Without the ugly spectacles to render them grotesque, he saw that her eyes were the velvety brown of rich chocolate, illumined at the centre with kaleidoscope flecks of iridescent gold. A scattering of freckles dusted the fair skin of her nose and cheeks, testament to an active outdoor life spent riding her father's horses. The dusky curls peeping out from under an elaborate cap of virulent purple velvet glowed auburn in the fading light of the autumn sunset.

Miss Denby's ugly puce 'disguise' was very effective, he realised with a something of a shock. She was in fact quite a lovely young woman, older than he'd initially calculated, and far more attractive than he'd thought upon first seeing her.

Which was even more reason not to destroy her future—or risk his own.

'You are certain?' she asked softly, interrupting his contemplation.

'I regret having to be so disobliging, but...yes.'

For the first time, her energy seemed to flag. Her shoulders slumped; weariness shadowed her eyes and she sighed, so softly that Max felt, rather than heard, the breath of it touch his lips.

Those signs of discouragement sent a surge of regret through him, ridiculous as it was to *regret* not doing them both irreparable harm. But before he could commit the idiocy of reconsidering, she squared her shoulders like a trooper coming to attention and gave him a brisk nod. 'Very well, I shan't importune you any longer. Thank you for your time, Mr Ransleigh.'

'It was my pleasure, Miss Denby,' he said in perfect truth. As she turned to go, though it was none of his business, he found himself asking, 'What will you do now?'

'I shall have to think of someone else, I suppose. Good day, Mr Ransleigh.' After dipping a graceful curtsy to his bow, she walked out of the conservatory.

He listened to her footfalls recede, feeling again that curious sense of regret. Not at refusing her absurd request, of course, but he did wish he could have helped her.

What an unusual young woman she was! He could readily believe her father had treated her like a son. She had the straightforward manner of a man, with her frank, direct gaze and brisk pace. She took disappointment like a man, too. Once he'd made his decision final, she'd not tried to sway him. Nor had she employed anything from the usual womanly arsenal of tears, pouts or tantrums to try to persuade him.

He'd always prided himself on his perception. But so well did she play the overdressed spinster role, it had taken an unaccountably long time for him to realise that she was a potently alluring female.

She didn't seem to realise that truth, though. In fact, it appeared she hadn't the faintest idea that if she wished to tempt a man into ruining her, her most powerful weapons weren't words, but that generous bosom and that kissable mouth.

Now, if she'd slipped into the conservatory and caught him unawares, still seated on the bench… pressed against him to whisper her request in his ear, leaning over to place those mounded treasures but a slight lift of his hand away…lowered her face in invitation…with the potent scent of jasmine washing over him, he'd probably have ended up kissing her senseless before he knew what he was doing.

At the thought, heat suffused him and his fingers tingled, as if they could already feel the softness of her skin. Damn, but it had been far too long since he'd last pleasured, and had been pleasured by, a lady. He reminded himself that he didn't debauch innocents—even innocents who asked to be debauched.

If only she were not gently born and not so innocent. He could easily imagine whiling away the rest of his time at Barton Abbey with her in his bed, awakening to its full potential the passion he sensed in her, tutoring her in every delicious variety of lovemaking.

But she *was* gently born and marriage was too high a price to pay for a fortnight's pleasure.

The ridiculousness of her request struck him again and he laughed out loud. What an outrageous chit! She'd made him smile and forget his own dissatisfaction, something no one had done for a very long time. He hoped she found a solution to her dilemma.

Her last remark echoed in his ears then, dashing the smile from his lips. Had she said she meant to try some*thing* else? Or some*one* else?

The last of his warm humour leached away as quickly as if he'd jumped into the icy depths of Alastair's favourite fishing stream. Her proposal could be considered merely outlandish…if delivered to a gentleman of honour. But Max could think of any number of rogues who'd be delighted to take the luscious Miss Denby up on her offer… and would be deaf to any pleas that they halt the seduction to which she'd invited them short of 'getting her with child'.

Were there any such rogues present at this gathering? Surely Jane and Aunt Grace would not have invited anyone who might take advantage of an innocent. He certainly hoped not, for he had no doubt, with the same single-minded directness she'd employed with him, Miss Denby would not flinch from making her preposterous offer to someone else.

He tried to tell himself that Miss Denby's situation was not his concern and he should put her, enchanting bosom and all, from his mind. But despite the salutary lesson of Vienna, he found he couldn't completely ignore a lady in distress.

Not that he meant to accept her offer, of course. But while he remained at Barton Abbey, shooting, fishing with Alastair, reading and contemplating his future, he could still keep an eye—from a safe distance—on Miss Caroline Denby.

Chapter Four

❧❧❧

Still brooding over her failed interview with Mr Ransleigh, Caroline rose at the first faint light of dawn, quickly donned the hidden boots and breeches, and crept silently to the stables before the tweenies were up to light the fires. She encountered only one sleepy groom, rousted from his bed above the tack room when she went in to retrieve Sultan's saddle.

After last night's dinner, the guests had stayed up playing interminable rounds of cards, so she felt fairly assured they would all be abed late this morning. Her peep-of-dawn start should give her at least an extra hour to ride Sultan before prudence required her to slip back to the house and change into more acceptable clothing.

He flicked his ears and nickered at her as she entered the stables, then nosed in her pockets for his usual treat as she led him from his stall. She fed him the bit of apple, quickly saddled him and led him to the lane, then gave him his head. Eagerly the gelding set off at a gallop, the calming effects of which she needed even more than the horse.

For the next few moments, she gave herself over to the unequalled delight of bending low over the neck of the magnificent animal beneath her, heart, mind and soul attuned to his effort as the ground flew by beneath his pounding hooves.

All too soon, it was time to pull up. Crooning her approval, she schooled him to a cool-down walk while her attention, no longer distracted by the pleasure of riding, returned inexorably to her dilemma.

Unwise as it was, it seemed she'd pinned her hopes on the mad scheme of being ruined. She hadn't realised until after he had turned her down just how much she'd been counting on coaxing Max Ransleigh to accept her offer and put an end to her matrimonial woes.

Though she had to admit to being a little relieved he *had* refused. Miss Claringdon had called him 'charming', but he exuded more than charm. Though she'd rather liked his keen wit, some prickly sense of awareness had flooded her as she'd stood under his gaze, some connection almost as real as a touch, that made her feel nervous and jittery as a colt eyeing his first bridle. When he'd asked her if she knew what he must do to compromise her, she'd blushed like a ninny, while visions of him drawing her close, covering her mouth with his, flashed through her mind. Thank heavens her garbled reply had made him laugh, but though the fraught moment had passed, she'd still felt his eyes examining her, heating her skin even as she walked away from him.

He certainly did not inspire her with the same ease and confidence Harry did.

Perhaps that's why she'd remained so tense and sleepless last night, tossing and turning in her bed as she ran through her mind all the gentlemen present at the house party who might be possible alternatives to Max Ransleigh.

Only Mr Alastair's reputation was scandalous enough to guarantee that being found in his presence would be enough to ruin her. She supposed she could try her luck with him, but she doubted he could be persuaded to throw his mother's house party into an uproar by compromising one of her guests.

She could approach him back in London next spring. But though she was fairly confident ruining herself here wouldn't create any long-lasting problems for her family, doing so at the height of the Season probably would, as Max Ransleigh had asserted. She certainly didn't wish to repay the kindness Lady Denby and Eugenia had always shown her by spoiling in any way the Season that her stepsister anticipated so eagerly.

Which brought her back to the guests at this house party.

Unless she could work out some way to turn one of them to account, the future stretched before her like a grimly unpleasant repetition of her curtailed London Season: evening after evening of dinners, musicales, card parties, balls and routs, crowded about by men eager to relieve her of her fortune.

Was there any way she could avoid being dragged through all that? Maybe she should write to Harry after all, proposing a long-distance engagement. But would Lady Denby consider such an informally made offer binding?

By the time they reached the end of the field bordering the paddock, she was no closer to finding an answer to her problem. Thrusting it aside in disgust, she turned her attention back to putting Sultan through his paces.

If only, she thought as she commanded him to a trot, life could be schooled to such perfection as a fine horse.

Blinking sleep from his eyes, Max shouldered creel and rod and followed Alastair to the stables. His cousin, having learned from his factor in the village that the fish were running well in the river, had dragged him from his bed before first light so they might try their luck at snagging some trout.

They were tromping in companionable silence down the path leading to the river when Alastair suddenly halted. 'By Jove, that's the finest piece of horseflesh I've seen in a dog's age, trotting there

in the paddock,' he declared, pointing in that direction. 'Whose nag is it, do you know?'

Max peered into the distance, where a stable
boy was guiding a showy bay hack in a series of
high-stepping motions. His eyes widening in appreciation, he noted the horse's deep chest, broad
shoulders, glossy sheen of coat and steady, perfect rhythm. His interest piqued as well, he said,
'I have no idea. The bay is a magnificent beast.'

'That's not one of our grooms, either. Horse
must belong to one of Mama's guests, who brought
his own man to exercise it.' Alastair laughed. 'I
might resent providing the food and drink these
man-milliners consume while they loiter here, but
an animal as magnificent as that is welcome to
my largesse.'

'Aunt Grace's largesse, to be fair.'

'Not that I truly begrudge Jane the expense of
their party. I just wish the guests were less tedious
and the timing not so inconvenient.'

At least one guest, Max thought, had not been
'tedious' in the least. He smiled as images of Miss
Denby ran through his head: staring up at him
with a grin, bug-eyed in her spectacles; the atrocious puce gown she'd employed to 'disguise' her
loveliness; and ah, yes, the luscious breasts whose
rounded tops enticed him above the low neckline
of her dinner dress...

Desire rose in him, surprising in its intensity.
Reminding himself that seducing Miss Denby was
not a possibility, he thrust the memories of her

from his mind and turned his attention back to the horse, now being put through several intricate manoeuvres.

Finally, the groom pulled up and leaned low over his mount's head, probably murmuring well-deserved compliments in his ear. Straightening, the lad kicked him to a trot across the paddock towards the lane leading back to the stables.

'I'd like a closer look at that horse,' Alastair said. 'If we cut back at the next crossing, we should reach the stable lane about the same time as the groom.'

Max nodding agreement, the two cousins set off. Confirming Alastair's prediction, after hurrying down the path, they emerged from behind a stand of trees just as the rider trotted past.

Apparently startled by their unexpected appearance, the horse neighed and reared up. With expert ease, the lad controlled him.

'Sorry to have frightened your mount,' Alastair told him. 'We've been admiring him from the other side of the paddock.'

Max was about to add his compliments when his assessing eyes moved from the horse to the rider. With a shock, he realised the 'groom' was in fact no groom at all, but Miss Caroline Denby.

Alastair, no sluggard where the feminine form was concerned, simultaneously reached the same conclusion. 'Devil's teeth! It's a girl!' he muttered to Max, even as he swept his hat off and bowed.

'Good morning, miss. Magnificent horse you have there!'

Miss Denby's alarmed gaze leapt from Alastair to Max. As recognition dawned in her eyes, her face flamed. 'Stepmother is going to be furious,' she murmured with a sigh. Apparently accepting that she'd been well and truly caught, she nodded to him. 'Good morning, Mr Ransleigh.'

Alastair's brows lifted as he looked enquiringly from Miss Denby back to Max, then gestured to him to perform the introductions. Bowing to the inevitable, Max said, 'Miss Denby, may I present my cousin, your host, Mr Alastair Ransleigh.'

She made a rueful grimace. 'I wish you wouldn't. I thought surely I'd be able to return before anyone but the grooms were stirring. Couldn't you just pretend you hadn't seen me?'

'Don't fret, Miss Denby,' Max said. 'We're not supposed to let *you* see *us*, either. Shall this unexpected encounter remain our secret?'

She smiled. 'In that case, I shall be pleased to meet you, Mr Ransleigh.'

'And I am absolutely charmed to meet you, Miss Denby,' Alastair replied, his rogue's eyes avidly roving her form.

Max restrained the strong desire to smack him. Hitherto he'd thought nothing could accentuate a lady's body like a silk gown, preferably thin and cut low in the bosom. But though he'd be delighted to see Miss Denby garbed only in the sheerest of materials, there was no escaping the fact that, in male riding attire, she looked entirely delectable.

Tight-knit breeches hugged her slender thighs and the curve of her trim *derrière* upon the saddle, while riding boots outlined her shapely calves. Beneath her unbuttoned tweed jacket, her shirt, open at the top since she wore no cravat, revealed a swan's curve of neck, kissable hollows at her throat and collarbones, and a lush fullness beneath that made his mouth water. Several lengths of the glossy dark hair she'd thrust up under her cap had tumbled down during the ride and lay in damp, tangled curls upon her face and neck— looking much as they might, he thought, if she were reclining against her pillows after a night of lovemaking.

The heated gleam in Alastair's eyes said he was envisioning exactly the same scene, damn him.

'Bargain or not, I'd best return immediately and get into more proper clothing,' Miss Denby said, pulling Max from his lusty imagining. 'Good day, gentlemen.'

'Wait, Miss Denby,' Alastair called. 'There wasn't a soul stirring when we left the house but a short time ago. Tarry with us a minute, please! I'd like to ask about your mount. You were training him, weren't you?'

She'd been looking towards the stables, obviously anxious to be away, but at Alastair's expression of interest, she turned back, her eyes brightening. 'Yes. Sultan is the most promising of our four-year-olds. Father bred him, Cleveland Bay with some Arabian for stamina and Irish thoroughbred for strength in the bone. Easy-going, with wonderful paces. He'll make a superior hunter or cavalry horse…although I've about decided I cannot part with him.'

'Your father…you mean Sir Martin Denby, of the Denby Stud?' Alastair asked. When she nodded, he said, 'No wonder your mount is so impressive. Max, you remember Mannington brought several of Sir Martin's horses to the Peninsula. Excellent mounts, all of them.'

'Lord Mannington?' Miss Denby echoed. 'Ah, yes, I remember; he purchased Alladin and Percival. Geldings who are kin to Sultan here, having the same dam, but a sire with a bit more Arabian blood. I'm so pleased to know they performed well.'

'Mannington said their stamina and speed saved his neck on several occasions,' Alastair said. After giving her a second, more thorough appraisal, he said, 'You seem very knowledgeable about your father's operation.'

'I've helped him with it since I mounted my first pony,' she responded, pride in her voice. 'In addition to training the foals, I kept the stud books and sales records, as Papa was more concerned with charting bloodlines than plotting numbers.'

Sympathy softened Alastair's face. 'You must miss him very much. My condolences on your loss.' While, her lips tightening, she nodded a quick acknowledgement, Alastair said, 'A sad loss for the stud as well. Who is running it now?'

'I am,' she replied, lifting her chin. 'Papa involved me in every aspect of the business, from breeding the mares to weaning the foals to breaking the yearlings and beginning the training of the two-year-olds.' Her chin notched higher. 'Denby Stud is my life. But…' she gestured toward the fishing gear looped across their shoulders '…I mustn't keep you from the trout eager to sacrifice themselves to your lures.'

She turned her mount's head towards the stable, then paused. 'I *can* count on your discretion, I trust?'

'Absolutely,' Alastair assured her.

Giving them a quick nod, she touched her heels to the gelding and rode off. Alastair, Max noted with disgruntlement, was following the bounce of her shapely posterior against the saddle as closely as he was, devil take him.

After she disappeared around the curve in the lane, Alastair turned to Max, grinning. 'Well, well, well. Don't think I've ever seen you so silent around a female. Here I thought you'd been moping about, mourning your lost career. Instead, you're been perfecting your credentials as a rogue, sneaking off to secret assignations with a tempting little morsel like that.'

Max struggled to keep his temper in check. 'Let me remind you,' he said stiffly, 'that "morsel" is one of your mother's guests and an innocent maid.'

'Is she truly innocent?' Alastair shook his head disbelievingly. 'Lord have mercy, riding astride in breeches like that! I can't believe I didn't immediately realise she was female. Just shows how one doesn't recognise what is right before one's eyes when one's not expecting it. Though she *is* an excellent rider: fine hands, great seat.' With a chuckle, he added, 'Wouldn't mind having her in the saddle, those lovely long legs wrapped around *me*.'

A flash of fury surging through him, Max whacked his cousin with his fishing pole. 'Stubble it! That's a *lady* you're insulting.'

'Fancy her for yourself, do you?' Alastair asked, unrepentant. 'With her going about like that, her limbs and bottom outlined for any red-blooded man to ogle, it's not my fault she evokes such thoughts. Nor are we the only ones watching.' He pointed toward the opposite side of the field. 'Some bloke over there is ogling her, too.'

His gaze following the direction of his cousin's extended arm, Max squinted into the morning sunlight. 'Who is it?'

'How should I know? Probably another one of those damned macaroni merchants hanging about, measuring up the female flesh on display. Not a man's man among them—petticoat-string dandies all,' he concluded in disgust. 'But this girl…she's truly an innocent, you say?'

'Absolutely.'

'How do you know so much about her?'

Knowing he'd have to explain, but not wishing to reveal too much—certainly not her scandalous proposition—Max gave Alastair an abbreviated version of his meeting with Miss Denby in the conservatory.

'Devil's teeth, she's a luscious armful in breeches. What a mistress she'd make!' Alastair exclaimed, then waved Max to silence before he could deliver another rebuke. 'Don't get your cravat in a knot; I know there's no chance of that. She is a "lady", amazing as that seems to a man seeing her for the first time garbed like that. If *marriage* is her stepmother's object, pulling it off is going to be difficult if word gets out of her offending the proprieties by riding about in boy's dress. Though it would almost be worth wedlock, to get one's hands on the Denby Stud.'

'So she fears. She doesn't want to marry, she said, and risk losing control over it.'

Alastair nodded. 'I suppose I can understand. One wouldn't wish to turn such a prime operation over to some hamfisted looby who couldn't housebreak a puppy.'

'How infuriating to see everything you'd worked on, worked for, the last ten years of your life given over to someone else. Ruined, perhaps, and you unable to do anything about it.'

Alastair gave him a searching look, as if he thought Max were speaking more about himself than Miss Denby. 'Well, I wish her luck. She's an odd lass, to be sure. But undeniably attractive, even without the inducement of the Denby Stud. Now, if we're going to catch breakfast, we'd better be going.' At that, Alastair kicked his mount into motion.

Lagging behind for a moment, Max studied the man across the field, who was now striding back toward the stables. He'd better find out who that was. And continue to keep an eye on Miss Denby.

Chapter Five

After a most satisfactory session at the stream, Max and Alastair returned the trout to the kitchen for Cook to turn into breakfast. While Alastair went on to change out of his fishing garb, Max hesitated by the door to his aunt's room.

All during their mostly silent camaraderie at the river, rather than concentrate on fish, Max had thought about his aunt's unusual guest. He'd had, he was forced to admit, to exercise some considerable discipline to keep his thoughts from turning from the serious matter of her situation and the man watching her to memories of her inviting gurgle of a laugh, that enticing bosom and the wonderfully suggestive up-and-down motion of her *derrière* on the saddle.

Making enquiries of Aunt Grace might seem odd, but while Alastair was otherwise occupied, he probably ought to risk it. If he discovered that the gentleman guests included none but paragons of honour and virtue, he could stop worrying about Miss Denby and dismiss her situation from his mind.

Decision made, he knocked and was bid to enter. 'Max! This is a pleasant surprise!' Mrs Ransleigh cried, her expression of mild curiosity warming to one of genuine pleasure. 'Will you take chocolate with me, or some coffee? I confess, I do feel terrible, I've been so poor a hostess to you.'

'Nonsense,' he said, waving away her offer. 'I'll not stay long enough for coffee; we're just back from the river, and I'm sure you'd as lief I not leave fish slime on your sofa. You know Alastair and I are quite able to keep ourselves well entertained.'

She flushed. 'I do appreciate your...discretion. Even as I absolutely deplore the necessity for it! Is there truly no hope of your finding another diplomatic position?'

'I have some ideas, but there's no point initiating anything yet while Father is still so angry. You know he has the influence to block whatever I attempt, should he wish to.'

'That's so *James*!' she cried. 'Brilliant orator and skilled politician your father may be, but he can be so bull-headed and unreasonable sometimes, I'd like to shake him!'

Though he appreciated his aunt's sympathy, he'd just as soon not dwell on the painful topic of his ruined prospects. 'I didn't stop by to talk about me,' he parried. 'How goes your party? Has Jane succeeded in leg-shackling any of the guests? Has Lissa found her ideal mate?'

'Felicity is enjoying herself immensely, which is all I wished for her, since I have no desire to give her up to a husband just yet! Among the other guests, there are some promising developments, though it's too early to tell yet whether they will result in engagements.'

Trying for a nonchalant tone, Max said, 'I happened to encounter one of your young ladies. No, nothing scandalous about it,' he assured her hastily before, her eyes widening in alarm, she could speak. 'I met her briefly and by chance one afternoon in the conservatory, where she darted in, she told me, to escape some suitor. A most unusual young woman.'

Aunt Grace laughed. 'Oh, dear! That must have been Miss Denby! Poor Diana—her stepmother, Lady Denby, an old friend of mine—is quite in despair over the girl. Perhaps you didn't notice in your quick meeting, but the lady is rather...old.'

Were he pressed to describe what he'd noticed about Miss Denby during that first meeting, Max thought, 'old' would not be among the adjectives that came to mind. 'I must confess, I didn't notice,' he replied in perfect truth.

'She should have had her first Season years ago,' his aunt continued. 'But she was her widowed father's only child. Now that I face having

my last chick leave home, I can perfectly understand why he didn't wish to lose her. She's a great
heiress, though, so Diana hasn't given up hope yet
of her making an acceptable match, even though
at five-and-twenty she's practically on the shelf.'

'A doddering old age, to be sure.'

'For a female of good birth and fortune to remain unwed at such an age *is* unusual,' his aunt
said reprovingly. 'With her being practically an
ape-leader, you'd think she'd be eager to wed, but
apparently it's quite the opposite! Though the poor
dear seems intelligent enough, she's terribly shy in
company and possesses not a particle of conversation unrelated to hunting and horses. To make
matters worse, though I hesitate to say something
so uncharitable about a guest, her taste in clothing
is atrocious. I expect, arbiter of fashion that you
are, you did notice the dreadful gown.'

'I did,' he said drily. *Though my attention focused more on the neckline than the trimming.*
'So, there is no one here who wishes to coax her
into matrimony?'

'I had high hopes of Lord Stantson. A very
knowledgeable horseman, he's a mature man with
a calm demeanour I thought might appeal to her.'
At Max's raised eyebrow, she said, 'Many young
ladies prefer to entrust their future to the steady
hand of an older gentleman, rather than risk all
with such dashing young rakes as *some* I might
mention! Mr Henshaw has also been pursuing her,

though I have to admit,' his aunt concluded, 'she has given neither man any encouragement.'

Henshaw! That was the man who'd been watching her in the paddock this morning, Max realised.

Aunt Grace sighed. 'Lady Denby is quite determined to get her settled before her own daughter Eugenia makes her début next spring. The poor girl's chances for making a good match will diminish drastically if she must share her Season with her stepsister, for Eugenia Whitman is nearly as wealthy as Miss Denby and far outshines her in youth, wit and beauty.'

Miss Denby was hardly an antidote, Max thought, indignant on her behalf before he recalled the great pains she'd been taking to ensure she created just the sort of negative impression his aunt was describing.

'If she seems so unwilling and unsuitable, I wonder that her stepmother keeps pushing her to wed. Why not let her remain at Denby Lodge, with her horses?'

'Well, she must marry *some time*,' Mrs Ransleigh said. 'What else is she to do? And she's very, very rich.'

'Which explains the gentlemen's pursuit of someone who gives them no encouragement.' Max had been feeling more hopeful, but some niggle of memory made him frown.

Having spent so much time away with the army, he hadn't visited London very often the last few years, but he vaguely recalled from his clubs the tattle that Henshaw was always pursuing some heiress or other. 'Is Henshaw a fortune hunter?'

Aunt Grace coloured. 'I should never describe him in such uncomplimentary terms. Mr Henshaw comes from a very good family and is perfectly respectable. If he wishes to marry a wealthy girl, such a desire is hardly unusual.'

Definitely a fortune hunter, Max concluded. 'Anyone else angling for the reluctant Miss Denby?'

His aunt fixed him with an assessing look. 'Did the young lady catch your interest?'

'Does she look like a lady who would attract me?' Max asked, feeling somehow guilty for disparaging a woman he admired even as he imbued his voice with the right note of disdain.

Fortunately, his previous flirts had always been acknowledged beauties, so the hopeful light in his aunt's eyes died. 'No,' she admitted.

'I merely found her amusingly unconventional.'

Aunt Grace laughed ruefully. 'She is certainly that! Poor Lady Denby! One can only sympathise with her difficulties in trying to get the girl married.'

Having discovered what he'd come for, he'd best take his leave, before Aunt Grace tried to spin some matrimonial web around *him*. 'I'll leave you to your dresser and return to my breakfast, which Cook is now preparing.'

'Go enjoy your fish, then. I'm so glad you stopped by. I do hope you'll stay long enough that

we can have a good visit, after all the guests leave.
Felicity and Jane are eager to have more from you
than a few hurried words.'

'I would like that.'

'Enjoy your day, then, my dear.'

Max kissed her hand. 'Enjoy your guests.'

After bowing himself out, Max walked towards
the study he and Alastair had turned into their
private parlour, running over in his mind what
he'd learned from Aunt Grace about Miss Denby.

So none but Stantson and Henshaw had set
their sights on the heiress. If Aunt Grace believed
both to be gentlemen, he had nothing to worry
about. He might enquire and see what Alastair
knew about the men, just to be sure, but unless
his cousin disclosed something to their discredit,
he had no reason to involve himself any further
in the matter of her future.

Though, as he'd assured his aunt, the lady was
nothing at all like the women who usually at-
tracted him, he had to admit to a feeling of regret
at the idea that he'd seen the last of Miss Denby,
the only unusual member of what was otherwise
a stultifyingly conventional gathering of females.

Several days later, while Alastair occupied
himself in the estate office, Max repaired to his
bench in the conservatory to while away the afternoon with some reading.

No sun gilded the tropical plants today, but the
morning's rain had left a soft mist dewing the

grass, greying the greens of the trees, shrubs and vines. Within the warm, heated expanse of the glasshouse, the soft swish of swaying palms and ferns and the sweet exotic scent of citrus and jasmine were infinitely soothing.

Alastair had informed him the previous evening that he'd heard the colonel of Max's former regiment had just returned from Paris. He'd recommended that Max speak with him about a position, sound advice Max meant to follow. The calm and beauty surrounding him here further lifted his spirits, filling him with the sense that much was still possible, if he were patient and persistent enough.

He was absorbed in his book when, some time later, a lavender scent tickled his nose. At the same moment, a soft 'Oh!' of surprise brought his head up, just in time to see Miss Denby halt abruptly a few yards away down the pathway.

A warm wave of anticipation suffused him, even as she hastily backed away. 'I'm so sorry, Mr Ransleigh! I didn't mean to disturb you!'

'Then you didn't come here to seek me out?' he asked, his tone teasing.

'Oh, no! I wouldn't have intruded on your privacy, sir. Your cousin Miss Felicity, who has become great friends with my stepsister, Eugenia, told her you and Mr Alastair would be away all day.'

'You truly are not pursuing me, then?' He

clapped a hand to his chest theatrically. 'What a blow to my self-esteem.'

For an instant, her brow furrowed in concern, before her ear caught his ironic tone and she grinned. 'I dare say your self-esteem can withstand the injury. But I told you I would not tease you and I meant it. I shall leave you to your book.'

It was only prudent that she leave at once...but he didn't want her to, not just yet.

'Since you've already interrupted my study, do stay for a moment, Miss Denby.'

She raised her eyebrows. 'For a chat that will become another of our little secrets?'

He grinned, pleased that she would joke with him. 'Exactly.' Come, sit.'

He motioned her to the bench...and found himself holding his breath, hoping she would come to him. Already his pulse had kicked up and all his senses sharpened, his body quickening at her nearness—which should have been warning enough that urging her to linger was not wise. He thrust the cautionary thought aside.

And then in a graceful swish of fabric, she sat down beside him. Max inhaled deeply as her faint lavender scent washed over him. It must be soap; he'd be astonished if she wore perfume. She was garbed against the misty chill in a cloak that covered her from head to toe, masking whatever hideous gown she'd selected along with, alas, that fine bosom. Even so, close up, he was able to drink in the fine texture of her face, the soft glow of her skin, the perfect shell of ear outlined by a mass of auburn-highlighted brown curls, tamed under her hat on this occasion. She tilted her face up to him and he lost himself in her extraordinary eyes, watching the golden centres shimmer within their dark-velvet depths.

Her lips, full and shapely, bore no trace of artificial gloss or colour. Would her mouth taste of wine, of apple, of mint?

Make conversation, he reminded himself, pulling back abruptly when he realised he'd been lowering his head toward their tempting surface. Devil's teeth, why did this young woman of no outstanding beauty evoke such a strong response from him?

'How goes your campaign?' he managed.

She made a moue of distaste, curving back the ripe fullness of her mouth. He wanted to trace the twin dimples that flanked it with his tongue.

'Not well, I'm afraid. As one might expect, all the men—the ones your aunt *invited*, in any event,' she added, tossing him a mischievous glance, 'are unmistakably gentlemen. I've considered each of them, but some are actively pursuing other ladies. Of the two pursuing *me*, neither is likely to refuse to marry, should I find some way to get myself compromised. Then there's the inhibiting presence of Lady Melross, whom I suspect Lady Claringdon inveigled to be present just to ensure that if any gentleman coaxed a maiden to stroll with him where she shouldn't, he'd be fairly caught—unless he was too dishonourable to do the proper thing and abandoned the girl to her ruin.' She sighed. 'Would that I might be!'

'Lady Melross is a dreadful woman, who delights in spreading bad news,' Max said feelingly. She'd been the first to trumpet the rumours of his disgrace, even before he reached London after leaving Vienna, then to whisper that his father had banished him. Though he knew she was zealous about reporting the failings of anyone of prominence whose missteps happened to reach her ears, it seemed to him she took a particularly malevolent interest in his affairs.

If he ever managed to secure a prominent position in government, hers would be the first name he would see struck from the invitation list at any function he attended.

Miss Denby drummed her fingers absently on the bench. 'I wish I could marry my horse. He's the most interesting male here, present company excepted, of course. Even if he has, ah, been deprived of the tools of his manhood.'

Surprised into a bark of laughter, Max shook his head. 'You really do say the most outlandish things for a lady.'

She shrugged. 'Because I'm not one, really. I wish I could convince all the pursing gentlemen of the fact that I'd make them a sadly deficient wife.'

With her seated there, tantalising his nose with her subtle lavender scent and his body by her nearness, Max thought that, for certain of a wife's duties, she would do admirably.

Before his thoughts could stampede down that lane, he reined himself back to more proper conversational paths. 'Still training your gelding every morning?'

'Yes.'

'In breeches and boots?' *A lovely image, that!*

'No more breeches and boots, alas; you and your cousin taught me to be more cautious. Though I still ride early, it's getting more difficult to avoid company. Lord Stantson has been pressing me to let him ride with me of a morning, but thus far has honoured my wishes when I firmly decline. He's a fine enough gentleman, but I've heard he came here specifically looking for a second wife. Since I'm not angling for the position, I'm trying to give him no encouragement.'

Wrinkling her nose in distaste, she continued, 'Mr Henshaw, however, not only requires no encouragement, he positively refuses to be *dis*couraged! He's turned up each of the last two mornings, despite my continued insistence that I prefer to ride alone. How am I to train Sultan properly, with him interrupting us?'

For a moment, her eyes focused unseeing on the glasshouse wall and she shivered. 'Though I was garbed in a stiflingly proper habit, he seems to be always *staring* at me. I don't care for his expression when he does so, either—as if I were a favourite pudding he meant to devour.'

Max frowned. She might have worn a proper habit every day since that first one, but she hadn't been the morning he'd seen Henshaw watching her. How close a look at her had the man got? Close enough to get an eyeful of the shapely form he and Alastair had so appreciated?

If so, Max could hardly fault any man for staring at her like a 'pudding one meant to devour'. Which didn't reduce one whit the strong desire rising in him to blacken both Henshaw's eyes for making her feel uncomfortable.

'He insisted on riding with me, despite the fact that I was quite obviously trying to work with Sultan,' Miss Denby continued. 'Honestly, he possesses terrible hands and the worst seat I've ever been forced to observe. I've taken to riding even earlier to avoid him.'

'I've never seen him astride, only observed his...remarkably inventive dress. He must make his tailors very rich.'

She chuckled. 'A man milliner indeed. One would think, with his exacting tastes in garments, sheer disgust over my atrocious gowns would be enough to dissuade him from pursuing me.'

She looked up at him, smiling faintly, those great dark eyes inviting him to share her amusement. Her lavender scent wrapped itself around him like a silken scarf, pulling him closer. He wanted to trace the scent to its origin, lick it from her neck and ears and the hollows of the collarbones he'd seen that day she'd ridden in an open-collared shirt and breeches.

As he gazed raptly, her dark eyes widened and her smile faded. She seemed as mesmerised as he, her lips parting slightly, giving him the tiniest glimpse of pink tongue within the warmth of her mouth.

Desire shot through him, pulsing in his veins, curling his fingers with the itch to cup her chin and taste her.

'Well,' she said, her voice a bit breathless, 'I suppose I should leave you now, lest someone come by and see us. Unless…' she smiled tremulously, brushing a curl back from her forehead as her cheeks pinked '…you'd like to…reconsider my proposition?'

Her cloak fell open at that movement. Beneath the fabric of another overtrimmed, pea-green gown, he saw the rapid rise and fall of her breasts as her breathing accelerated.

His certainly had. All over his body, things were accelerating and rising and pulsing. The need to kiss her, learn the taste of her mouth, the contour of her ears and shoulders and the hollow of her throat, thrummed in his blood. His gaze wandered back to the mesmerizing shimmer of gold in her eyes and halted.

In his head, that persistent fly of temptation buzzed louder, almost drowning out good sense.

Almost.

It took him a full minute to shoo it away and find his voice.

'A tempting offer. But I fear I must still decline.'

Despite the words, he couldn't make himself stand, bow, put an end to this interlude, as prudence demanded.

She, too, remained motionless, her eyes studying his, the current of attraction pulsing between them almost palpable. As he watched intently, the embarrassment she'd displayed upon repeating her offer changed to uncertainty and then, yes, he was certain, to desire. Confirming that assessment, slowly she leaned towards him and tilted her face up, bringing her lips tantalisingly close.

Max forced himself to remain motionless, while every nerve and sense screamed at him to lower his head and take her mouth. In some distant corner of his brain, honour and common sense was nattering that he should move away, end this before it began.

But he couldn't. He would not cross that slight boundary and touch her first, but, shutting out the little voice insisting this was madness, he waited, aflame with anticipation, confident she would close the distance between them and kiss him.

Her eyelashes feathered shut. His eyes closed, too, as her warm breath washed over him, the first tentative wave from an incoming tide of pleasure.

Just as his eager body whispered 'now, now',

she straightened abruptly and scooted backwards on the bench.

'I—I should go,' she said unsteadily.

Max shook his head, trying to drown out the buzzy little voice that urged him to lure her into remaining.

And he could do it; he knew he could.

Over the protest of every outraged sense, he wrestled his desire back under control. 'That would be wisest…if not nearly so pleasant.'

'Wisest…yes,' she repeated and belatedly bobbed to her feet. 'Thank you for the, ah, chat. Good day, Mr Ransleigh.'

He stood as well and bowed. 'Good day, Miss Denby.'

Regretfully, while his body yammered and scolded at him like a disgruntled housewife cheated by a market vendor, he watched her retreat down the pathway. Just before turning the corner to exit the glasshouse, she halted.

Looking back over her shoulder, she said softly, in tones of wonder, 'You tempt me too, you know.'

A surge of delight and pure masculine satisfaction blazed through him. Before he could reply, she turned and hurried out.

He jumped to his feet and paced after her. Fortunately, by the time he reached the door to the glasshouse, sanity had returned.

Good grief, if he couldn't rein in his reaction to her, he'd better avoid her altogether, lest he find himself being quickstepped to the altar. Had he not committed idiocies enough for one lifetime?

So he made himself stand there, watching her trim figure retreat through the mist down the pathway back to the house. But as she took the turn leading to the drawing-room terrace, a man stepped out.

Henshaw.

Max gritted his teeth. Frowning, he watched the exchange, too far away to hear their voices, as Henshaw bowed to Miss Denby's curtsy. Offered his arm, which she declined with a shake of her head and a motion of her hand in the direction of the stables. Henshaw, giving a dismissive wave, offered his arm again, which, after a few more unintelligible words, she reluctantly accepted.

They'd just set off on the path to the house when Alastair came striding up. Putting a hand to his forehead, he peered into the distance and declared, 'That looks like the chap who was watching Miss Denby ride the other morning.'

'It is. David Henshaw. Do you know him?'

'Ah, yes, that's why he looked familiar. He's a member at Brooks's. Too concerned with the cut of his coat and the style of his cravat for my taste. He the front runner for Miss Denby's affections?'

'Not if she has anything to say about it.'

'Ah, had another little chat with the lady, did you? Sure you don't fancy her for yourself?'

He made himself give Alastair a withering look. 'Does she look like a woman I'd fancy?' he drawled, feeling more uncomfortable about uttering the disparaging remark this time, after he'd practically devoured her on the greenhouse bench, than when he'd been trying to throw Aunt Grace off the scent.

'Not in your usual style,' Alastair allowed, 'but there is *something* about her. Devilishly arousing in her own way…like when riding astride in breeches! What a shame she's an innocent; don't forget, my friend, that the price for tasting *that* morsel is marriage.'

'So I keep reminding myself,' Max muttered, grimly aware that the moment she'd sat down beside him, his instincts for self-preservation had gone missing.

'I'm not surprised Henshaw is on the scent,' Alastair continued. 'The latest word at the London clubs was he's run so far into debt, he can't even go back to his town house for fear of meeting the bailiffs. The Denby girl's fat dowry would put all his financial problems to rest.'

Max had never given much thought to the fact that a husband gained control over all his wife's wealth, but after hearing Miss Denby lament the fact, such an arrangement now struck him as little short of robbery. 'Doesn't seem quite sporting that he could float himself down River Tick and then use her money to paddle out of danger.'

Alastair shrugged. 'It's done all the time.'

The fact that it was didn't make it any more

palatable, Max thought. 'Does Aunt Grace know about Henshaw's current monetary difficulties?'

'I don't know. But he's been angling to marry a fortune ever since he came up from Cambridge, so there's nothing new about it, except perhaps the degree of urgency. Come now, enough about Henshaw. The man's a pretentious, ill-dressed bore. How about a game of billiards before dinner? If any guests approach the room, I'll have Wendell scare them off.'

Absently Max agreed, but as they walked back to the house, he couldn't get out of his mind the image of Henshaw compelling Miss Denby to take his arm.

Were Henshaw's circumstances difficult enough that he'd be willing to coerce an heiress into matrimony?

Most likely, he was letting his dislike for the dandified Henshaw colour his perceptions. The man *was* a gentleman of good family and Aunt Grace would never have invited him if there were any doubt about his integrity.

However, just to be safe, he'd ride out early tomorrow and warn Miss Denby to be on her guard with him.

Feeling better about the matter, he followed his cousin into the house and focused his mind on the best strategy for beating Alastair for the third evening in a row.

Chapter Six

The next morning, Max rose before dawn and headed to the stables before even a glimmer of dawn lightened the treeline, determined not to risk missing Miss Denby. But though he trotted his mount up and down the stable lane for so long that the grooms must have wondered what in the world he was doing, she did not appear.

Perhaps she was being prudent, abstaining from her morning ride so as not to be pounced upon by Henshaw. Alastair had told him over billiards the previous evening that his mother said the party was wrapping up; Jane had boasted to him of its successes, two matrons having managed to get offers for their daughters. Felicity, she added, had made a great new friend of Miss Denby's stepsister, Eugenia Whitman, and was giddy about the prospect of sharing her upcoming Season with the girl.

The same Miss Whitman who, his Aunt Grace had informed him, 'far outshines her stepsister in youth, wit and beauty'. Max still resented that comment on Miss Denby's behalf.

In any event, it appeared she would soon be relieved of Mr Henshaw's pursuit, Max concluded, turning his probably puzzled mount to the stable and returning to the house. But what of next spring? Would she, as she feared, have to suffer through another Season, dragged off to participate in a round of social activities for which she had no inclination, forced to neglect her beloved horses?

What a shame her childhood beau Harry was so far away. She deserved to marry a man who appreciated her unique talents and interests, who supported rather than discouraged her desire to carry on her father's legacy.

He toyed with the idea of trying to seek her out and bid her goodbye, but couldn't come up with a way to do so that would not shock the gathering by revealing she was well acquainted with a man she wasn't supposed to know. Perhaps, once he had his life sorted out, he could call on her in London, maybe even seek her out at Denby Lodge and purchase some of her horses.

With Alastair away on another of his lord-of-the-manor errands, Max fetched his book and headed for what might be his last afternoon hidden away at the conservatory. He'd rather miss the place, whose warm scented air and soothing palm murmurs he would probably never have discovered had he not been forced to vacate the house. With the guests soon departing, he and Alastair would have free run of the estate again.

He halted just inside the threshold of the glasshouse, inhaling the tangy-sweet scent of jasmine that seemed always to hang in the air, insubstantial as a whisper. He was about to proceed to his usual bench when a murmur of voices reached his ears, the words as indistinct as the gurgling of a brook over rocks.

He halted, trying to identify the speakers. Aunt Grace, conferring with the gardener? Or one of the affianced couples, stealing one last tryst before the party broke up?

In either case, his presence would be an impediment. He was silently retracing his steps when a feminine voice reached his ears, its increased volume making the words suddenly clear.

'Mr Henshaw, I *do* appreciate the honour of your offer, but I'm absolutely convinced we will not suit!'

Miss Denby's voice, Max realised, halting in mid-step. Had Henshaw tracked her there?

His first impulse was to set off in her direction, but she'd probably not thank him for interfering. Still, though he felt confident she could handle her disappointed suitor without his assistance, some deep-seated protective instinct made him linger.

After a masculine murmur whose words he could not make out, Miss Denby said, 'No, I shall not change my mind. You must admit, sir, that I have tried in every possible way to discourage you, so my refusal can hardly come as a surprise. You will oblige me by leaving now.'

'Waiting here for someone else, were you?' Henshaw replied, his angry tones now comprehensible. 'Max Ransleigh, perhaps? He'd never marry you. Despite his father's banishment, he has money enough, and if he ever does wed, it will be a woman from a prominent society family. In any event, his taste runs to sophisticated beauties, which you, I'm forced to say, are not. Nor are you getting any younger. If you've any hopes at all of marrying, you'd better accept my offer.'

Why, the mercenary little weasel, Max thought, incensed. Only the certainty that Miss Denby would not appreciate having him witness this embarrassing scene kept him from setting off down the pathway to plant a fist squarely on the jaw of that overdressed excuse for a gentleman.

'You're quite correct,' she was saying. 'I possess none of the virtues and talents a gentleman looks for in a wife. As you so kindly noted, I'm hardly a beauty and am hopeless at making the sort of polite chat that makes up society conversation. Worst of all, I fear I have no fashion sense. You can do so much better, Mr Henshaw! Why not wait until the Season and find yourself a more suitable bride?'

Despite his ire, Max had to grin. Had any female ever so thoroughly disparaged herself to a prospective suitor?

'I'm afraid, my dear, the press of creditors don't allow me the luxury of waiting. Though admittedly you possess neither the style nor the talents I would wish for in a wife, you do have...a certain charm of person. And wealth, of which I'm in desperate need.'

No style? No talent? His mirth rapidly dissipating, Max reconsidered the prospect of cornering Henshaw, shaking him like a dog with a ferret and then tossing him out of the glasshouse like the refuse he was.

But alerting them to his presence would not only distress Miss Denby, it might give the thwarted suitor an opportunity to claim he'd caught *Max and Miss Denby* alone together. His self-protective instincts on full alert now that Miss Denby wasn't within touching distance, Max didn't want to risk that.

His decision not to intervene, however, wavered when he heard a sharp, cracking sound that could only be a slap.

'Keep your hands to yourself,' Miss Denby cried. 'You followed me without my leave or encouragement. If you will not quit this place, then I will do so. Since I do not anticipate seeing you again before the party ends, I will say goodbye, Mr Henshaw.'

'Not so hasty, my dear. It might not be an arrangement either of us want, but you *will* marry me.'

'Let go of my arm! It's useless for you to detain me, for I promise you, nothing on earth would ever induce me to marry you!'

'I'd hoped you would consent willingly, but if you will not, you force me to employ…other measures. Before you leave this spot, you'll be fit to be no one's wife but mine.'

At that threat, Max abandoned discretion and set off at a run. If he hadn't already been prepared to tear Henshaw limb from limb, the scuffling, panting sounds of a struggle that reached him as he rounded the last corner, followed by the unmistakable rip of fabric, had him ready to do murder.

Seconds later, he lunged over a potted fern to find Henshaw trying to pin a wildly struggling Miss Denby down on the bench, his free hand clawing up her skirts. As a clay pot fell over and shattered, Henshaw looked up, his hands stilling.

The smirk on his face and the lust in his eyes turned to surprise, then alarm as he recognised Max. But before Max could seize him, Miss Denby, taking advantage of Henshaw's distraction, kneed him in the groin, then caught him full on the nose with a roundhouse left jab of which Gentleman Jackson would have been proud.

Howling, Henshaw released Miss Denby and staggered backwards, one hand on his breeches front, the other holding his nose. Blood oozing through his fingers, he snarled, 'Bitch! You'll regret that!'

Max grabbed him by the arm and slammed him against the wall, regrettably with less force than he would have liked, but he didn't want to break a glass panel in Aunt Grace's conservatory.

Securing him against it with a stranglehold on his cravat, Max growled, 'Miss Denby will not regret her rejection. But you, varlet, will regret this episode for the rest of your life unless you do exactly what I say. You will apologise to Miss Denby, then pack your bag and leave immediately, before I tell the world and Lady Melross how you tried to attack an innocent and unwilling young lady.' Giving Henshaw's cravat a final twist, he released the man.

Henshaw shook his arms free and retreated several steps, trying to repair his ruined cravat before giving it up as hopeless. 'You dare to threaten me?' he blustered. 'Who will believe you? A flagrant womaniser, sent away from Vienna in disgrace, disowned by your own father!'

'Who will believe me?' Max echoed, his voice silky-soft. 'Your hostess, my aunt, perhaps? Or Lady Melross, seeing your elegant attire as it now appears?'

Fury and desperation might have briefly clouded Henshaw's judgement, but the reference to his dishevelled clothing snapped him back to reality. Obviously realising he could not hope to prevail over the nephew of his hostess, especially in his present incriminating state of disorder, he clamped his lips shut and looked down the pathway, eyeing the exit.

More concerned with assisting the lady, Max

resigned himself to letting him go. 'Are you un-harmed, Miss Denby?' he asked, stepping past Henshaw to her side.

'Y-yes,' she replied, her voice breaking a little.

The path to the doorway free, Henshaw backed cautiously away, his wary gaze fixed on Max. After retreating a safe distance, he tossed back, 'I won't forget this, Ransleigh. I'll have retribution some day…and on the bitch, too.'

'You don't follow instructions very well,' Max said softly, an icy contempt filling him. 'Now I'm going to have to thrash you like the cur you are.'

But before he could take a step, abandoning any pretence of dignity, Henshaw bolted for the door. Much as he would have liked to give chase and thrash the man, Max concluded his more urgent duty was to see to Miss Denby, who stood trembling by the bench, holding together the ripped edges of her bodice.

Her cloak had fallen off during the struggle and her pelisse, now lacking its buttons, gaped open over her white-knuckled hands. Her beautiful dark eyes, wide with shock and outrage, looked stricken.

Max cursed under his breath, wishing he'd tossed the bounder through the glass wall after all. 'I entered a few minutes ago and heard voices, but didn't realise what was transpiring until…it was almost too late. I'm so sorry I didn't intervene earlier and spare you that indignity. Say the word and I'll track down Henshaw and give him the drubbing he deserves.'

'Beating him further will serve no useful purpose,' she said, attempting a smile, which wobbled badly. 'Though I might wish to hit him again myself. He has ruined one of my best ugly gowns.'

Thankfully, some colour was returning to her pale cheeks and her voice sounded stronger, so Max might not have to pursue the man and rearrange his skeleton after all. 'You did quite a capital job on your first round, though I don't believe you succeeded in breaking his nose, more's the pity. Who taught you to box? That roundhouse jab was worthy of a professional.'

'Harry. He took lessons with Jackson in London while he was at Winchester. Satisfying as it was to land the blow exactly where I wished— on both parts of his anatomy—that won't help my biggest problem now, which is how to get back to my chamber and out of this gown. My stepmother would have palpitations if she saw me like this. Not that I would mind being ruined, but I should be indignant if anyone were to try to force me to marry *Henshaw*.'

'That sorry excuse for a man?' Max said in disgust. 'I should think not.'

'A sorry excuse indeed, but stronger than I anticipated,' she said, looking down at the fingers clutching her torn bodice. 'I thought I could handle him, but…' She took a shuddering breath, as if shaken by the evidence of how close she'd come to being ravaged. 'If only *you* had accepted my first offer! I'm certain you would have c-compromised me much more g-genteelly.'

She was trying to put on a brave face, but tears had begun slipping down her cheeks and she started to tremble again.

Making a vow to seek out Henshaw wherever he went to ground and pummel him senseless, Max abandoned discretion and drew Miss Denby into his arms. 'If *I* were to compromise you, I would at least make sure you *enjoyed* it,' he said, trying for a teasing tone as he cradled her, gently chafing her hands and trying to use his warmth to heat her chilled body. 'And it would have been done with much more expertise and finesse. Like this,' he said and kissed just the freckled tip of her nose.

The last time he'd encountered her in the conservatory, he'd burned to plunder her mouth and let his lips discover every wonder of nose, chin and eyelids. As indignant as his aunt would be that a guest of the Ransleighs had been assaulted, all he wished for now was to erase from her memory the outrage that had just been perpetrated against her.

To his relief, she gave herself into his hands, snuggling with a broken little gasp against his chest. For long moments, he simply held her, one finger gently stroking her cheek, until at last the tremors eased and she pulled back a bit, still resting in the circle of his arms.

'You do compromise a lady most genteelly,' she said. 'Thank you, Mr Ransleigh. I shall never forget your kind assistance.'

'Max,' he corrected with a smile. 'I should be honoured to have you call on me at any time.'

Before she could reply, a loud shriek split the air. *'Miss Denby!'* a shrill female voice exclaimed. 'Whatever are you about?'

A sense of impending disaster stabbing in his gut, Max looked over Miss Denby's head to see Lady Melross hurrying toward them.

Chapter Seven

Clutching the ragged edges of her bodice, Caroline stared in horror as Lady Melross marched up to them, her eyes widening with shock, then malicious glee as she perceived Caro wrapped in Ransleigh's arms, her bodice in ruins.

A sick feeling invaded Caro's stomach. How could things have gone so hideously wrong? In Lady Melross's accusing eyes, Mr Ransleigh, who had protected and comforted her, must now appear to be the one who'd tried to ravish her. And the old harpy would lose no time in trumpeting the news to all and sundry.

'This isn't what you think!' Caro cried, furious, frustrated, knowing the denial was hopeless. Oh, that she might run after Henshaw and rake her fingers down his deceitful face!

Ransleigh had never wanted to compromise her. Now, through the hapless intervention of the detestable Henshaw, the scandal he'd scrupulously avoided would fall full upon him.

It was all her fault…and she couldn't think of a single way to stop it.

'Not what I think?' Lady Melross echoed. 'Gracious, Miss Denby, do you believe me a simpleton, unable to comprehend what I see right before my eyes? No wonder a little bird told me I might find something interesting in the conservatory.'

'A little bird?' Caro echoed. 'What do you mean?'

'Oh, I had a note…from someone who knew about your rendezvous. Or maybe you sent it yourself, Miss Caroline?'

'Henshaw,' Caro whispered, her eyes pleading with Max, who'd already stepped away from her, his face going grim and shuttered the moment he saw Lady Melross charging toward them down the glasshouse path, Lady Caringdon trailing behind.

Henshaw must have sent the note, wanting Lady Melross to find them with her gown in tatters, ensuring a scandal public enough that they'd be forced to marry.

Surely Max Ransleigh understood that?

'You, Ransleigh,' Lady Melross said, turning to Max, 'I wouldn't have expected something this lacking in taste and finesse…although after Vienna, I suppose maybe I should have. What a sly thing you turned out to be, Miss Denby,' she continued as she snatched up Caroline's cloak and tossed it over her shoulders. 'There, you're decent again.'

Lady Caringdon stared at them both accusingly. 'Aren't you a rum one, Ransleigh, sneaking around, keeping your distance from the company while you plotted to seduce an innocent right under the nose of her chaperone! And you, young lady, have got exactly what you deserve!'

'Indeed!' Lady Melross crowed. 'Don't you understand, you stupid girl? Ruining yourself with Ransleigh won't earn you the elevated position in society you expect, for his father isn't even receiving him! While you were immured in the country at that dreary horse farm, he was creating a scandal—'

'Lady Melross,' Max broke in on the lady's tirade, 'that is quite enough. Abuse me as you will, but I cannot allow you to harass Miss Denby. She has suffered a shock and should return to the house at once to recover. Miss Denby,' he continued, turning to Caroline, his voice gentling, 'will you allow these ladies to escort you back to your chamber? We will talk of this later.'

'I should like to settle it now—' Caro said.

'No, in this at least, Ransleigh has the right of it,' Lady Melross broke in. 'You cannot stand there chatting in that disgrace of a garment! Come along, both of you. Though I cannot imagine what you could say that might excuse your behavior, Ransleigh, before you present yourself to Lady

Denby, you'd best go and make yourself respectable.'

'Perhaps it would be better if I talk with Stepmother first,' Caroline conceded. Poor Lady Denby would be close to hysterics if the outcry about this disaster reached her before Caro did. She'd need to explain and calm her down before Max called on her.

Lady Caringdon sniffed. 'Poor Diana. What a tawdry, embarrassing predicament—and with dear Eugenia set to make her bow next spring! Dreadful!'

'Dreadful indeed,' Lady Melross said, sounding not at all regretful. 'Come along now, and wrap that cloak tight about you, miss. I shouldn't want to shock any of the *proper* young ladies we might encounter on the way. Doubtless Lady Denby will summon you later, Ransleigh. Perhaps you'd better go and acquaint your aunt with the débâcle you've created in the midst of her party.'

'Don't worry,' Ransleigh said to Caro, ignoring Lady Melross's disparaging remarks. 'Get some rest. I'll see you later and make everything right.' Giving her an encouraging smile, he stepped back to allow Lady Melross to take her arm.

Having a sudden change of heart, Caroline almost reached out to snag his sleeve and beg him to walk in with her. If only they could face Lady Denby now, together, and explain what had happened, surely they could sort it out and keep the dreadful Lady Melross from spreading her malicious account of the events!

But she suspected Ransleigh wouldn't deign to explain himself with Lady Melross present, and there was no chance whatsoever that the lady would let herself be manoeuvred out of escorting her victim into the house.

'I will call on Lady Denby soon,' he told Caro, then moved aside to let them pass.

'Speak with me first!' she tossed back as, Lady Caringdon seizing her other arm, the two women half-led, half-dragged her down the path.

They marched her into the house and up the stairs, relentless as gaolers. Initially they peppered her with questions, but her refusal to provide any details eventually convinced them she intended to remain silent.

With a final warning that it was useless to turn mute now, as her character was already ruined, they ignored her and spent the rest of the transit speculating about how devastated Lady Denby and Mrs Ransleigh would be and how fast the scandalous news would spread.

While they chattered, Caro's mind raced furiously. Should she ask Max Ransleigh to seek out Henshaw, drag him in so they might jointly accuse him? Was Henshaw still at Barton Abbey to be accused?

Trapped between the two dragons, she had no way of determining that. Should she try to explain

immediately to Lady Denby, or wait until after
she'd consulted with Mr Ransleigh?

She had only a short time to figure out what *she*
wanted, while her whole life and future hinged on
her making the right decision.

When she reached her rooms and her erstwhile
'rescuers' discovered neither her stepmother nor
her sister was present, they finally stopped plagu-
ing her and rushed off. Doubtless anxious to com-
pete over who could convey the interesting news
to the most people the fastest, Caro thought sar-
donically.

She hoped her stepmother would not be one of
those so informed, vastly preferring to break the
dismal story herself. In any event, Lady Denby's
absence gave her the opportunity to summon Dulcie and change before the tattered evidence of the
disaster could further upset her stepmother. Reassuring her maid, who gasped in alarm upon seeing her in the ruined gown, that she was quite
unharmed and would explain later, Caro sent her
off to dispose of the garment.

Watching the girl carry out the shreds, Caro
smiled grimly. It certainly wasn't the way she
would have chosen to do it, but the escapade in
the glasshouse *had* effectively ruined her. At least
now she'd be able to purchase gowns that didn't
make her wince when she saw her image in a mir-
ror. With that heartening thought, she scrawled

a note asking Mr Ransleigh to meet her in Lady Denby's sitting room at his earliest convenience.

As she waited for her stepmother to return, she tried to corral the thoughts galloping about in her mind like colts set loose in a spring meadow. How could she turn Henshaw's despicable conduct to best advantage, managing the scandal so she would be able to return to Denby Lodge and her horses, while leaving Mr Ransleigh's good name unblemished?

Only one thought truly dismayed her: that having heard Lady Melross testify that she'd received a note bidding her come to the conservatory, Max might think, in blatant disregard of his wishes, *she* had arranged for Lady Melross to find them, trapping him with treachery into compromising her after persuasion had failed.

Trapping herself?

How to avoid that fate? Too unsettled to remain seated, she paced the room. In the aftermath of Henshaw's unexpected attack, her still-jangled nerves were hampering her ability to think clearly. The bald truth was she'd underestimated the man, dismissed him as a self-indulgent weakling she could easily handle.

It shook her to the core to admit that, had Max Ransleigh not rushed to her rescue, she probably could not have successfully resisted Henshaw.

How understanding Max had been, lending her his warmth and strength as she had struggled to compose herself. Bringing her back from the horror of what might have been to a reassuring normalcy with his gentle teasing. Renewed gratitude suffused her.

They must find some way out of this conundrum. She refused to repay his generosity by trapping him in a marriage neither of them wanted.

But when she recalled his parting words, a deep sense of unease filled her.

'I'll make everything right,' he'd said. Initially, she'd thought he meant to track down Henshaw and force him to confess his guilt. However, if Henshaw had already scuttled away from Barton Abbey, leaving Max bearing the blame for her disgrace, Ransleigh's sense of honour might very well force him into making her an offer.

And that wouldn't do at all. For one, he'd told her quite plainly he had no wish to marry and she could think of few things worse than being shackled to an uninterested husband. The image of her cousin Elizabeth came forcefully to mind.

Nor did she want to cobble her future to a man with whom she had little in common, whose wit engaged her but who agitated and discomforted her every time she was near him, filling her with powerful desires she had no idea how to manage.

Before she could analyse the matter any further, a rapid patter of footsteps in the hallway and the buzz of raised voices announced the imminent return of her stepmother.

Praying Lady Melross had not accompanied her, Caro braced herself for the onslaught.

A moment later, the door flew open and Lady Denby burst into the room, Eugenia at her elbow. 'Is it true?' her stepsister demanded. 'Did Mr Ransleigh truly…debauch you in the conservatory, as Lady Melross claims?'

'He did not.'

'Oh, thank heavens!' Lady Denby exclaimed. 'That dreadful woman! I knew it had to be naught but a malicious hum!'

'There was an…altercation,' Caro allowed. 'But events did not unfold as Lady Melross supposed.'

'Surely she didn't find you wrapped in Mr Ransleigh's arms, your gown in disarray, your bodice torn?' Eugenia asked.

'My gown had been damaged, but it was not—'

'Oh, no!' Eugenia interrupted with a wail. 'Then you *are* ruined. Indeed, we are *both* ruined! I shall never have my Season in London now!' Clapping a hand to her mouth, she burst into tears and rushed into her adjoining room, slamming the door behind her.

Lady Denby stood pale-faced and trembling, tears tracking down her own cheeks as she looked at Caro reproachfully. 'Oh, Caro,' she said faintly, 'how *could* you? Even if you had no concern about your own future, how could you jeopardise Eugenia's?'

'Please, ma'am, sit and let me explain. Truly, it is not as bad as you think. I'm certain that virtually nothing the detestable Lady Melross told you is accurate.'

Lady Denby allowed herself to be shown to a seat and accepted a glass of sherry, which she sipped while Caro related what had actually transpired. When she got to the part about how Mr Ransleigh's timely arrival had prevented Henshaw from overpowering her, Lady Denby cried out and leapt to her feet, wrapping Caro in her arms.

'Oh, my poor dear, how awful for you! Bless Mr Ransleigh for having the courage to intervene.'

'I owe him a great debt,' Caro agreed, settling her stepmother back in her chair. 'Which is why we need to somehow stop Lady Melross from circulating the falsehood that he compromised me. I can hardly repay Mr Ransleigh's gallantry by forcing him to offer for me, a girl he hardly knows. That would not be fair, would it?'

'It doesn't seem right,' Lady Denby admitted. 'But if you don't marry *someone*…how are we to salvage anything? And my dear, the truth is, this scandal could ruin Eugenia's Season as well!'

'Surely not! She's not even a Denby! Once Lady Gilford and Mrs Ransleigh learn the truth, I'm certain they will enlist their friends to ensure my difficulties do not reflect badly on my stepsister.'

That hope seemed to reassure Lady Denby, for she nodded. 'Yes, perhaps you are right. Grace and Jane would think it monstrous for poor Eugenia to suffer for Henshaw's villainy. But how are we to salvage your position, my dear?'

'I don't know yet,' Caro evaded, guiltily aware that she had no desire to 'salvage' it. 'Will you allow me to discuss this alone with Mr Ransleigh first, before he speaks with you? I expect him at any moment.'

'Very well,' Lady Denby agreed with a sigh. 'It's all so very distressing! I must go and comfort Eugenia.'

After giving her a final hug, Lady Denby walked out. Knowing that she would be meeting Max Ransleigh again any moment set every nerve on edge.

The fact that, despite her agitation, an insidious little voice was whispering that wedding Max might not be so disastrous after all filled her with a panicky agitation that drove her once again to pace the room.

From the very first, he'd affected her differently than any other man she'd ever met. Being near him filled her with a tingling physical immediacy, a consciousness of her breasts and lips and body she'd never previously experienced.

Yesterday in the conservatory, that strange but powerful attraction had urged her to touch him, kiss him, feel his mouth and hands on her. Thought and reason vaporised into heat and need, into a burning, irresistible desire to know him, to let him know her. She'd *craved* that contact with a force and single-mindedness she would never have believed possible.

Even with the threat of the Curse hanging over her, she wasn't sure she would have been able to bring her rioting senses under control and walk away if he'd made any move at all to entice her to stay.

The power Henshaw had exerted over her while she struggled to escape him had frightened her, but what Max inspired in her was even more terrifying…because she hadn't wanted to escape it. Indeed, recalling him poised motionless on the bench, inviting her kiss, making no move to cajole or entice, letting her own desire propel her to him, was more coercive than any force he could have employed.

She'd been as powerfully in his thrall as…as her cousin Elizabeth had once been to Spencer Russell, the reprobate she'd married. The man who'd charmed and wed and betrayed, and almost bankrupted her cousin before a fortuitous racing accident had brought to an end Elizabeth's humiliating existence as a disdained and abandoned wife.

Caro did not want to be ensnared by an emotion that dazzled her out of her common sense, nor be held captive by a lust so strong it paralysed will and smothered rational thinking.

Just as she reached that conclusion, a rap sounded at the door.

Her heartbeat stopped, then recommenced at a rapid pace as a stinging shock rippled through her, setting her stomach churning. Wiping her suddenly sweaty palms on her gown, she took a deep breath and walked to open the door.

Chapter Eight

A<small>s</small> expected, Max Ransleigh stood on the threshold. Looking solemn, he took her hand and kissed her fingers.

A second wave of sensation blazed through her. Clenching her fists and jaw to try to dampen the effect, she mumbled an incoherent welcome and led him to a chair. Though she was still too agitated to want to sit, knowing he would not unless she did so, she forced herself into the place opposite him.

'I'm so sorry to have involved you in this,' she began before he could speak. 'Though I did invite you to compromise me, I hope you realise I had no part in setting up the situation in the conservatory today! I would never have gone behind your back to create a scandal in which you'd already assured me you wanted no part.'

'I believe you,' he said, calming her fears on

that matter, at least. 'I expect it was Henshaw who sent Lady Melross the note, wanting her to find you with him in a state dishevelled enough to ensure you'd be coerced to wed him.'

'Thank you. I would hate to have you think I'd use you so shabbily. Lady Denby has agreed to let me speak with you privately before she comes in, so shall we discuss what is to be done?'

'Let us do so. You did get your wish, you know. You are quite effectively ruined.'

'Yes, I know. I certainly didn't enjoy being mauled by Henshaw, but it might turn out for the best. We need only tell people what really happened, establishing that you had no part in it, and all will be well. I'll still be ruined, but with Henshaw showing his character to be so despicable, no one could fault me for refusing to marry him.'

Frowning, Ransleigh shook his head. 'I'm afraid that is not the case. Society would still believe the only way to salvage your reputation would be for you to marry your seducer. However deplorable his present conduct, Henshaw was *born* a gentleman, so much would be forgiven as long as you end up wed.'

'But that's appalling!' Caro cried. 'The *victim* is expected to marry her attacker?'

'Rightly or wrongly, the blame usually attaches itself to the female. But it won't come to that. Accusing Henshaw isn't possible; he's already left Barton Abbey. Any evidence that might confirm he was your attacker—bloody nose, ruined cravat—will have been put to rights by the time I could run him to ground. Since he can now have no doubt that you'd refuse to marry him, he has no reason to corroborate the truth, especially since Lady Melross is circulating a version of events that relieves him of responsibility. Indeed, he will probably think it a fine revenge to see me blamed for his transgressions.'

Caro nodded, distressed but not surprised that Ransleigh's assessment of Henshaw's character matched her own. 'I imagine he would, though I have no intention of allowing him the satisfaction. Whether he admits his guilt or not, I still intend to accuse him. Why should you, who intervened only to help me, suffer for his loathsome behaviour?'

'I don't think accusing him would be wise.'

Puzzled, Caro frowned at him. 'Why not?'

'You were discovered in *my* embrace. I'm the son of an earl who exerts a powerful influence in government; you are the orphaned daughter of a rural baron. If you accuse Henshaw, who will justly claim he was in his room, preparing to depart when Lady Melross found us, there will be many who will whisper that I coerced you into naming another man to cover up my own bad conduct. Lady Melross in particular will be delighted to embellish the details of my supposed ravishment and assert such behaviour is only to be expected after my…previous scandal.'

'You really think no one would believe me if I tell the truth?' Caro asked incredulously.

'What, allow such a salacious act to be blamed on some insignificant member of the *ton* rather than titillate the masses by accusing the well-known son of a very important man? No, I don't think anyone would believe you. I can see the scurrilous cartoons in the London print-shop windows now,' he finished bitterly.

'But that's so…unfair!' she burst out.

He laughed shortly, no humour in the sound. 'I have learned of late just how unfair life can be. Believe me, I like the solution as little as you do, but with your reputation destroyed and the blame for it laid at my door, the only way to salvage your position is for you to marry me.'

Alarmed as she was by his conclusion, Caro felt a flash of admiration for his willingness to do what he saw as right. 'A noble offer and I do honour you for it. But I think it ridiculous to allow society's expectations—based on a lie!—to force us into something neither of us desire.'

'Miss Denby, let me remind you that you are *ruined*,' he repeated, his tone now edged with an undercurrent of anger and frustration. 'Fail to marry and you risk being exiled altogether from respectable society. Being cast out of the company of those with whom you have always associated is not a pleasant condition, as I have good reason to know.'

'First, I've never really "associated" with the *ton*,' she countered, 'and, as I've assured you several times, polite society's opinion does not matter to me. Certainly not when compared with losing the freedom to live life how—and with whom—I choose.'

'But Lady Denby does live and move in that society and Miss Whitman's future may well depend upon its opinions. We may be far removed from London here, but I assure you, Lady Melross will delight in dredging up every detail of this scandal when your relations arrive in London next spring.'

Caroline shook her head. 'I've already discussed that problem with my stepmother. If they band together, I'm certain Lady Denby, your aunt and Lady Gilford can manage this affair so that no harm comes to Eugenia's prospects. Since you are already accounted a rake, it shouldn't much affect your reputation and ruining mine has been my goal from the outset.'

She'd hoped to persuade Max to accept her argument. Far from looking convinced, though, his expression turned even grimmer and his jaw flexed, as if he were trying not to grit his teeth.

'Miss Denby,' he began again after a moment, 'I don't mean to seem overbearing or argumentative, but the very fact that you have not much associated with society means you are in no position to accurately predict its reaction. I have lived all my life under its scrutiny and I promise you, once Lady Denby has thought through the matter, she will agree with me that our marriage is the only solution that will safeguard the reputations of everyone involved.'

He paused and took a deep breath, as if armouring himself. 'So you may assure her that I have done the proper thing and made a formal offer for your hand.'

If the situation had not been so serious, Caro might have laughed, for he spat out the declaration as if each word were a hot coal that burned his tongue as he uttered it. His obvious reluctance might even have been considered insulting, if her own desire to avoid marriage hadn't exceeded his.

But then, as if realising that his grudging offer was hardly lover-like, he shook his head and sighed. 'Let me try this again,' he said, then reached over to tangle his fingers with hers.

Immediately, heat rushed up her arm, while her heart accelerated so rapidly, she felt dizzy.

'Won't you honour me by giving me your hand?' he said. 'I know neither of us came to Barton Abbey with marriage in mind. But during our brief acquaintance, I've come to admire and respect you. I flatter myself that you've come to like me, too, at least a little.'

'I do like and…and admire you,' she replied disjointedly, wishing he'd release her fingers. They seemed somehow connected to her chest and her brain, for she was finding it hard to breathe and even harder to think as he retained them.

His thumb was rubbing lazy circles of wonderment around her palm, setting off little shocks of sensation that seemed to radiate straight to the core of her.

She should pull free, but she didn't seem able to move. So he continued, his touch mesmerising, until all the clear reasons against marriage dissolved into a porridge-like muddle in her brain. She couldn't seem to concentrate on anything but the press of his thumb and the delights it created.

'I think we could rub together tolerably well,' he went on, obviously not at all affected by the touch that was wreaking such havoc in her. 'I admire you, too, and from what I've seen of your Sultan, you are excellent with horses. You could run Denby Stud with my blessing.'

That assurance was as seductively appealing as the thumb caressing her palm, which was now making her body hot and her nipples ache. An insidious longing welled up within her, a yearning for him to kiss her, for her to kiss him back.

Without question, he knew society better than she did, and, for a moment, her certainty that she ought to refuse him wavered. She struggled to recapture her purpose and remember why marrying him was such a bad idea.

Unable to order her thoughts in Max's disturbing presence, she pulled her fingers free, sprang up and paced to the window.

How could she become his wife and not let him touch her? Was she really ready to test the power of the Curse for a man who merely 'admired' her? Besides, the experience of their last two meetings suggested that her ability to resist him, if he did make overtures toward her, would be feeble at best, regardless of how tepid his feelings for her might be.

She could tell him why she was so opposed to marriage. But after his courage in rescuing her and resolutely facing the consequences, she really didn't wish to appear a coward by admitting that it was the strong probability that she would die in childbed, as so many of her maternal relations had, that made her leery of wedlock.

No, the very fact that he affected her so strongly was reason enough not to marry Max Ransleigh.

Reminding herself of her conviction that Lady Denby could protect Eugenia, she said, 'I know you make your offer hastily and under duress. If you will but think longer about it, you will agree that it isn't wise to take a step that will permanently compromise our futures in order to avoid a scandal that will soon enough be overshadowed by some other.'

'It will have to be some scandal,' he said drily.

'Only think if I were to accept you!' she continued, avoiding his gaze in the hope that not meeting his eyes might lessen the disturbing physical hold he exerted over her. 'I'm not being modest when I assert that a huge divide exists between Miss Denby, countrified, unfashionable daughter of minor gentry, and Max Ransleigh, an earl's son accustomed to moving in the first circles of society. I have neither the skills nor the background to be the sort of wife you deserve.'

Before he could insert some patently false reassurance, she rushed on, 'Nor, frankly, do I wish to acquire them. My world isn't Drury Lane, but the lane that leads from the barns to the paddocks. Not the odour of expensive perfume, but the scent of leather polish, sawdust and new hay. Not the murmur of political conversation, but the jingle of harness, the neighing of horses, the clang of the blacksmith's hammer. I have no desire to give that up for your world, London's parlours and theatre boxes and its endless round of dinner parties, routs and balls.'

His expression softened to a smile. 'You are quite eloquent in defence of "your world", Miss Denby.'

'I don't mean to disparage yours!' she said quickly. 'Only to point out how different we are. All I want is to remain at Denby Lodge, where I belong, sharing my life with someone who loves and appreciates that world as I do.' *Someone to whom*, she added silently, *I have long been bound by a comfortable affection, not a man as disturbing and far-too-insidiously appealing as you.*

Turning from the window, she said, 'Though I am fully conscious of the honour of your offer, as I told you from the beginning, I wish to marry Harry. By the time he returns from India, this furore will have calmed. And even if it has not, Harry will not care.'

'I don't know that you can be certain about that,' he objected. 'If it doesn't, and he marries you, he will share in your notoriety. Being banished from society is no little thing. Would you choose exile for him? Would he suffer it for you?'

'Harry would suffer anything for me.'

'How can you commit Harry to such a course without giving him a choice?'

'How can you ask me to give him up without giving him a chance? No, Mr Ransleigh, I will not do it. I will leave it to ladies better placed than I to protect my stepsister and to Harry to settle my future when he returns. And lest you think to argue your position with her, Lady Denby would not compel me to marry against my will.'

Hoping to finally convince him, she chanced gazing into his eyes. 'It really is more sensible this way, surely you can see that! Some day you, too, will encounter a lady you *wish* to marry, one who can be the perfect helpmate and government hostess. You'll be happy then that I did not allow you to sway me. So, though I am sorry to be disobliging, I must refuse your very flattering offer.'

He studied her a long moment; she couldn't tell from his face whether he felt relief or exasperation. 'You needn't give me a final answer now. Why not think on the matter for a few days?'

'That won't be necessary; I am resolved on this. As soon as my stepmother recovers from the shock, we will pack and leave for Denby Lodge.'

For another long moment he said nothing. 'I am no Henshaw to try to force your hand, even though I believe your leaving here without the protection of an engagement is absolutely the wrong course of action. However, if you insist on refusing it, know that if at any time you decide to reconsider, my offer will remain open.'

Truly, he was the kindest of men. The shock and outrage and dismay of the day taking its toll, she felt an annoyingly missish desire to burst into tears.

'I will do so. Thank you.'

He bowed. 'I will send a note to Lady Denby, offering to call and tender my apologies if she permits. Will you let me know before you leave, so I might bid you goodbye?'

'It would probably be wiser if we go our separate ways as quickly as possible.'

'As you wish.' He approached her then, halting one step away. Her body quivered in response to his nearness.

'It has been a most…interesting association, Miss Denby.' He held out his hand and reluctantly she laid hers in his as he brought her fingers to his lips. Little sparks danced and tingled and shivered from her fingernails outwards.

'I will remain always your most devoted servant.'

Snatching back the hand that didn't want to follow her instructions to remove itself from his grasp, she curtsied and watched him stride out of the room, telling herself this was for the best.

And the sooner she got back to Denby Lodge, the better.

Chapter Nine

Max stalked from Lady Denby's sitting room towards the library, anger, outrage and frustration churning in his gut. Encountering one of the guests in the hallway, avid curiosity in his eyes, Max gave him such a thunderous glare, the man pivoted without speaking and fled in the opposite direction.

Stomping into his haven, he went straight to the brandy decanter, poured and downed a glass, then poured another, welcoming the burn of the liquor down his throat.

What a calamity of a day.

Throwing himself into one of the wing chairs by the fire, he wondered despairingly how everything could have gone so wrong. It seemed impossible that, just a few bare hours ago, he'd halted on the threshold of the conservatory and breathed deeply of the fragrant air, his spirits rising on its scented promise that life was going to get better.

Instead, events had taken a turn that could end up anywhere from worse to disastrous.

Reviewing the scene in the glasshouse, he swore again. Hadn't Vienna taught him not to embroil himself in the problems of females wholly unrelated to him? Apparently not, for though, unlike Madame Lefevre, he acquitted the Denby girl of deliberately drawing him into this fiasco, by watching over her he'd been dragged in anyway.

And might very well be forced into wedding a lady with whom, by her own admission, he had virtually nothing in common.

True, Miss Denby had turned down his offer. But he placed no reliance on her continuing to do so, once her stepmother brought home to her just how difficult her situation would be if they didn't marry.

His wouldn't be as dire, but the resulting scandal certainly wouldn't be helpful. With a sardonic curl of his lip, he recalled Miss Denby's blithe assumption that since he already had a reputation as a rake, the scandal wouldn't affect him at all. He'd been on the point of explaining that, even for a rake, there were limits to acceptable behaviour and ruining a young lady of quality went rather beyond them.

But if the danger to her own reputation wasn't enough to convince her, he wasn't about to whine to her about the damage not wedding her would do to his own.

There might be some small benefit to be squeezed from disaster: if he were thought to be a heartless seducer, he'd no longer be a target for the schemes of matchmaking mamas and their devious daughters. However, for someone about to go hat in hand looking for a government posting, the timing couldn't be worse. Being branded as a man unable to regulate his behaviour around women certainly wouldn't help his chances of finding a sponsor…or winning back Wellington's favour.

He seized his empty glass and threw it into the fireplace.

He was still brooding over what to do when Alastair came in.

'Devil's teeth, Max, what fandango occurred while I was out today? Even the grooms are buzzing with it—some crazy tale of you trying to ravish some chit in the conservatory?'

Max debated telling Alastair the truth, but his hot-headed cousin would probably head out straight away to track down Henshaw and challenge him to a duel, pressing the issue until the man was forced to face him or leave the country in disgrace.

Of course, being an excellent shot as well as a superior swordsman, if Alastair prevailed upon Henshaw to meet him, his cousin would kill the weasel for certain—and then *he*'d be forced to leave England.

He'd complicated his own life sufficiently; he didn't intend to ruin Alastair's as well.

'I…got a bit carried away. Lady Melross and her crony came running in before I could set the young lady to rights.'

Alastair studied his face. 'I heard the chit's bodice was torn to her bosom, the buttons of her pelisse scattered all over the floor. Devil take it, Max, don't try to gammon me. You've infinitely more finesse than that…and if you wanted a woman, you wouldn't have to rip her out of her gown—in a public place, no less!'

Wishing he hadn't tossed away his perfectly good glass, Max rummaged for one on the sideboard and poured himself another brandy. 'I'm really not at liberty to say any more.'

'Damn and blast, you can't think I'd believe that Banbury tale! Did the Denby chit deliberately try to trap you? Dammit, I *liked* her! Surely you're not going to let her get away with this!'

'If by "getting away with it", you mean forcing me to marry her, you're out there. I made her an offer, as any gentleman of honour would in such a situation, but thus far, she's refused it.'

Alastair stared at him for a long moment, then poured himself a brandy. 'This whole story,' he said, downing a large swallow, 'makes no sense at all.'

'With that, I can agree,' Max said.

Suddenly, Alastair threw back his head and laughed. 'Won't need to worry about the Melross hag blackening your character in town. After bringing her party to such a scandalous conclusion, *Jane*'s going to murder you.'

'Maybe I'll hand her the pistol,' Max muttered.

'To women!' Alastair held up his glass before tossing down the rest of the brandy. 'One of the greatest scourges on the face of the earth. I don't know what in hell happened today in the conservatory and, if you don't want to tell me, that's an end to it. But I do know you'd never do anything to harm a female and I'll stand beside you, no matter what lies that dragon Melross and her pack of seditious gossips spread.'

Suddenly a wave of weariness come over Max…as it had in the wake of the Vienna disaster, when he'd wandered back to his rooms, numbed by shock, disbelief and a sense of incredulity that things could possibly have turned out so badly when he'd done nothing wrong. 'Thank you,' he said, setting down his glass.

Alastair poured them both another. 'Ransleigh Rogues,' he said, touching his glass to Max's.

Before Max could take another sip, a footman entered, handing him a note written on Barton Abbey stationery. A flash of foreboding filled him—had Miss Denby already reconsidered?

But when he broke the seal, he discovered the note came from Lady Denby.

After thanking him for his offer to apologise

and his assurance that he stood by his proposal to marry her stepdaughter, since Miss Denby informed her she had no intention of accepting him, there was really nothing else to be said. As both Miss Denby and her own daughter were most anxious to depart as soon as possible, she intended to leave immediately, but reserved the privilege of writing to him again when she'd had more opportunity to Sort Matters Out, at which time she trusted he would still be willing, as a Man of Honour, to Do The Right Thing.

An almost euphoric sense of relief filled Max. Apparently Lady Denby hadn't managed to convince her *stepdaughter* to 'Do the Right Thing' before leaving Barton Abbey. With Miss Denby about to get everything she wanted—a return to her beloved Denby Lodge and a ruination that would allow her to wait in peace for the return of her Harry—Max was nearly certain no amount of Sorting Things Out later would convince Miss Denby to reconsider.

He'd remain a free man after all.

The misery of the day lightened just a trifle. Now he must concentrate on trying to limit the damage to his prospects of a career.

'Good news?' Alastair asked.

Max grinned at him. 'The best. It appears I will not have to get leg-shackled after all. Amazingly, Miss Denby has resisted her stepmother's attempts to convince her to marry me.'

Alastair whistled. 'Amazing indeed! She must

be dicked in the nob to discard a foolproof hand for forcing the Magnificent Max Ransleigh into marriage, but no matter.'

'There's an army sweetheart she's waiting to marry.'

'Better him than you,' Alastair said as he refilled their glasses. 'Here's to Miss Denby's resistance and remaining unwed!'

'Add a government position to that and I'll be a happy man.'

Max knew the worst wasn't over yet. Whispers about the scandal in the conservatory would doubtless have raced through the rest of the company like a wildfire through parched grass. At some point, Aunt Grace would summon him in response to the note he'd sent her, wanting to know why he'd created such an uproar at her house party.

The two cousins remained barricaded in the library, from which stronghold they occasionally heard the thumps and bangs of footmen descending the stairs with the baggage of departing guests. But as the hour grew later without his aunt summoning him, Max guessed that some guests had chosen to remain another night, doubtless eager to grill their hostess for every detail over dinner, embarrassing Felicity, making Jane simmer and contemplate murder.

Alastair, ever loyal, kept him company, playing a few desultory hands of cards after he'd declined the offer of billiards. He wasn't sure he'd trust himself with a cue in hand without trying to break it over someone's head.

Probably his own.

So it was nearly midnight when a footman bowed himself in to tell him Mrs Ransleigh begged the indulgence of a few words with him in her sitting room.

Max swallowed hard. Now he must face the lady who'd stood by him, disparaging his father's conduct and insisting he deserved better. And just like Vienna, though all he had done was assist a woman in distress, this time he'd ended up miring not just himself, but also his aunt, in embarrassment and scandal.

He'd not whined to Miss Denby about the black mark that would be left on his character by her refusal to wed; he wasn't going to make excuses to his aunt, either. Girding himself to endure anger and recriminations, he crossed the room.

Alastair, who knew only too well what he'd face, gave him an encouraging slap on the shoulder as he walked by.

He found his aunt reclining on her couch in a dressing gown, eyes closed. She sat up with a start as the footman announced him, her eyes shadowed with fatigue, filling with tears as he approached.

His chest tightening, he felt about as miserable as he'd ever felt in his life. Rather than cause his aunt pain, he almost wished he'd fallen with the valiant at Hougoumont.

'Aunt Grace,' he murmured, kissing her outstretched fingers. 'I am so sorry.'

But instead of the reproaches he'd steeled himself to endure, she pushed herself from her seat and enveloped him in a hug. 'Oh, my poor Max, under which unlucky star were you born that such trouble has come into your life?'

Hugging her back, he muttered. 'Lord knows. If I were one of the ancients, I'd think I'd somehow offended Aphrodite.'

'Come, sit by me,' she said, patting the sofa beside her.

Heartened by her unexpectedly sympathetic reception, he took a seat. 'I'd been prepared to have you abuse my character and order me from the house. I cannot imagine why you have not, after I've unleashed such a sordid scandal at your house party.'

'I imagine Anita Melross was delighted,' she said drily. 'She will doubtless dine out for weeks on the story of how she found you in the conservatory. Dreadful woman! How infuriating that she is so well connected, one cannot simply cut her. But enough about Anita. Oh, Max, what are we to do now?'

'There isn't much that can be done. Lady Melross and her minions will have already set the gossip mill in motion, thoroughly shredding my character. Frankly, I expected you to take part in the process.'

'Frankly, I might have,' his aunt retorted, 'had Miss Denby not insisted upon speaking with me before she left.'

Surprise rendered him momentarily speechless. 'Miss Denby spoke with you?' he echoed an instant later.

'I must admit, I was so angry with both of you, I had no desire whatsoever to listen to any excuses she wished to offer. But she was quite adamant.' His aunt laughed. 'Indeed, she told Wendell she would not quit the passage outside my chamber until she was permitted to see me. I'm so glad now that she persisted, for she confessed the whole to me—something I expect that you, my dear Max, would not have done.'

'She…told you everything?' Max asked, that news surprising him even more than his aunt's unexpected sympathy.

His aunt nodded. 'How Mr Henshaw made her an offer, so insistent upon her acceptance he was ready to attack her to force it! I was never so distressed!' she cried, putting a hand on her chest. 'Is there truly no way to lay the blame for that shocking attack where it belongs, at Henshaw's feet?'

'If Miss Denby disclosed the whole of what happened, you must see that there is virtually no chance we could fix the responsibility on him.'

'Poor child! I feel wretched that someone I invited into my home would take such unspeakable liberties! With her shyness and lack of polish, she would never have found much success in the Marriage Mart, but to have her ruined by that... that infamous blackguard! And then, to have *you* wrongfully accused for her disgrace! 'Tis monstrous, all of it!'

Max sat back, his emotions in turmoil. Though he hadn't truly blamed Miss Denby for what had happened, he'd resented the fact that, at the end of it all, *she* had got what she wanted, while *he* was left a position that made obtaining his goal much more difficult.

Still, he could work relentlessly until he achieved what he wanted; her ruination couldn't be undone. It had taken courage to insist on braving the contempt of her hostess so she might explain what had really transpired, thereby exonerating him to a woman whose good opinion she must know he treasured.

In refusing to allow herself to be forced into something she did not want, regardless of the personal cost, and in remaining steadfastly loyal to her childhood love, she'd displayed a sense of honour as unshakeable as his own. He couldn't help admiring that.

'I hardly expected her to tell you the truth... but I'm glad she did,' he said at last.

'Oh, Max, you would have said nothing and simply shouldered all the blame, would you not?' she asked, seizing his hands.

He shrugged. 'With Henshaw showing himself too dishonourable to admit to his actions, I don't see how I could avoid it. There was no point making accusations we have no way of proving.'

'Are you certain that's the right course? It seems monstrous that you both must suffer, while the guilty party escapes all blame!'

'We'll have to endure it, at least for the present. I intend to quietly search for evidence that might incriminate Henshaw, but I'm not hopeful anything useful will turn up. In the interim, I'd rather Alastair not learn the truth. He's already suspicious of Lady Melross's story. If he were to find out what really happened, he might go after Henshaw and—'

'—tear him limb from limb, or something equally rash,' Mrs Ransleigh finished for him. 'Although it will chafe him to be kept in the dark, I appreciate your doing it. Ever since…That Woman, he's been so reckless and bitter. Even after all those years in the army, he's still spoiling for a fight, still heedless of the consequences.'

'It shall remain our secret, then.'

She sighed. 'If there is any way I might be of assistance, let me know. I can think of little that would give me more pleasure than being able to show up Anita Melross for the idle, malicious gossip she is.'

'If the opportunity arises, I will certainly call on your help. By the way…did Miss Denby also tell you I'd asked for her hand and she'd refused me?'

'She did. Bless the child, she even said that

after you had been everything that was gentle-manly, preventing Henshaw from ravishing her and comforting her afterwards, she simply could not repay your kindness by shackling you to a girl you didn't want. She insisted you must remain free to take a wife of your own choosing, who would be the suitable hostess and companion to a man in high position that she could never be.'

Max smiled, his spirits lightened by the first glimmer of amusement he'd felt since Lady Melross burst into the conservatory. 'Difficult to be angry with someone who rejects you with such glowing compliments.'

'And such absolute sincerity! It was the longest and most eloquent speech I've got from her since her arrival. Perhaps she isn't quite as hopeless as I'd thought.'

Max resisted the impulse to defend Miss Denby. How well she'd cultivated the image of an awkward, ill-spoken spinster! If only his aunt could have seen her, fierce determination in her eyes as she'd vividly described her world at Denby Lodge.

She'd been quite magnificent. Even had he wished to wed her, he would have felt compelled to let her go.

'I must say, I was relieved to discover she has an army beau who will marry her when he returns,' Mrs Ransleigh continued. 'Having been the unwitting instrument of her disgrace, it makes me feel a bit better to know she won't be condemned for ever to live without the care and protection of a good man.'

Max nodded. 'That's the only reason I didn't push her harder to marry me. Not that I'd ever force myself on a woman.'

'Of course you would not. Well, I'm off to bed. Calamities such as the events that transpired today exhaust me! But I did not wish to sleep before telling you I knew everything, lest you take it in your head to lope off somewhere in the night, still believing I thought ill of you.'

'I'm so glad you do not. And I've no plans to take myself off as yet.'

'Stay as long as you like,' his aunt said as she offered him her cheek to kiss. 'By the way, I should like to reveal the truth to Jane. She is perfectly discreet and, as she is now quite an influential hostess in London, she might find the means to be of some help.'

'Miss Denby already mentioned that Lady Denby hoped to enlist you and Jane in defending her stepsister; I'd appreciate anything you might do to assist Miss Denby as well. Of all the unwilling participants in this débâcle, she is the one who loses the most.'

Mrs Ransleigh nodded. 'We will certainly give it our best efforts.'

'I'll leave you to your slumber, then. Thank you, Aunt Grace. For still believing in me.'

'You're quite welcome,' she replied with a

smile. 'You might want to thank Miss Denby, too, for believing in you as well.'

Bidding her goodnight, Max walked out. Though he hadn't yet worked out how he was going to work around this check to his governmental aspirations, he felt immeasurably better to know that he had not, after all, disappointed and alienated his aunt.

That happy outcome he owed to Miss Denby. He found her courage in risking censure to defend him to his family as amazing as her fortitude in refusing a convenient marriage.

Aunt Grace was right. He did owe her thanks. But given the disastrous events that seemed to happen when she came near him, he didn't think he'd risk delivering it in person any time soon.

Chapter Ten

$\infty\!\!\sim\!\!\sim\!\!\sim\!\!\infty$

In the late afternoon a month later, Caroline Denby turned the last gelding over to the stable boy and walked out of the barn. After returning from the disaster at Barton Abbey, she'd thrown herself into working with the horses, readying them for the upcoming autumn sale. But as she'd suspected, though she'd left the scandal behind, its repercussions continued to follow her.

In the last two weeks, several gentlemen who'd not previously purchased mounts from the stud had journeyed into Kent, claiming they wished to view and evaluate the stock. Since the gentlemen had spent more time gawking at her than at the horses, she suspected their real interest had been to inspect for themselves the subject of Lady Melross's most titillating gossip—the hoyden who'd been discovered half-naked with Max Ransleigh.

If they'd been expecting some seductive siren, she'd doubtless sent them away disappointed, Caro thought with a sigh.

At least there was no question of her returning to London for another Season, and after a week of fruitless attempts, Lady Denby had given up trying to convince her to marry Max Ransleigh as well. Though Eugenia still hadn't entirely forgiven her for the débâcle which had put such an unpleasant end to the house party, when Caro had explained during the drive home what had really happened, her stepsister had been first shocked, then indignant, then had wept at the outrage she had suffered.

So it now appeared, Caro thought with satisfaction as she paced up the steps into the manor and tossed her gloves and crop to the butler, that she'd gained what she'd wanted all along: to be left in peace to run her farm.

She was hopeful that Eugenia would also get what she wanted, the successful Season she'd dreamed of for so long. While Caro worked with her horses, Lady Denby had been busy with correspondence, consulting with Lady Gilford and Mrs Ransleigh and writing to her many friends to ensure enough support for Eugenia's début that her prospects would not suffer because of Caro's scandal.

Grateful for that, Caroline refused to regret what had happened. And if she sometimes woke in the night, her soul awash with yearning as she recalled being cradled against a broad chest, while a strong finger gently caressed her cheek and a deep masculine voice murmured soothingly against her hair, she would, in time, get over it.

Garbed in her usual working attire of breeches and boots, she intended to tiptoe quietly up to her chamber and change into more conventional clothing before dinner. But as she crept past the parlour, Lady Denby called out, 'Caroline, is that you? I must speak to you at once!'

Wondering what she could have done now to distress Lady Denby, she changed course and proceeded into the room. 'Yes, Stepmama?'

In her agitation, Lady Denby didn't so much as frown at Caro's breeches. 'Oh, my dear, I fear I may have inadvertently done you a grave disservice!'

Foreboding slammed like a fist into her chest. 'What are you talking about?'

Lady Denby gave her a guilty look. 'Well, you see, after the events at Barton Abbey, I wrote to the trustees of your father's estate, informing them you were to be married and asking that the solicitors begin working on marriage settlements.' Before Caroline could protest, she rushed on, 'I was so very sure you would, in the end, be convinced to marry! Then last week, after finally conceding there would be no wedding, I wrote back to them, telling them you had refused Mr Ransleigh's offer. In today's post, I received a reply from Lord Woodbury.'

'Woodbury?' Caro gave a contemptuous snort. 'I can only imagine what *he* had to say about it. How I wish Papa had not made him head of the trustees!'

'Well, dear, he was one of your papa's closest friends and his estate at Mendinhall is very prosperous, so it's not unreasonable that Papa thought Woodbury would take equal care of yours.'

'I won't deny that he's a good steward,' Caro replied, 'but Woodbury never approved of my working the stud. The last time they met, he told Papa he thought it well past time for me to put on proper dress and start behaving like a woman of my rank, instead of racketing about the stables, hobnobbing with grooms and coachmen.'

When Lady Denby remained tactfully silent—probably more in agreement with Lord Woodbury's views than with her own—Caroline said, 'What did Lord Woodbury write, then?'

Her stepmother sighed. 'You're not going to like it. Apparently he heard about the events at Barton Abbey. He claims the shock of it must have unbalanced your mind for, he wrote, no young lady of breeding in her right senses, caught in such a dire situation, would ever turn down a respectable offer of marriage. He's convinced your, um, "unnatural preoccupation" with running the stud has made you unable to realise how badly the scandal reflects upon you and the entire family. So, to protect you and the Denby name, he's convinced the other trustees to agree to something he's long been urging: the sale of the stud.'

Shock froze her in place, while her heart stood still and blood seemed to drain from her head and limbs. Dizzy, she grabbed the back of a wing chair to steady herself. 'The sale of the stud?' she repeated, stunned. 'He wants to sell *my horses*?'

'Y-yes, my dear.'

It was impossible. It was outrageous. Aside from Lady Denby's generous widow's portion, the rest of the estate, including Denby Lodge, the Denby Stud and the income to operate it, had been willed to her. Papa had always promised the farm and the land would remain hers, for her use and then as part of her dowry.

She shook her head to clear the faintness. 'Can they do that?' she demanded, her voice trembling.

'I don't know. Oh, my dear, I'm so sorry! I know how much the stud means to you.'

'How much… Why, it means *everything*,' Caro said, feeling returning to her limbs in a rush of fury. 'Everything I've worked for these last ten years! Has it been done yet? May I see the note?'

Silently, her stepmother held it out. Caroline snatched and read it through rapidly.

'It does not appear the sale has gone through yet,' she said, when she had finished it. 'There must be some way to stop it. The stud belongs to me!'

But even as she made the bold declaration,

doubt and dread rose up to check her like a ten-foot gate before a novice jumper.

Did she have control of the stud? Numb, shocked and trying to cope with the immensity of her father's sudden death, she'd sat silent and vacant-headed during the reading of his will. Thinking back, she knew the assets of the estate had been turned over to trustees to manage for her, but no details about how the trust was to be administered, or the extent of the powers granted the trustees, had penetrated her pall of grief and pain.

'What will you do?' Lady Denby asked.

'I shall leave for London tomorrow at first light and consult Papa's solicitor. Mr Henderson will know if anything can be done.'

Lady Denby shook her head. 'I'm so sorry, Caroline. I would never have written if I'd had any suspicion Lord Woodbury would do such a thing.'

Absently Caroline patted her hand. 'It's not your fault. According to the note, Woodbury has been trying to convince the other trustees to sell the stud for some time.'

Anguish twisted in her gut as the scene played out in her head: some stranger arriving to lead away Sultan, whom she'd eased from his mother's body the night he was born. She'd put on him his first halter, his first saddle. Turning over Sultan, or Sheik's Ransom or Arabian Lady or Cleveland's Hope or any of the horses she'd worked with from foal to weaning to training, would be like having someone confiscate her brothers and sisters.

'Thank you for telling me at once,' she said, brisk purpose submerging her anxiety—at least for the moment. 'Now, you will please excuse me. I must confer with Newman in the stables, so he may continue the training while I'm gone.' She dismissed the flare of panic in her belly at the thought that when she came back, she might no longer be giving the orders. 'Would you ring Dulcie for me and ask her to pack some things?'

'While you're at the stables, be sure to tell John Coachman to ready the travelling barouche.'

Already pacing towards the door, Caro shook her head impatiently. 'No, I'll go by mail coach; it will be faster.'

'By mail coach!' Lady Denby gasped. 'But… that will not be at all proper! If you don't wish to take the barouche, at least hire a carriage.'

'My dear Stepmama, I don't wish to make the journey in the easy stages required if I'm forced to hire horses along the way! I'll take Dulcie to lend me some countenance,' she added. Despite her agitation, she had to grin at the dismay the maid would doubtless feel upon being informed she would be rattling around in a public vehicle, probably stuffed full of other travellers, that broke its journey at the inns along the route only for the few minutes required to change the horses.

'Where will you stay in London?' Lady Denby cried, following her out into the passage.

'With Cousin Elizabeth. Or at a hotel, if she's not in town. If necessary, Mr Henderson will find me something suitable. Now I must go. I have a hundred things to do before the Royal Mail leaves tomorrow.'

Giving her stepmother's hand a quick squeeze, Caro strode through the entry, trotted down the steps and, once out of her stepmother's sight, set off at a run for the stables.

It was long past dark by the time she'd concluded her rounds of the stalls with Newman, her head trainer, reviewing with him the regimen she wished him to follow with each horse.

'Don't you worry, Miss Caroline,' he told her when they'd finished. 'Your late father, God rest 'im, trained me and every groom at Denby Stables. We'll do whatever's needful to carry on. You go up to London and do what you must. And, miss...' he added gruffly, giving her arm an awkward pat, 'best of luck to you.'

With a wisp of a smile, Caro watched him go. Even after so many years of living in a large household, it never ceased to amaze her how quickly news travelled through invisible servants' networks. Although she'd told Newman nothing beyond the fact that urgent business called her away to London, somehow he must have discovered the true reason behind her journey.

Her final stop before returning to the house was Sultan's box. 'No, my handsome boy, I'll not take you with me this time,' she told him as she stroked the velvet nose. 'You're too fine a horse to risk having you turn an ankle in some pothole, racing through the dark to London. Though you would fly to take me there, if I asked you.'

The gelding nosed her hand and nickered his agreement.

The darkness seemed to close around her, magnifying the fear and anxiety she'd been struggling to hold at bay. Sensing her distress, Sultan nosed her again and rubbed his neck against her hand. Trying to give her comfort, it seemed.

What comfort would she have, if she lost him, lost them all? She had no siblings, no close neighbours other than Harry, and he was off in India. All her life, her horses had been her friends and playmates. She'd poured out her problems and told them her secrets, while they listened, nickering encouragement and sympathy.

Denby Lodge was a vast holding, its wealth derived from farms, cattle and fields planted in corn and other crops. Like her father, she'd been content to let the estate manager—and then the trustees in London—concern themselves with the other businesses, as she let the housekeeper manage the manor itself and its servants, while she focused solely on managing the stud.

She'd not been dissembling when she told Henshaw she possessed no feminine talents. She didn't sew or embroider, paint, sing, or play an instrument. What was she to do with herself without her horses to birth, raise and train?

It was all she knew. All she had ever done. All she had ever wanted to do. What could she find to replace the long hours spent in these immaculately kept barns with their rows of box stalls, where every breath brought the familiar scents of hay and bran and horse, saddle leather and polished brass? What could replace the thrill of feeling a thousand pounds of stallion thundering under her as he galloped across a meadow, responding to signals she'd ingrained in him after hours and hours of patient, careful training?

After all she had done to keep the stud, it was intolerable that some self-important peer, who wished to dictate to her what a woman's place should be, might have the power to strip it all from her.

What was to become of her if Woodbury succeeded?

Weary, anxious, desperate, she wrapped her arms around Sultan's neck and wept.

Chapter Eleven

Little more than thirty hours later, Caroline climbed down from the hackney that had brought her back from the solicitor's office and walked slowly up the stairs into her cousin Elizabeth's modest town house. A house that been part of her cousin's marriage settlements, fortunately, Caro thought, making it one of the few assets her profligate husband hadn't been able to squander.

Oh, fortunate Elizabeth.

A dull ache in her head, she felt the weariness of every sleepless hour she'd endured, from her last night at Denby Lodge, briefing the trainer and preparing for the journey, to the long dusty, uncomfortable transit into London. She'd barely taken the time to greet Elizabeth and inform her about her urgent mission before leaving for Mr Henderson's office.

Where she was met with the chilling news that

her trustees, approved by the Court of Chancery under her father's will to care for her inheritance, definitely had the legal right to sell off any land or assets they saw fit, for the good of the estate.

Lady Elizabeth was out, the butler told her as he let her in. Her chest so tight with pain and outrage she could barely breathe, too exhausted to sleep, Caroline went to the small study, took paper and scrawled a letter to Harry, pouring into it all her anguished desperation.

Not that it would make any difference; she probably wouldn't even post it. By the time the letter reached Harry, even if he wrote back immediately, agreeing to marry her by proxy, it would be too late. The sale, Mr Henderson had advised her this afternoon, was already near to being concluded.

She was going to lose the stud.

That awful fact echoed in hollowness of her belly like a shot ricocheting inside a stone building, chipping off pieces that could wound and maim. She felt her heart's blood oozing out even now.

She might as well shoot herself and get it over with, she thought bleakly.

A rustling in the passageway announced her cousin Elizabeth's return. Not wishing to leave the letter there, where some curious servant might read her ramblings, she quickly sanded and folded it and scrawled Harry's name on the top. Setting it to the side of the desk, she rose to meet her cousin.

Elizabeth took one look at her face and gathered her into a hug.

'Men!' she said bitterly, releasing Caro before linking arms and leading her to the sofa. 'They shape our world, write its laws and pretend we are helpless creatures who cannot be trusted to manage our own lives. So they can take it all.'

'At least you have your house. Maybe I can come and reside with you, once…once it's gone. I don't think I can bear to live at Denby Lodge, afterwards.'

'You'd certainly be welcome. I don't have nearly the income I once did, but it's enough for us to manage.'

'Oh, I should have wealth aplenty for us both, especially after the sale. My kind trustees are managing the estate so brilliantly, I should be awash in guineas. Lord Woodbury would doubtless approve my buying every feminine frippery under the sun…as long as I don't do the only thing in life I care about.'

Elizabeth poured them wine and handed Caro a glass. 'Come and live with me, then. We'll be two eccentric bluestockings, keeping pugs, reading scientific tracts and nattering on about the rights of working women and prostitutes, like that Mary Wollstonecraft creature.'

Caro attempted a smile, but with her whole world disintegrating around her, she didn't have the heart to appreciate her cousin's attempt at humour. 'You should think twice before making such an offer. I'm a social pariah now, remember.'

Her cousin merely laughed. 'Oh, yes, I've heard the fantastical tale Lady Melross has been spreading. You, baring your bosom to snag a gentleman? Max Ransleigh, rake though he be, mauling a gently born girl in his own aunt's conservatory? No one who knows either of you could possibly believe it.'

In no mood to recount the story again, despite the curiosity in her cousin's eyes, Caro merely shrugged.

Tacitly accepting her reluctance, Elizabeth sighed. 'Is there no way to get around Lord Woodbury?'

'Only if I could find a fortune hunter desperate enough to escort me to Gretna Green tonight.'

Elizabeth shuddered. 'Don't even joke of such a thing! Besides, wouldn't Woodbury put a stop to that, too?'

'He couldn't; I'm of age. And, once married, my new husband would take ownership of everything from the trustees, with the power to cancel the sale.'

'I trust you are only jesting,' Elizabeth said, looking at her with concern. 'Gaining a husband would give you no more control over your wealth than your trustees do, as I learned to my sorrow. Oh, if only Harry were not so far away in India!'

'I know,' Caro said, feeling tears again prick her eyes. She'd never expected that at the most desperate hour of her life her closest childhood friend would be too far away to help her. 'I wrote to him tonight, useless as that was. But the plain fact is he's not here, nor could he possibly return before the sale goes through…and then the stud is lost to me for ever.'

Merely saying the words sent a knife-like pain slashing through her. Lips trembling, she pushed the image of Sultan from her mind.

'That soon?' Elizabeth was saying. 'I'm almost willing to draw up a list of eligible gentlemen.'

'He could have all my money, as long as he left me enough to maintain the stud. If only I knew someone besides Harry who'd be honourable enough to make such a bargain and keep—' Caroline broke off abruptly as Max Ransleigh's words echoed in her ears: *You could run the stud with my blessing…*

A near-hysterical excitement blazing new energy into her, she seized her cousin's arm. 'Elizabeth, you are acquainted with the Ransleighs, aren't you?'

'I haven't moved in their circles since my début Season, but I still count Jane Ransleigh as a friend. She's Lady Gilford now, one of society's most important—'

'Yes, yes, I know her,' Caroline interrupted. 'Is she in town? Could you get a message to her?'

'I suppose so. What is it, Caro? You're as white as if you were about to faint—and you're hurting my arm.'

'Sorry,' she mumbled, releasing it at once. Lightheaded, desperate, feeling every hour she'd gone without food and sleep and rest, she said, 'I must get a message to her cousin, Max Ransleigh. Tonight, if possible.'

'Max Ransleigh? Ah, the man who...' Comprehension dawned in Elizabeth's eyes. 'Are you sure?'

'I am. Though I'm not at all sure, after the scandal I dragged him into, that Lady Gilford would agree to give me his direction.'

'You don't have to ask her. Max is here now, in London. Jane told me at tea last week that he'd come to town to meet with the colonel who used to command his regiment.'

'Do you know where he is staying?

'No, but Tilly, my maid, could find out. A friend of hers is the housekeeper's assistant for Lady Gilford.'

'Could you ask her to go to Lady Gilford's at once?'

Elizabeth studied her. 'Are you sure you want to do this?'

'No,' Caro replied, panic and hope coursing through her in equal measure. 'Nor have I any assurance he would even agree to see me, if I can locate him. But it's the only chance I've got. The sale will be final before the month's end.'

'What about the Curse? Your mother, aunt, cousin, grandmother—every female on your mother's side, for the last two generations has died in childbed. I thought you intended never to risk that.'

Putting out of her mind the heat that had flared between them in the glasshouse, Caro said, 'Mr Ransleigh's only seen me in atrocious gowns and in breeches, so maybe he won't want that from me. By all accounts, he prefers beautiful, sophisticated women and I'm hardly that. I'd give him free rein, with my blessing, to pursue and bed any other woman he wished.'

Elizabeth's eyes shadowed; Caro knew her husband had availed himself of that privilege without his wife's blessing. And despite her passionate love for him.

Maybe there was something to be said for wedding with cool calculation, with no emotions involved.

'Even if he took his pleasure elsewhere, he'd want to couple with his wife. Like every other man, he'll want an heir.'

'Perhaps. I'll worry about that later, after I save the stud.'

'What about Harry?' Elizabeth persisted.

A bittersweet pang went through her. She'd never imagined a future that did not include working the stud with Harry, the two of them linked by the same companionable affection they'd shared since childhood.

Pushing away the doubts, she said, 'What good would it be to have Harry, with no stud to run? Once the horses are sold and scattered, it would be nearly impossible to reassemble the breeding stock. As for the Curse, what good is hanging on to life if I've already lost what I love the most? No, Elizabeth, if there is a single chance of saving my horses, I simply must take it.'

Elizabeth hesitated another moment, frowning. 'I'm not at all sure this is wise, but…very well, I'll send Tilly to Lady Gilford's.'

Caroline crushed her cousin in a hug, hope and fear and desperation racing through her with the speed of a thoroughbred galloping towards the finish line at Newmarket. 'I'm not sure it's wise either. But ask her to hurry.'

On the other side of Mayfair, Max Ransleigh was sharing a brandy with the colonel of his former regiment at his lodgings at Albany.

'I appreciate your support, sir,' Max told him.

Colonel Brandon nodded brusquely. 'Can't trust these civilians not to muck things up. Foreign Office!' He snorted. 'If any of them had ever faced down fire in the heat of battle, they'd know the mettle of the men who fought beside them beyond any doubt. The very idea that you could have anything to do with that attempt against Wellington would be considered insulting and ridiculous by any soldier who ever served with you. As the scurvy diplomats should have realised.'

'If my own father wasn't willing to go to my defence, I don't suppose I can complain about the

Foreign Office's lack of support,' Max countered, trying to keep the bitterness from his tone.

'Your father's a political type and they are even worse than the Foreign Office. I suppose policy making requires compromise, but hell's teeth, give me a battlefield any day! No wrangling over this clause or that provision, just the enemy before you, your men around you, and duty, clear and simple.'

'After my brief time in Vienna, I must agree,' Max said.

'I've no doubt we can find you some position where you belong, in the War Department. Though I must warn you, Ransleigh, you've certainly muddied the waters with this heiress business. Not that I credit any of the wild stories floating about, but the fact that you are believed to have compromised a well-born girl and then refused to marry her won't make finding a post any easier. Especially not coming on the heels of that Vienna affair.'

So, just as he'd feared, he was being blamed for the fiasco. The anger, resentment and frustration with his situation—and Caroline Denby—that simmered just beneath the surface fired hotter and Max had to rein in the strong desire to explain what had happened and defend himself.

But the colonel wasn't interested in excuses. 'I'm well aware of that,' he said shortly.

'I cannot help but advise that it would improve your prospects if you'd just marry the chit. Or you might try to locate that damned female who tried to cozen up to you in Vienna.'

'I intended to do so right after I returned from Waterloo. But the Foreign Office gave me to understand it wouldn't make any difference.

'The Foreign Office prefers concealing dirty linen to laundering it,' the colonel said acidly. 'No, I'm convinced that if you could get her to confess to the plot, it would go a long way towards redeeming your reputation. I might even be able to talk Wellington around.'

'Do you think so?' Max tried to stifle the hope that flared within him. 'It would mean a lot to know I'd regained his trust.'

'Old Hookey is notoriously intolerant of error, but he has a soft spot for the ladies. He might be induced to see there was no other course that you, as a gentleman, could have taken but to help a female in distress.'

Max tried to curb a rising excitement. 'Then perhaps, while you look around for a posting, I'll head back to Vienna and see what I can turn up.'

'Couldn't hurt,' the colonel said. 'Those lackwits in the Foreign Office bungled their chance to have you, the fools. The War Office's a better place for the man who led the counter-charge and saved the colours at Hougoumont! Had the chateau fallen, we might have lost the whole damn battle, and now be watching Bonaparte march through Europe again. Report back to me in a month and I'll see what I can do.'

'Thank you, Colonel. I'm much in your debt.'

Brandon waved off Max's thanks. 'It's a commander's job to watch out for his men. Only wish I'd returned to London sooner, so you'd not have been left twisting in the wind for so long. Drinking and wenching is all good and well, eh?' he said, giving Max a wink. 'But a man of your talents should occupy his time with something more challenging.'

Max grinned. 'Amen to that, sir.'

After an exchange of courtesies, Max bowed and took his leave, fired with more purpose than he'd felt since leaving his unit after Waterloo. The colonel's optimism provided him the first real glimmer of hope he'd had since that awful day in Vienna, when the world as he'd known it had shattered around him like the windows of Hougoumont under French artillery fire.

After nearly a year of drifting idly about—drinking and wenching, as the colonel had said—he might finally be on the threshold of the new career for which he longed.

He might even win back Wellington's approval.

That happy thought cheered him as the hackney he'd hailed carried him towards the lodgings in Upper Brook Street that, being barred from his own family's home in London, he'd borrowed from Alastair.

With a respectable position, he'd be able to hold his head up again when he visited his mother.

He wasn't sure when, or if, he'd seek out his

father. The earl had made clear during their one meeting that his son was no longer of any use to him in the Lords and a person of no use to the earl was no longer of any importance either. The truth of that fact stung less now than it had when he'd first had to face it, after Vienna.

A short time later, the hackney halted in front of Alastair's town house. Paying off the driver, Max paced to the entry, the cold sharp night air as invigorating as the renewed hope within him.

He was about to mount the steps when, in the darkness beside the entry stairs, something stirred. Reflexes honed by years on a battlefield had him instantly whipping out the blade hidden in his boot. Half-crouched and prepared to strike, he called out, 'Who's there? Come out where I can see you!'

While he poised, knife extended, a shadow straightened and walked toward him. In the dim illumination of the streetlamp, she pulled off the hood of her cloak.

For a shocked moment he thought he must be hallucinating. 'Miss *Denby*?' he said incredulously.

'Mr Ransleigh,' she acknowledged with a nod. 'Although I may be the last person in England you wish to see, may I beg a moment of your time?'

Max blinked, still not quite believing she was standing beside his doorstep. What could have possessed her to come alone to his lodgings and wait for him in the fair middle of night?

A strong protective instinct surfaced, warning whatever brought her would likely mean yet more scandal and he'd had enough already.

'You shouldn't be here,' he said flatly, his eyes sweeping the street, which mercifully appeared to be deserted. 'Where are you staying? Give me your direction and I'll call on you tomorrow.'

'I know it's highly irregular to come here, but it's not as if I have any reputation left to lose. The matter about which I must consult you is so pressing I don't want to wait until tomorrow. That is, if…if you will consent to speak with me.'

Whatever it was, his first imperative was to get her away from his front door and out of sight of the neighbours or any passers-by returning home from some *ton* party.

'Very well. Please, do come in,' he urged, hurrying her up the stairs and through the doorway.

The sleepy footman within snapped to attention, closing his gaping mouth at Max's warning frown when he perceived Max was accompanied by a female. At Max's pointed glance, he stepped out of the way and handed over his candle.

Just what he needed, Max thought, his anger and frustration surfacing again, Miss Denby turning up to cause more problems just when Colonel Brandon was about to begin delicate negotiations to secure his future.

Max hustled her past the servant down the hall

and into the back sitting room, where the glow of the light wouldn't be visible to any neighbours on the other side of Upper Brook Street. Now to discover her mission and hustle her back out again before she caused any more damage.

Chapter Twelve

Torn between irritation and curiosity over Miss Denby's audacity in sitting beside his steps like a forgotten parcel, Max tried to muster up a cordial tone. 'Perhaps you'd better explain and be on your way.'

She took a deep breath. 'When I refused your offer at Barton Abbey, you assured me that if I should ever change my mind, I should let you know.'

Max swallowed hard, her words like a noose tightening around his neck. Now, when it finally looked like he might work out the future he wanted, was she suddenly going to hold him to that honour-coerced offer?

Grasping at something to deflect her, he said, 'I seem to remember that you were quite adamant about refusing it. You insisted you would marry no one but your Harry.'

'So I was, but I've just encountered circumstances that force me to revise those plans. Upon my father's death, trustees were appointed to oversee the management of the estate he bequeathed to me. As long as they did not interfere in the running of the stables, I was perfectly content with the arrangement.'

He recalled the great lengths she had gone to, willing to sacrifice her reputation—and sully his—to maintain control over the stud. 'And now they are interfering?' he guessed.

'Worse than interfering. I've just learned they intend to sell it. A buyer has been found and, unless something happens to prevent it, in about two weeks' time the estate will no longer own the stud.'

'And you can do nothing to stop this?' he asked, appalled despite himself and keenly aware of what the loss of Denby stables would mean to her.

'Lord Woodbury, the head trustee, has never approved of my involvement with the stud. When he learned that, despite becoming embroiled in a scandal that threatened my reputation, I refused to marry, he convinced the other trustees that my unnatural position running the stud had so corrupted my feminine nature, they should sell it to "protect" me and the good name of the family from further harm. Believing that, he's unlikely to listen to any plea I might make begging him to halt the sale. The only way—'

'—is to marry and have control over your assets

pass to a husband,' Max finished, understanding now why she had come to him.

'I'm desperate, or I would never be going back on my promise to leave you free to wed a woman of your choice. But you did once tell me you thought we might rub along well together, so if you would consider renewing your very kind offer, wedding me could offer you a few advantages.'

Her words tumbled over each other, as if she'd stood there in the dark rehearsing the speech over and over. Pausing only to drag in a ragged breath, she continued, 'I know you are already comfortably circumstanced, but I am a very wealthy woman. As long as you guarantee me sufficient funds to maintain the stud, you are welcome to the rest. Buy a higher rank in the army, purchase an estate, make investments on the 'Change. Travel to Vienna and hunt down the conspirators who engineered the attack on Lord Wellington. Whatever you wish that coin can buy, it can be yours.'

As if she didn't dare give him the opportunity to utter a syllable, she rushed on, 'Wedding me would also help to re-establish your reputation since, as you asserted from the first and I now recognise, my refusal to marry has most unfairly layered blame upon you. Indeed, if you truly wish to spike the guns of Lady Melross's malicious gossip, you might have Lady Gilford put it about that we've been acquainted for some time and the wedding long planned. No one would think it remarkable that the son of the Earl of Swynford,

discovered caressing his almost-betrothed in a se-
cluded conservatory, would feel no need to justify
his actions or explain the nature of his relationship
to a mere Lady Melross.'

The idea was so ingenious that, despite the turmoil of thoughts whirling in his brain, Max had to
laugh. 'Brilliant! An audacious lie—but plausible.'

'We'd have to wed by special license, but many
prominent individuals do so, to avoid the vulgar
publicity of having the banns called. If Lady Gilford and her friends seemed to find nothing ex-
ceptional about it, society would accept it as well.'

'You mis-spoke, Miss Denby,' Max said, shaking his head with rueful admiration. 'You are quite
diabolical. I begin to believe you'd make a master politician.'

That earned him a wisp of a smile before,
clutching her hands together, she dropped her
eyes, avoiding his gaze. 'As for intimacy,' she
continued, her cheeks colouring, 'I should prefer a marriage in name only, for reasons I would
rather not discuss. Since you aren't the eldest son,
there's no title to pass along. Having already asked
so huge a favour, I should make no other claim
upon your time or your affections. Although, obviously, you would not be free to marry, I will
neither interfere in nor protest at any other relationship you choose to enter. Although if…if
you felt for some reason that you *must* exercise
your marital rights…well, I realise I would have
no grounds to refuse you.'

Taking another deep breath, she raised her chin and faced him squarely. 'So that is the bargain. I don't expect you to give me an answer tonight, but I will need your reply within a few days. I know I have no right to intrude upon you with my dilemma…but the stud is my life. With everything I am and everything I love about to be stripped away, I simply had to seize any possible chance to prevent it.'

She fell silent, watching him, her dark eyes huge and imploring in a face lined with weariness. Tears had gathered at the corners of her eyes, he noted, sparkling like brilliants in the candlelight.

A host of questions crowded to his lips, even as his startled wits tried to sort out the preposterous new scheme she'd just laid in front of him. But before he had a chance to ask any of them, she sighed and hoisted herself unsteadily to her feet.

'I'll go now, through the kitchen if the footman will lead me out, so it's less likely any of your neighbours might see me and make matters worse. If such a thing is possible.'

But as she took a step, she stumbled and fell forwards. Max jumped up to catch her before she tumbled to the floor, her slight frame swaying in his hands.

'You're not well,' he exclaimed, all the questions swirling in his mind slamming to a halt at that observation. 'Here, sit back down.'

He eased her into the chair, sure she would have

collapsed had he not supported her weight. 'Where is Lady Denby? When did you arrive in London?'

She gave her head a small shake, as if the answer to so simple a question was a profound mystery. 'I arrived…this afternoon? Yes, it was this afternoon. Just myself and my maid. Stepmother got Lord Woodbury's letter two days ago; I travelled post yesterday and last night, arriving today to consult with Papa's solicitor and see if anything could be done.'

'You travelled post yesterday?' he repeated with a frown. 'When did you last sleep? Two nights ago? Three?'

'I don't recall.' She scrubbed a hand over her eyes, as if trying to clear the exhaustion from them. 'Something like that.'

'When did you last eat?'

'I'm not sure. The Royal Mail stops only to change horses, you know, not long enough to order a meal. Upon reaching London, I went directly to the solicitor's office, then back to my cousin Elizabeth's. And when I thought maybe you could help me, I came here.'

'Sit back in that chair before you fall out of it,' he ordered, pacing over to throw open the door. The footman he'd intended to call stood just beyond the threshold; from the flush on the man's face and his half-bending stance, Max suspected he'd been listening through the keyhole.

'Fetch some bread, cheese and ham,' he instructed. 'Brandy for me and some water.'

'No, you needn't entertain me,' Miss Denby protested as he closed the door. 'I've already trespassed enough on your time. I will await your reply at my cousin's house. Lady Elizabeth Russell, in Laura Place.'

She made another wobbly attempt to rise; gently he pushed her back into her chair. 'Miss Denby, there is no way I am sending you out of the kitchen door like some Whitechapel purse-snatcher to creep home through the midnight streets. By the way, please assure me you didn't walk here alone in the dark.'

'No, I did not.'

'Thank heavens for that!'

'I took a hackney to Hyde Park and walked from there. I didn't want the neighbours to see a carriage pull up and a female alight from it before your front door.'

Which meant she had traversed quite a distance through the London night. Though Mayfair was one of its more prosperous sections, no area of the city was entirely safe after dark for a young woman alone.

Max uttered an exasperated oath. 'Are you always this much trouble?'

'I'm afraid so,' she replied, with an apologetic look that almost made him chuckle.

'Well, your nocturnal wanderings are over,' he pronounced, curbing his humour. 'You will sit by that fire and warm yourself, then take some nourishment while I consider what is to be done.'

A ghost of a smile touched her weary lips. 'So masterful, Mr Ransleigh. Spoken like an earl's son indeed.'

Despite himself, he had to grin—was there any situation into which he'd got with this girl that didn't become absurd? 'It's the army officer in me,' he corrected.

'I knew it couldn't be the diplomat. Never make up their minds about anything without debating it for weeks.'

But, too distressed and weary, he suspected, to give more than token protest, she settled into the wing chair with a sigh, leaning her head back and closing her eyes.

Wilson returned a moment later with the refreshments, nearly goggle-eyed with curiosity. Instructing the footman to venture out into the night and find a hackey, Max closed the door in his face. Probably not even Wilson's scandalous employer Alastair had ever escorted an obviously gently bred female into the house after midnight.

'So, let me see if I understand you correctly,' he said after she'd begun dutifully nibbling on some ham and a biscuit. 'You propose that we wed immediately so that I may take charge of your assets before Lord Woodbury can sell off the stud. I would agree to allow you sufficient funds to run it and go my own way, with the rest of your dowry to invest as I see fit.'

'Correct.'

'In addition, I am free to engage in such… relationships as I choose, with your full approval.'

'Yes,' she confirmed, meeting his eyes steadily, though a hint of a blush coloured her cheeks.

He turned away, considering. Though he found her unusual and quite attractive in an unconventional way, he had no more inclination to marry now than when honour had forced him to make her an offer at Barton Abbey. Sympathetic though he was to her dire situation, his first impulse was to refuse.

But then he recalled Brandon's advice that the most helpful thing he could do to speed the colonel's efforts would be to redress the scandalous situation with the heiress.

Wedding her would rub out the tarnish on his honour, especially if he prevailed upon Jane to circulate the myth of their prior relationship that Miss Denby had just invented. His lips twitched again with appreciation at that blatant falsehood. Oh, how satisfying it would be to rout the noxious Lady Melross!

More importantly, wedding Miss Denby was the only way she could salvage *her* reputation. Though he wanted to remain angry with her for embroiling him in this mess to begin with, in truth, she was as much an innocent victim of the scandal Henshaw had unleashed upon them as he was.

As a gentleman of honour, he didn't see how he could refuse her plea that they marry now, any more than he could have avoided making her an offer after the escapade in the glasshouse at Barton Abbey.

Dismayed by that conclusion, he stared into the fire, his mind furiously casting about for any feasible way out…and finding none. It seemed he might have to marry her after all. Could he make himself do it?

If he did, he vowed the relationship would have to be more than the cold-blooded alliance of convenience his parents had made. He already knew that even if they had nothing else in common, there was passion between them.

He stole a covert look at Miss Denby, who had, after presenting her first proposition, having laid out all her arguments, left him alone to ponder his decision, with no further effort to entreat or cajole.

Though she was certainly far lovelier than she gave herself credit for being, there was no getting around the fact that she was nothing like well-connected society beauty Lady Mary Langton, whom he'd vaguely imagined marrying back when he was thought to have a brilliant political future.

But there might be advantages to that. Since Miss Denby wanted to remain in the country, he would not have to torture himself escorting his wife through endless rounds of society amusements, when he'd much prefer being at the nearby political gatherings from which he was now barred.

But she would never bore him. Unless he was

much mistaken about her character, she'd never beg him for trifles, demand that he dance attendance upon her, sulk or pout or importune him to get her way over some matter upon which they disagreed. Like a man, she'd discuss and reason and agree to compromise.

He'd be passing up his only chance to marry for love, but he wasn't sure he really believed in that poetic nonsense anyway. Of his closest friends, only Alastair had experienced it, and all that had got him was a desire to blow himself up on the nearest battlefield.

By now, Miss Denby had stopped eating and sat gazing glassy-eyed into the distance. Since she appeared too weary to notice, he indulged himself by openly inspecting her.

He'd thought it angular, but in fact her face was all soft curves and planes crowned by high cheekbones and finished with a determined little chin below full, soft lips he remembered all too well. Above that graceful arch of neck, another stray auburn curl caressed the edge of a delicious little shell of an ear.

How far down her back and breasts would that thick mass of curls tumble when he removed it from its pins? His fingers tingled and desire stirred, thick and molten in his blood.

She wore another of her dreadful, over-trimmed dresses. He imagined the kind of gown he might buy for her, that would show off to perfection her slender form…and luscious bosom.

His mouth grew dry as he remembered that, too.

This current appraisal confirmed his previous assessment that she was far lovelier than anyone at Barton Abbey had realised. Having gone about all her life thinking of herself almost as her father's son, she treated her womanly attractions as negligible. She seemed to have no inkling whatsoever of their potent power.

He could teach her that. Awaken her.

The zeal with which she pleaded for her horses, the fire he'd seen in her as she rode, the energy and determination that had driven her to travel halfway across England by coach and halfway across London by night all bespoke a passionate nature.

That passion and loveliness could be his, to arouse and enjoy. But, no, hadn't she also requested a marriage in name only?

Why would a woman of such obvious fire wish to enter a marriage without any? he wondered. Had one of her father's buyers cornered her in a stall one night, frightened her, manhandled her, as Henshaw had?

Anger boiled up at the thought. If she had been attacked, she'd not been violated; forthright as she was, she would have told him if she were not a virgin. He would certainly never force himself on her, but he had no right whatsoever to his reputation as Magnificent Max, able to charm any woman and persuade any man, if he couldn't manage to seduce his own bride. The fiery young woman who, he recalled with satisfaction, had already admitted in the conservatory at Barton Abbey that he tempted her.

A more unpleasant explanation occurred, chilling his ardour like the splash of a North Sea wave. Did she spurn fulfillment because she wanted to 'save herself' for the absent Harry? He was willing to risk many things, but not the possibility of being cuckolded.

'Despite our marriage vows, you offered me freedom of conduct if I agree to wed you, did you not, Miss Denby?' he asked, breaking the long silence.

Startled out of her abstraction, she looked up. As the meaning of his words penetrated, surprise widened her eyes. 'You might actually…consider doing this?'

'If I do, I'm afraid I'm not prepared to be as generous about your conduct. I require unquestioned faithfulness in my wife. What of Harry, when he eventually returns?'

'I promise you, upon my most solemn honour, that if you agree to marry me, I will pledge you my loyalty as well as my hand. I would never betray you with anyone else. Not even Harry.'

Another woman, seeing what she most desired within grasp, might dissemble at such a moment, but Miss Denby had never told him less than the absolute truth. Even when it didn't flatter her, he recalled ruefully.

He remembered her soldier's bearing as she

straightened her shoulders and marched off with no tears or pleading after he refused her first offer. How she'd backed away, apologising for intruding upon his peace, when they'd met by accident in the conservatory the second time. How she'd stationed herself outside his aunt's door at Barton Abbey, refusing to leave until she had spoken with Mrs Ransleigh and exonerated him.

He knew in his bones she meant every word of her promise and intended to keep it.

That fact sealed his fate. Perhaps on some level he'd known, ever since they'd been caught by Lady Melross in the glasshouse, that eventually it would come to this, for his initial fury had subsided to a calm resignation.

Never one to put off what must be done, once he'd truly decided to do it, Max dropped to one knee before her. 'Miss Denby, would you do me the honour of accepting my hand in marriage?'

Her eyes widened further. 'Don't you want to consider this further?'

'I have considered it. I'm quite willing to proceed at once.'

A look of befuddled wonder came over her face. 'You'll really marry me, Mr Ransleigh?'

'If you will have me, Miss Denby,' he replied, amused and a little touched by the enormity of her surprise. It seemed she hadn't truly believed her last-minute, desperate appeal would succeed.

Did she count the wealth she brought him, her intriguing personality, that ferocious honour and sense of loyalty…that luscious body, of such little worth?

Max would have to show her differently. Marriage to Caroline Denby might even be…fun.

If she'd been so unprepared for his acceptance, though, maybe she hadn't considered the consequences very carefully. 'Are you sure *you* don't need to think it over further?'

'Absolutely!' she cried, one of the tears still lingering at the corners of her eyes spilling down her cheek. Tentatively, as if she couldn't quite believe she now had the right, she laid her hand on his. 'I should be honoured to accept your offer, Mr Ransleigh.'

'Please, my friends call me Max.'

'Yes, friends. I believe we can be very good friends…Max.'

Friendship was a beginning, he thought. But with any luck and a full measure of his celebrated charm, he hoped to become a good deal more. If he must wed, by heavens, he intended his union to be a passionate one.

'If you've finished, let me escort you back to your cousin's house—by way of the front door, if you please. Now that we are to marry, I'll have no more skulking alone about the back streets of London.'

She nodded, 'And if we're to wed without delay, there is much to be done.'

'I'll set about obtaining a special licence, but there doesn't need to be unseemly haste.'

'But we only have—'

'I'll speak with Lord Woodbury and the trustees, telling them I don't wish the stud to be sold. Once they know we are to wed, I'm sure they will respect that choice.'

Her lips twisted in distaste. 'I expect you're right. *My* desires mean nothing, but the trustees will bow to the wishes of my intended husband.'

'Who also happens to be the son of a powerful member of government, someone they would not want to offend. Might as well use Papa's position to our benefit.' *Since it has done me little other good of late*, Max thought cynically. 'Besides, I suspect Lady Denby would be hurt were we to rush off and marry without even informing her.'

To his satisfaction, her eyes lit at that observation. 'You are right again, of course. She's harangued and cajoled me toward matrimony so frequently, I know she would be disappointed not to be present when her fondest wish is finally realised.'

'Exactly. Once I obtain the licence, we can be married at Denby Lodge, if you prefer.'

'I'd rather do so here, as soon as Stepmama and Eugenia can get to London. I don't trust Lord Woodbury.'

'Would you like to accompany me when I call on him?'

'Only if you intend to make him grovel,' she retorted.

He grinned at her. 'That could probably be arranged.'

Her eyes scanned his face, weighing the seriousness of his offer. Finally realising he meant every word, she said, 'That, I would very much like to witness—galling as it will be to watch him treat you with every solicitude, when he has always dismissed my opinions out of hand.'

'He will never do so again,' Max promised. Having a female, especially a young female, run a horse farm might be unusual, but since it was Lord Woodbury's interference that had forced this situation upon them, Max was not inclined to be forgiving.

She smiled with genuine gratitude. 'Though I sorely wish I might be able to do it on my own, watching you vanquish Lord Woodbury will still be satisfying. Thank you for being so considerate. And waiting until I can have my family present for the wedding. It will make it seem more…real.'

'Legally, it's absolutely real, wherever it takes place.' Pushing away the faceless image of an army lieutenant serving in far-off India, he continued, 'You must be very certain this is what you want; there'll be no going back later.'

'No going back for you, either,' she countered soberly. 'I only hope you won't hate me one day… as you might well, should you ever fall in love with a woman you then can't marry.'

'I think I will be quite satisfied with our bargain,' he assured her…and, to his surprise, realised that if wedding her made obtaining a posting easier, he might actually mean those gallant words.

'I shall do my best to make sure you never regret it.'

Max brought the hand she'd given him to his lips. As he brushed them against her knuckles, he heard her quick intake of breath, felt the shiver that moved through her.

Desire rose in him, sharp, sudden. He wanted to taste her skin, take her mouth, trace his thumb over the outline of her breasts, sure he would find the nipples taut and pebbled.

But not yet, not now, while fatigue clouded her eyes and worry over the loss of her home and her horses consumed her thoughts.

She tugged at her hand, confirming that caution. At once he released her.

At that moment, there was a knock at the door. Wilson peeked in to inform Max that a hackney awaited them.

'I'll return you to your cousin's, then,' Max said, helping her to her feet. 'You need your rest. Can't have my bride looking haggard, letting Lady Melross claim she had to be coerced into marrying me.'

'No, I must be radiant—if only to confound Lady Melross.'

Max escorted her out, reflecting that over his time as a privileged son, he'd had women from Diamonds of the *ton* to experienced courtesans try to entice him. None of them had sparked in him the combination of curiosity and desire inspired by the plain-spoken Caroline Denby—who'd made no attempt at all to entice him.

He had a sudden, lowering thought that he was about to marry a woman who might well fascinate him for the rest of his life…and she was marrying *him* to save her horses.

He'd just have to be up to the challenge of fascinating her, then. He might not be able to coerce an apology from the Foreign Office, but surely he could make one slip of a girl never regret marrying him.

Chapter Thirteen

Two days later, Max collected Caro at Laura Place and escorted her to the offices of Mr Henderson in the City, where Lord Woodbury, as spokesman for her father's trustees, was to meet them.

The solicitor, to whom Caro had already sent a note apprising him of her new status, greeted her warmly and treated Max, she thought, with just the right amount of deference, respectful of his status as an earl's son, but not fawning over him. After offering congratulations on their imminent nuptials, he said, 'I'm assuming you wanted to consult Lord Woodbury about transferring control over Miss Denby's inheritance?'

'Yes. Most urgently, though, I want to inform him that I do not wish for Denby Stud to be sold.'

'I'm so very glad to hear it!' Mr Henderson exclaimed. 'Having Miss Denby assume so active a role in the business might have been uncommon, but knowing how well she discharged those duties, I very much regretted the trustees' decision, an action I had no authority to countermand. I'm delighted you intend to retain ownership.'

'Anything that pleases my intended, pleases me as well,' Max said. 'I've been impressed by how highly Miss Denby has spoken of your services, Mr Henderson. If you will, I'd like you to work with my solicitors in drawing up the wedding settlements. We're both anxious to be wed as soon as possible,' he added, giving Caro a warm, lover-like look so believable that her face heated…and her body hummed.

Observing that glance, the lawyer smiled. 'So I see. I'm honoured by your confidence and will begin the necessary paperwork at once. Now, if I may show you into my private office? Lord Woodbury awaits you.'

Max offered his arm; Caro took it and together they walked into the office.

Lord Woodbury rose from his chair as they entered. After looking at Caro with some surprise, he recovered to say, 'Ah, the affianced couple! Allow me to wish you both every happiness.'

'Thank you,' Max said. 'As I mentioned in my note, I wish to briefly review the status of Miss Denby's estate.'

'Of course. Miss Denby, I'm sure Mr Henderson will make you comfortable elsewhere whilst Mr Ransleigh and I discuss these matters.'

'No, I wish her to be present,' Max said. 'The

first item under review is halting the sale of the Denby Stud and Miss Denby knows the details of its operation much better than I.'

Woodbury looked as if he'd like to assert she knew them far too well—but after viewing Max's expression, swallowed those words and said instead, 'You wish the estate to retain ownership?'

'I don't want any major changes made to the estate's assets before my man of business and I have the opportunity to review the whole.'

To Caro's mingled outrage and chagrin, without a syllable of protest, Woodbury replied, 'Quite understandable, Mr Ransleigh. I must confess some surprise, however, that you have an interest in running the stud. I assumed you would prefer to return to a government post.'

'I probably shall accept another position. Since my bride has overseen the stud's operation with great competence for years, I see no reason to make any changes in its management.'

Though the approving light in Woodbury's eyes dimmed, to Caro's added irritation, whether out of respect for the Earl of Swynford's son or because a *man* made the statement, Woodbury did not argue. After a moment, he said only, 'I suppose you may order things as you like in your own household.'

'Indeed I shall. I shall also see that my bride is never again slighted or insulted by those into whose safekeeping her inheritance was entrusted.'

Woodbury had the grace to look a bit uncomfortable. 'Certainly not.'

'I regret to say I am most disappointed in your stewardship, my lord. Nay—' Max held up a hand when Woodbury, eyes widening in surprise, began to sputter a protest. 'I appreciate that, in the main, the estate has prospered. But I must wonder at the character of a man who would so carelessly injure the delicate sensibilities of a female under his protection.'

Woodbury stared at him. 'Delicate sensibilities of a female…you mean *Caro*?'

After a warning glance from Max, Caro stifled the protest automatically rising to her lips. Following his lead, she sighed heavily and dropped her gaze, trying her best to look like a fragile maiden in distress.

'I understand you were a close friend of Sir Martin. I cannot imagine he would have been happy to learn you intended to strip away from his poor orphaned daughter the great project upon which the two of them had worked closely for so many years, the sole reminder she possessed of the father for whom she still grieves.'

'Well, I certainly—' Woodbury sputtered.

'Then there's the matter of the letter you wrote to Lady Denby, making rather…regrettable remarks about my betrothed. I'm shocked that a gentleman of your standing would have given so much heed to scurrilous rumour, rather than discreetly enquiring of the families involved. Surely you don't expect the Earl of Swynford to post details about private family matters on a handbill in every print-shop window! Or that he would stoop to correct common gossip.'

'But Lady Denby herself wrote me that you were not to wed!' Woodbury protested.

Max shook his head pityingly. 'Perhaps you did not read her letter aright. She merely meant to inform you that, at the time of her missive, we were not planning an immediate wedding. We subsequently decided to advance the date of our nuptials. In any event, I was quite disappointed by the unnecessary haste with which you set about disposing of a major component of my betrothed's estate without even the courtesy of consulting me. As was my father, the earl.'

'Your father, the earl?' Woodbury echoed, his indignation visibly wilting at Max's mention of his father's disapproval.

'I suppose you were only doing what you thought best—'

'Indeed, I was!' Woodbury inserted hastily.

'Still, I think you owe Miss Denby an apology.'

Woodbury opened and closed his lips several times, indignation seeming to vie with prudence as he attempted to dredge up the appropriate words.

'My father, the earl, would think it a handsome gesture,' Max added softly.

The expression on his face as sour as if he had just swallowed a large bite of green apple, Woodbury turned to Caro. 'My apologies, Miss Denby, if I have given offence,' he said woodenly. 'It was certainly unintended.'

She nodded. 'Apology accepted, Lord Woodbury. We may have had our…disagreements, but I know you tried to serve the best interests of the estate.'

'Since your trusteeship will end within days anyway, you may consider yourself relieved of your duties now,' Max announced. 'Mr Henderson can oversee whatever needs to be done until our marriage. Thank you for your efforts on Miss Denby's behalf, Lord Woodbury, and a good day to you.' Gesturing towards the door, Max gave him a regal wave of farewell.

Caro doubted the Prince Regent himself could have sounded more dismissive. Stifling any reply he might have wished to make, Woodbury bowed and departed, looking like a resentful schoolboy who'd just been caned by the headmaster.

After he'd exited, Max turned to Caro. 'Satisfied?'

Caro jumped up and sank before him into a curtsy deep enough to do justice to the Queen's Drawing Room. 'Completely, my lord. How perfectly you play the "earl's son" when you wish! I was nearly intimidated myself.'

'I did study at the feet of a master,' Max said drily.

'You tell a falsehood with as much skill as I do.' She chuckled. 'I can only imagine the outrage of your father, could he have heard you invoking his name in this case! To give Lord Woodbury his due, he did manage the *other* assets of the estate quite competently.'

'Yes, but while doing so, he deeply wounded the delicate sensibility of the female under his protection. Made her desperate enough to travel through the night to reach London and then endanger herself crossing the city alone in darkness. She even offered herself in a marriage she did not want, to undo the damage he had done. That's not an injury I will easily forgive.'

She was about to protest the 'delicate sensibility' description…but, in truth, she *had* been desperate. Looking up to admit that, she met his gaze, so full of concern that it sent a shock through her.

The rout he'd just made of Lord Woodbury was more than a clever demonstration of his rhetorical power; it showed he was indeed prepared to defend what mattered to her. That he took seriously his promise to protect it, and her.

For the first time since her father's death, Caro felt…safe. A wave of affection and gratitude swept through her, brought the sting of tears to her eyes, made her want to throw her arms around his neck.

'Thank you for standing behind me to save the stud.' The last part of his comment suddenly registering, she added softly, 'As for that marriage, I'm daily coming to believe proposing to you was the wisest decision I've ever made.'

He took her hand and kissed it. 'I hope so. You

are mine to protect now, Caro. I intend to do that to the very best of my abilities.'

As soon as he touched her, the clarity of her thoughts muddied, her mind disturbed by a rush of sensation, like the clash when the foam of a receding breaker meets the thrust of an incoming wave. Staring down at the hand he still held, distracted by the feelings coursing through her, she stuttered, 'I—I will t-try to prove myself worthy of that care.'

Then she looked up from her tingling fingers, became caught by his ardent gaze...and was lost.

She couldn't seem to either speak or look away. The attraction between them intensified, throbbing in her veins, humming in her ears, drowning out sound, paralysing thought.

That same strange, powerful compulsion she had felt in the conservatory at Barton Abbey welled up again, pulling her towards him. As if hypnotised, she found herself lifting her chin, stripped of everything but the need to feel his lips against hers.

He placed his warm, strong hand under her chin, drawing a murmur from her as she angled her head to feel the slide of his fingers against her skin. A maelstrom of desire began churning in her belly, tightening in her chest, as she raised her lips towards his.

Just as her eyelids fluttered shut, the door swung open. The sound acting upon her taut nerves like the crack of a whip, she pushed away from Max with a gasp, her heart pounding.

Henderson walked in, a stack of documents in his hands. 'I've begun the preliminary paperwork, Mr Ransleigh. If you'll have your solicitors contact me, I'm sure we can sort everything out quickly. If you have no further business here, may I offer you some refreshment before you leave?'

'Thank you, but we must be going. Let me again express my gratitude for the advice and support you have given my fiancée.'

Henderson bowed. 'Having known and esteemed Miss Denby since she was a child, I'm pleased to find that you intend to honour her wishes…and her.' Surprising Caro, he added, 'You might just be worthy of her.'

Grinning, Max returned the bow, the earl's son seeming not at all offended to have his conduct judged by a mere solicitor. Her nerves still jangled, Caro let him lead her back to the carriage, trying to stifle the yearning of a body that stubbornly regretted not getting that kiss.

Max had been not nearly as affected by it, she scolded herself. He'd probably kissed a score of girls, many of them prettier, every one of them more skilled in allurement than she. A simple little kiss was not for him the soul-shattering experience it promised to be for her.

Oh, this would never do. She simply had to wrestle this unruly attraction under control. Certainly before the wedding…after which she would suddenly be cast into significantly closer proximity to him for a much longer interval.

She really was getting married. A *frisson* of alarm, underscored by a deeper, hot liquid excitement licked through her. Once she truly belonged to him, body and soul, how was she to resist the force driving her to yield to him?

By recalling that the power of the Curse loomed a mesmerised moment of forgetfulness away.

Caro sighed. If she had any hope of resisting him, she must concentrate more on that real danger and learn to deal better with his maddening, bewitching allure. And with the wedding a mere few days away, she'd better learn quickly.

Chapter Fourteen

A little over a week later, Caro stood before the glass in a guest bedchamber of Lady Gilford's London town house. Lady Denby stood behind her, instructing the maid who was adjusting the skirts of her pale-green wedding gown.

Wishing she could soothe away the anxiety in her stomach as easily as the maid smoothed down the soft silken skirts, Caro studied her reflection critically. She couldn't remember ever owning so flattering a garment. At home, she'd ordered a few gowns each year from the village seamstress, but they had been adequate rather than stylish, and during her aborted Season, she'd taken care to choose cuts and colours as unsuited to her as possible.

For her wedding, she'd wanted to wear something that at least wouldn't make Max regret his decision the minute he saw her at the altar.

Would he find her appealing? Anticipation and unease skittered across her skin. In the few rushed days since their trip to Mr Henderson's office, she'd not made any progress in bringing her response to him under control. She felt attraction curl in the pit of her stomach every time he handed her into a carriage or took her arm up the stairs. Each time, she longed to extend and lengthen the contact.

In fact, the more time she spent with him, the more powerful his allure seemed to become, to the point that she feared if he made any move to make their marriage a real one, even the threat of the Curse might not be enough to armour her against him.

Which made it all the more imperative for her to get this marriage business finished as soon as possible and leave him in London to tend his career while she returned to Denby Lodge.

'Enough, Dulcie, you may go,' Lady Denby was saying. As the maid departed, Lady Denby gave her a reproving look. 'How lovely you are! I can't believe you hoodwinked me into wearing those atrocious dresses!'

'You have forgiven me, I hope.'

'With you mending matters by marrying Mr Ransleigh after all, of course I have. I do hope you'll be very happy.'

'I hope to make him so,' Caro said, thinking guiltily how robbing him of the chance to marry a lady he truly loved would make that goal more difficult. With society holding him responsible for her ruin, honour had given him little choice but to agree to her bargain.

'You mustn't worry about tonight,' Lady Denby said, obviously noticing Caro's nervousness. 'You may know everything about breeding horses, but the human animal is quite different. I'm sure Mr Ransleigh will be gentle and careful with you.'

Would he? They'd said nothing more since the first night about that part of their agreement. Legally, she couldn't deny him if he decided to ignore her request that theirs be a marriage in name only. Would he choose to do so…or not?

She came back from her reverie to find Lady Denby staring at her. 'I'm not worried,' she said a bit too heartily.

'You must put out of your mind that silly business about "the Curse",' Lady Denby said, patting her hand soothingly. 'I admit, the experience of some of your relations was unfortunate, but your mama, Sir Martin told me, had always been delicate. You are young and in robust health; there's no reason not to believe your own experience won't be much happier. Indeed, when the midwife places that first babe in your arms, you'll know it was worth all the discomfort and danger.'

Not if the hands receiving the babe were dead and cold, Caro thought.

'In any event, Mr Ransleigh will hope for an heir, as all men do, and you can't mean to deny him,' Lady Denby concluded, with a sharp glance at Caro.

Having no intention of confessing her bargain to her stepmother, Caro said meekly, 'No, of course not.'

Blessing again the fact that Max bore no responsibility for passing on his father's title, Caro hoped, for the present at least, that he'd be content to dally with the ladies sure to flock about such a dynamic, handsome, charismatic man—especially once he'd been restored to some important government position. She squelched a little niggle of jealousy at the thought.

It was ridiculous for her to be jealous that he would doubtless share with other women the intimacy she needed to avoid—and had actively *encouraged* him to pursue elsewhere.

She had about as much luck banishing the emotion as she had at controlling her responses to Max. Sighing, she shook her head at her own idiocy. Her inability to think coolly and logically about this matter was yet another indication that the sooner they parted after the wedding, the better.

Before they could walk out, a beaming Eugenia hurried in. 'Caro, how lovely you look! Oh, Mama, I've just had the most wonderful talk with Lady Gilford and Miss Ransleigh. Lady Gilford said she was going to speak with you about having us stay with her for the whole Season, so Felicity and I can share the experience! How kind she is, inviting us and allowing Caro and Mr Ransleigh to have their wedding breakfast at her house.'

As well as quietly putting out the taradiddle Caro had constructed about a previous attachment between herself and Max Ransleigh. 'We owe her a great deal,' Caro said. 'I'm glad everything is going to work out for your Season.'

'How much better everything looks now than when we left Barton Abbey! Though…I am sorry about Harry, Caro. I hope you are not too unhappy about marrying Mr Ransleigh instead. Not that I can imagine any girl being unhappy to marry someone so handsome, charming and well connected! But I know Harry was your best and dearest childhood friend.'

'I am quite content to marry Mr Ransleigh,' Caro answered, trying to keep her voice even and mask the frantic agitation the mere thought set fluttering in her veins.

The busyness of the last week had made it possible for her to put out of mind the fact that she'd traded away the ease, long friendship and wordless understanding she'd always shared with Harry for the edgy uncertainty of marriage to a man whose mere presence in a room made her pulse race.

But though she might refuse to *think* about it, the fierce attraction continued to simmer between them, driving her at once to try to stay near him and to flee his hold over her. With her nerves constantly on edge, she'd barely slept and, despite

Lady Denby's assurances, could scarcely contemplate the wedding night without a panicky feeling in her gut. Would he come to claim her? Could she make herself resist him if he did?

Oh, how much easier this would have been had Harry been the bridegroom with the right to enter her chamber tonight! A vision of his dear face rose up before her and she felt tears prick her eyes.

But it wouldn't be Harry tonight. It would never be Harry. Facing the dilemma before her, she'd made the only choice she could. There was no use looking back; she could only go forwards.

As she reaffirmed that conclusion, Lady Gilford opened the door and beckoned to them.

'How charming you look, Miss Denby! Shall we go? Max and the clergyman will be awaiting us at the church.'

In the nave of St. George's, Hanover Square, Max paced, trying to settle down a few nerves of his own. Once the decision to wed Caro Denby had been finalised, he'd experienced surprisingly few qualms and only one minor regret. Despite his vaunted charm, he hadn't made much headway in seducing his bride; if anything, she seemed more skittish than ever.

Perhaps it was only maidenly nerves and inevitable; knowing nothing about virgins, Max couldn't tell. An experienced man did have the advantage; he knew what to expect of intimacy, where his innocent bride could only speculate.

The stories reaching her ears must be lurid indeed, Max reflected, for as the day of their wedding grew nearer, Caro had grown as unsettled
as a green-broke colt sidling in a paddock, eyeing the saddle about to be placed on its back. Each
time he took her arm to assist her into a carriage
or walk her into a room, she jumped as if scalded
by his touch.

He shook his head ruefully and laughed. Bless
her, did she think he was going to drag her into
the bedchamber tonight and mount her with no
regard for her fears or her comfort, like a stallion
covering a mare?

The door to the sanctuary opened and his
senses sprang to the alert. But instead of the priest
leading in the bridal party, the figure striding in
was his father, the Earl of Swynford.

Max sent a swift prayer of thanks that he had
the space of several rows between them to col-
lect his thoughts before he must greet the man
with whom he'd had no contact since the morning he'd been dismissed from Ransleigh House.
He'd taken Caro to call briefly on his mother—
after making sure his father would be out. He'd
left his sire only a terse note to inform him of his
upcoming nuptials.

The man whose approval he'd once sought to
win before all else halted before him. 'My lord,'
Max said, bowing. 'I didn't expect you'd have the
time to attend.'

'I shan't stay for the wedding breakfast, but I

thought it wise to appear for this, so society would know I approved your choice. Despite the recent scandal over this girl, it seems you managed to land on your feet after all. "A previous attachment", indeed,' the earl said with a snort. 'I hope you thanked your aunt and Jane Gilford for their assistance in promoting that falsehood.'

'Yes, I've much appreciated all the efforts they expended on my behalf,' he said drily.

That barb hit home; his father frowned. 'You mean to imply that I have done nothing? You must remember, my son, at the time of your ill-advised liaison in Vienna, I was in the midst of very delicate negations to—'

Max held up a hand. 'I understand, Father.' The hell of it was, he *did* understand, though he still couldn't help resenting the fact that his father had not tried harder to find a way to intervene on his behalf.

'Well, however odd the path you followed to settle on this girl, it's a good choice. Better to have had a bride from a political family, but after Vienna, there's not much chance of that. At least you found yourself an heiress. Being rich will go a long way toward reconciling society to your lapses in judgement.'

Angry words rushed to his lips, but arguing with his father wouldn't set the proper tone for his wedding day. Restraining himself with effort, he said instead, 'I'm glad you approve my choice.'

'I expect you'll get her breeding and leave her

in the country. I don't recall meeting her last Season, but Maria Selfridge told me she wasn't up to snuff, with little to recommend her beyond a good pedigree and a better dowry.'

'Indeed?' Max said, annoyed by this cavalier dismissal of Caro, even though he knew she'd taken great pains during her brief Season to create exactly that impression. 'I find her both intelligent and lovely. But, yes, I expect we will settle at her property in Kent, to which she is very attached.'

His father nodded. 'Probably a wise move. Live retired for a year or two, breed some sons, let the memory of the scandals die down. By that time, when you come back to London, I'll probably be able to find a position for you.'

A cold anger rose in him, surprising in its intensity. 'There's no need, Father. I'm sure whichever flunky with whom you're now working is performing quite adequately, else you'd have turned him off, too. In any event, Colonel Brandon is soliciting a post for me in the War Department. If you'll excuse me, I must see what is keeping the priest.'

With a nod to his father, Max strode across the room and out into the foyer.

He closed the door, his hands still shaking with the force of his fury and, acknowledging that, his lips curved in a wry smile. Apparently the resentment and hurt over his father's abandonment ran far deeper than he'd thought.

Taking a shaky breath, he was wondering if

he should hide out in the gardens until the priest summoned him for the ceremony when the bridal party appeared at the entry door.

Then he saw Caro and his anger at his father was swept away by wonder.

He'd known since first discovering her 'disguise' that she was attractive. He'd been anticipating seeing her garbed in a more flattering gown—and taking her out of it. Still, he was not prepared for the enchanting vision that now met his appreciative eyes.

Vanished with the ugly gowns was any chance her unusual activities could lead one to find her mannish or unfeminine. Sunlight shining through the open doorway haloed her in gold, while its beams burnished to copper the artful arrangement of her auburn curls. The soft sage colour of her gown set off the cream of her shoulders and the rounded tops of her breasts that swelled up from beneath the fashionably low neckline. The long skirt and demi-train, mercifully unadorned, draped and flowed about her waist and hips, showing off her shapely, slender figure to perfection.

While he drank in the sight of her, she must have seen him, for she froze in mid-step on the threshold, her hand clutching at her stepmother's arm. With her dark eyes staring at him, she looked as uncertain and wary as a startled doe poised to flee.

This was no creature of salons and ballrooms, skilled in meaningless chat and empty flattery, but a pure, untamed soul whose words mirrored her actions and showed her to be exactly what she claimed: a woman who emanated a fierce independence and a feral energy that triggered a primitive response in him.

He wanted to devour her in one gulp.

But that would be for later…if the time was right. Max sighed. Nervous as she'd been this last week and still looked, that time probably wouldn't be tonight.

The priest entered and nodded at them both. 'Are you ready to proceed?'

Max walked over to claim her hand. He wasn't surprised to find it cold. 'Shall we do this?' he murmured, half-expecting her to say 'no'.

Taking a deep breath, she seemed to gather her composure. 'Yes. I'm ready.'

'Let us begin, then, Father Denton,' Max told him.

Within moments, they had taken their places before the altar. For Max, unable to wrench his wondering gaze from Caro, the ceremony afterwards was a blur. He barely registered his father watching sombrely, Lady Denby dabbing at her eyes, the delight on Felicity and Caro's stepsister's faces, the pleasure on Jane's and Aunt Grace's.

In some miraculous transformation, the nervous bride had disappeared, replaced by a serene lady lovelier than he could have imagined, who repeated her vows in a calm voice. From time to time, she glanced up at him shyly, golden motes dancing in huge dark eyes he could lose himself in.

Then the priest clasped hands together, pronouncing them husband and wife, and led them off to sign the parish register.

'Well, it's done,' she said quietly as she wrote her name in a firm hand.

'You look enchanting.'

She angled her head at him, apparently assessing the genuineness of his compliment. 'You truly think so?'

'I do.'

She smiled. 'Then thank you. Was that your father, glowering at us? I would think he'd approve of your marrying a fortune, at least. Will he be at the wedding breakfast?'

'No, thankfully. Mother should be and a handful of Jane's friends. I hadn't expected him here, either, or I would have warned you.'

She shrugged. 'I'm more nervous about your mother. Shock doubtless limited her conversation during the brief call we made on her; I fear she will want to corner me for a proper grilling this time, trying to discover how some country nobody made off with her son.'

'You needn't fear that. Aunt Grace has already told her what happened at Barton Abbey. She wants only to see me happy. Since you are now my wife, that means she wants you to be happy too.'

Caro gave him a dubious look, but had no time to reply before Lady Gilford came over to give them each a hug. 'A splendid wedding! Shall we return to the house? I expect guests will be arriving for the wedding breakfast soon.'

Looking a bit alarmed, Miss Denby—no, *Mrs Ransleigh*, a title it was going to take Max some time to adjust to, he admitted—said, 'There won't be many, will there? Stepmama said it was to be just a small reception.'

'Of course. In keeping with the story already circulating—which, Max tells me, was your invention, and very clever!—I thought it best to keep it very select, just immediate family and a few close friends.'

Caro nodded. 'Fewer people to gossip.'

Lady Gilford gave a peal of laughter. 'Oh, no, quite the opposite! With only the *crème de la crème* in attendance, those who weren't present will envy those who were and want to know everything about it…so they can discuss it as if they, too, had been invited. It will be quite the talk of the town.'

'Approving talk?' Caro asked.

'Definitely. Without wishing to sound arrogant, I do have a fair amount of influence. Where I and my friends approve, others follow…especially now that Max has done the sensible thing and got himself wed to a lady of intelligence and breeding.'

'And beauty,' Max said, pulling Caro's hand up for a kiss that set his lips—and other parts—tingling.

Blushing a bit, she pulled her hand free. 'And

large dowry,' she added. 'How much more sensible could any gentleman be?'

So completely had Max concentrated on Caro's flustered reaction—and the brief moment when her hand had tightened on his before pulling away—the sound of his father's voice startled him.

'Congratulations, Mrs Ransleigh, and welcome to the family,' the earl was saying.

'It was good of you to attend, my lord,' Caro said, dipping him a curtsy.

'I wanted all of London to know I approve of my son's choice.'

'This time, you mean?'

In the sudden hush, Max could almost hear the gasp of indrawn breath; no one who knew the Earl dared risk inciting his famous temper. Max tensed, mentally scrambling for words to deflect what would probably be a stinging rejoinder.

It must be bridal luck, for the earl merely gave a thin smile. 'This choice, no one could dispute.'

'I'm glad you think so and I'm sure he appreciates your taking the time to attend the service. I'm sorry we shall not see you at Lady Gilford's breakfast, but as I understand your duties keep you excessively busy I shall bid you farewell here. Thank you again for attending, my lord.' She made the earl another graceful curtsy.

It was almost a...*dismissal*! Max thought, shocked. He'd assumed her initial, rather confrontational greeting to his sire was perhaps an awkward choice of words due to nervousness.

But she didn't appear nervous—quite the opposite. Her poised figure and cool manner seemed to indicate she neither feared, nor desired to impress, the powerful earl whose behaviour, her tone suggested, she disapproved of. Astounded, Max had to conclude she'd said exactly what she had wanted to say.

Since he wasn't sure how he might deflect a tongue-lashing from his father, thankfully the earl chose to be forbearing. With only a surprised lift of his eyebrow in Max's direction, he bowed and kissed Caro's hand. 'Let me wish you both happy.'

Max watched his father walk away. Still somewhat awed, he offered Caro his arm and led her to their waiting coach. As she settled into her seat, he said, 'I should warn you not to tweak my father. Few who do so emerge unbloodied.'

Caro merely shrugged. 'Unless the earl can sell off my stud, I've nothing to fear from him. His approval means nothing to me—nor are your future prospects held hostage to his patronage any longer. Which is fortunate, since it's certainly done you little enough good so far. I'm sorry if I sounded… ungracious; I do appreciate his recognition of you, however belated.'

A flush of gratitude warmed Max at this unexpected avowal of support. Before he could summon a reply, Caro continued, 'But how could he not approve? He'd look rather foolish if he refused to bless his son's marriage to a girl of impeccable birth who brought a fortune into the family. As I possess no ties of childhood affection that make me anxious for his favour, I'll not easily forgive him for refusing to assist you when you needed him most.'

She halted the protest he'd been about to utter with a lift of her hand. 'Oh, I understand he is a busy man with heavy responsibilities. But to my mind, there is no responsibility more important than helping your own kin.'

'Being his son has brought me many advantages,' Max replied, finding himself in the odd position of defending the man who'd hurt and angered him so deeply.

'He gave you the advantages of birth and his approval when it cost him nothing...but didn't lift a finger when assisting you might have made his own position more difficult,' she retorted. 'That is not what I call "affection" or "loyalty". One deserves better from one's family.'

Like watching a stable mongrel run out to bite a pure-bred hunting dog twice its size, Max couldn't quite get his mind around the audacity of little Caro Denby nipping at the mighty Earl of Swynford with her disapproval.

'You intend to offer me better,' he asked, bemused.

Looking up at him, her face still fierce, she said, 'Of course. I told you I would when you agreed to wed me. I just promised it again before God and those witnesses.'

'My little warrior,' he said. But her unexpected

loyalty penetrated deep within him, soothing a place still raw and aching. He'd thought to protect and defend her from his father; he'd never expected *her* to defend *him*.

'I know you must still want his approval; he is your father, after all. But you are no longer a puppet dancing as he pulls the strings, forced to settle for whatever he decrees. You have wealth of your own, a patron in Colonel Brandon who is independent of his influence. You can meet him on *your* terms now.'

He'd never before considered it, but she was right. The idea of being truly out of his father's shadow was...liberating. 'You really are ferocious,' he said, half-amused, half-serious. 'Remind me never to cross you.'

Her fierceness vanished in a grin. 'That's probably wise. I suppose I am passionate about those things I believe in.'

'Like your horses.'

'And your future. But I can't disapprove of the earl completely. If he *had* supported you as he should, you wouldn't have been exiled and at Barton Abbey to rescue me.'

'I've become more thankful by the hour that I was.'

As the coach bowled along, a gallery of the ladies he'd squired on one occasion or another suddenly ran through Max's mind. All had been practically quivering with eagerness when he introduced them to the earl, echoing his father's opinions, anxious to win his favour. His bride not only had made no such effort, she'd practically tweaked his father's nose.

Because the mighty earl had not stooped to stand by him.

Max shook his head anew. He'd known from the moment they'd met that Caro was unique; how she continued to surprise him!

Having traversed the short distance between parish church and his cousin's house, the coach halted and a footman ran up to let down the steps.

Caro took a deep breath. 'Well, here we are. I hope Lady Gilford spoke the truth when she promised there would be only a few close family and friends at the reception.'

'If you can face down my father,' Max said as the footman helped her out, 'you can face down anyone.'

She gave him a rueful smile. 'I'm better at facing people down when I'm angry. Unless your family and friends incite my hostility by criticising you or the quality of the Denby Stud, I'd rather avoid conversation. I communicate much better with horses.'

'Tell them to neigh,' he suggested, eliciting a giggle as he led her in.

Chapter Fifteen

Caro paused uncertainly beside Max on the threshold of Lady Gilford's reception room as the butler announced the bride and groom, to the applause of the assembled guests. Lady Gilford had told the truth; probably not more than thirty people stood within a spacious room that could have easily had many more.

Their hostess immediately took Caro's arm and led them along, introducing friends and relations. Caro tried to do her part, nodding, smiling, dredging up names to match faces from her vague memories of her brief London Season. She didn't want to embarrass her hostess or Max by appearing to be the gauche, country bumpkin she truly was.

She even managed to do tolerably well, she thought, when meeting again Max's mother and his aunt, Mrs Grace Ransleigh, two ladies who had little reason to like her.

Hiding whatever chagrin she must be feeling to find her splendid son married to a woman so lacking in all the society graces, Lady Swynford congratulated her and pronounced her charming. The hostess of Barton Abbey, whose house party she'd marred with scandal and whose private rooms she'd invaded, was equally forbearing when she begged that lady's forgiveness.

'I may have initially resented your actions, but your insistence on revealing the truth about you and Max won my gratitude in a moment,' Mrs Ransleigh told her. 'I'm delighted to wish you both very happy.'

Thinking guiltily how disappointed both his mother and aunt would be if they knew the true terms of the bargain she'd made with Max, she said, 'I hope to make him so.'

Mrs Ransleigh gave her a shrewd glance. 'I think he's luckier than he knows.'

'Indeed I am,' Max agreed, reclaiming her arm, which set little shivers vibrating deep within her. 'I can't wait to discover just how much,' he added in a murmur meant for her ears only, accompanying the words with a look that whispered of warm sheets and intimate caresses.

The vibrations magnified, making her hands and lips tremble as a surge of both desire and panic washed through her. Her cheeks heating, she mumbled an incoherent reply to Mrs Ransleigh.

Turning away from Max, who continued chatting with his mother, she found herself face to face with Alastair Ransleigh.

After all the good will and compliments, his sardonic expression was a reviving slap, for which she uttered a silent thanks. Seductive innuendo confounded her, but the patent disapproval on his face she could deal with.

'Mr Ransleigh,' she acknowledged him with a curtsy. 'I'm sure Max is happy you journeyed to London to celebrate with him.'

'But you are not?' he shot back.

Shrugging, she raised her chin. 'Whether or not you approve of my wedding him is a circumstance over which I have no control. I could assure you I meant the best for your cousin, but only time will prove the truth of that.'

He inclined his head. 'A clever response and correct on both counts, *Mrs Ransleigh*. I must warn you, there are four of us who have guarded each other's backs since we were children. Play my cousin false, and you will have not just me, but three other Ransleighs to deal with.'

Caro laughed. 'Do you think to frighten me? I realise your opinion of ladies is very low, Mr Ransleigh, but not all women are cut from the same cloth. Just as appearances in Vienna are not proof your cousin bears any blame in the attempt made on Lord Wellington.'

'We agree on one point, then,' Alastair replied.

At that moment, Max turned back to her and discovered Alastair's presence. After exchanging greetings, the two cousins shared a few moments of handshaking and hearty, man-to-man congratulations.

Watching them, Caro had to smile. Their deep mutual affection was so obvious that, knowing Alastair Ransleigh's sad history, she supposed she could forgive him his suspicions.

But it had been a long, exhausting week; so weary was Caro that she silently rejoiced as the guests paid their respects to their hostess and began drifting out. For a short, cowardly moment, she wished she could go back upstairs to the chamber she'd shared last night with Eugenia and listen to her stepsister's eager chatter until they both fell asleep.

But she'd made a bargain and it was now time to begin fulfilling it. Instead of sleeping upstairs, she'd spend the night in a suite at the Pultney Hotel…with her new husband.

She swallowed hard. Max had shown her nothing but kindness, had suffered scandal on her behalf, had been the instrument of saving her beloved horses. He'd given her much; now she must respond by doing the hardest thing that had ever been required of her: placing control of herself and her body in his hands.

She wasn't going to do it trembling like a coward.

So she nodded with an appearance of cool self-possession as they took their leave of the party. Tried not to flinch when Max took her arm, too acutely conscious of his presence beside her to make any sense of the thanks he offered Lady Gilford.

Then they were out of the door, down the steps and he was handing her into the hackney. As he climbed in after her, she tried to think of some polite and amusing topic of conversation. But the courage necessary to keep herself from trembling sapped all the strength she had left, leaving her mind an utter blank.

Embarrassed, she hoped her nervousness was not as apparent to Max as it was to her. But since she jumped every time he touched her and he was not a stupid man, she figured miserably that he was probably only too aware of it.

When his voice came out of the darkness, she braced herself for some reproof about her timidity. Instead, he said, 'I must admit, in all the rush to finish up the details necessary for the wedding, I've not thought much beyond today. We could take a bridal trip, if you like. I'm ashamed to admit, I have no idea where you might wish to go. Do the wonders of ancient Rome appeal to you? The mountains of Switzerland?'

Seizing on that safe topic, she said, 'Have you visited them?'

'Rome, yes, and some other parts of Europe during my travels to and from Vienna.'

'What did you find most interesting about Rome?'

Fortunately, he'd found the city fascinating and

was quite willing to describe it. Caro needed only to insert an enquiry here and there to prompt him to elaborate on his observations.

After a few minutes during which nothing more was required of her than to listen, Max said, 'But enough of my travels. Would you like to visit the city?'

'Perhaps some day. For now, I wish to return to Denby Lodge as soon as possible. As you may recall, the winter sale takes place—'

Before she could finish her remarks, the carriage braked and slowed to a halt. Max hopped out and waited by the steps for her to alight. A mix of dread and anticipation accelerating her heartbeat, she put a cold hand on his arm and followed him into the hotel.

Chapter Sixteen

⁓⁓⁓⁓⁓

Acutely conscious of the powerful, virile man beside her, Caro responded with mechanical civility to the manager's greeting. Her nerves tightened as if turned upon a vice with each step up the stairway as a servant led the way and ushered them into an elegantly appointed sitting room. In her super-sensitised ears, the soft snick of the door as he exited echoed as if he'd slammed it.

Numbly Caro noted the trunk Dulcie had packed for her sitting inside the adjoining dressing room. Opposite that, beyond a partially opened door, was a bedchamber dominated by an enormous, four-poster bed.

Images danced through her mind…Max's warm, strong hands stroking her skin as he removed her gown…his hard lean body, naked in the candlelight.

A wash of heat coursed through her. Jerking

her gaze away from the bed, she tried to shut the thoughts out of her mind.

She turned to find Max, with an amused smile that said it must not have been his first request, asking if she'd like a glass of wine.

Seizing upon anything that might calm her nerves, Caro accepted gratefully. Beneath the anxiety, eddies of excitement were building. Her body whispered its hope that tonight Max would ignore their bargain and claim his marital rights. Lead her into the bedchamber, press her against the softness of the mattress, caress and kiss her as he removed her gown and bared his own body to her touch and admiration.

Her hands tingled at the thought of running the pads of her fingers over his arms, his legs, the flat nipples of his chest.

In another part of her brain, a near-panicked awareness shouted she must avoid that outcome at all costs…or she was lost.

Hoping he would make that decision soon and remove her from this agony of speculation, she walked to the sofa and perched on the edge, her back to the bedchamber door.

He brought her the wine and took a seat beside her.

'Before we arrived, you were saying you wished to go home?'

'Y-yes,' she said distractedly. Heavens, how was she to think when he sat so close beside her she could feel the heat emanating from his body, his soft exhales of breath?

'As you may remember,' she forced herself to begin again, 'the winter sale will take place in less than a month. There's much work that must be done.'

'I can well imagine.'

She looked down, unwilling to meet his gaze as she continued, 'It's not…necessary that you come to Denby, too. You've lived all your life in a hectic political household, took part as diplomats from every nation met to decide the future of Europe, then fought against Napoleon at Waterloo in the greatest army ever assembled. I wouldn't expect you to be content rattling about a horse farm in Kent.'

Even as she uttered the words, she felt a completely illogical pang of regret. She'd come to hope they might pursue the friendship begun these last few days, she suddenly realised. In the moments when his imposing physical presence was not setting her nerve endings afire and turning her mind to mush, she'd enjoyed his companionship. Life without his intoxicating presence would seem somehow…tamer, less vital and exciting.

'Would you miss me if I don't accompany you?' he murmured. Before she could decide how to reply, he distracted her by placing one warm, strong hand on the back of her neck.

Though she jumped at first contact, she soon found the gentle massage of his fingers on the tightly corded muscles wonderfully soothing. Oh, how she wanted to lean in and give herself up to the pleasure of his touch!

Soon, she might have to give up everything... perhaps even her very life. The tension retightening, she leaned away from his hand.

'I will miss you,' she answered honestly. 'But I gave you my pledge not to interfere in your life and I meant it.'

'I see. I could escort you home, at least. Unless...you don't want me to meet your neighbours?'

That question was so absurd she had to laugh. 'Nonsense—I shall be proud to introduce you in the neighbourhood!' Envisioning the probable reaction, she added with a grin, 'I'm sure many in the county will be astonished to discover that mannish scapegrace Caro Denby, who could scarcely make it to church with her skirts unmuddied and her gloves clean, managed to land an earl's son. I'm afraid there are several matrons whose opinions of my running the stud matched Lord Woodbury's.'

'In my guise as the elevated son of an earl, would you like me to snub them?'

'I think you'd find them difficult to snub! Even the prospect of having to be pleasant to me wouldn't be distasteful enough to discourage those with marriageable daughters from seizing the opportunity to have their girls flirt with you, so they may claim acquaintance with your family when they go to London.'

To her dismay, at the prospect of having the lovely, blue-eyed Misses Deversham or the curvaceous brunette Miss Cecelia Woodard make eyes at Max, she felt a sharp pang of what could only be jealousy.

The ambitious mothers of local maidens were not the only ladies who would be happy to claim Max's acquaintance in London. Now that he once again had the promise of high position, all sorts of women would be throwing out lures, hoping to entice a handsome earl's son with a conveniently absent wife.

Was letting him go a mistake?

She shook her head. This was ridiculous. Max was not hers to hold. Even if he cared for her, under the terms of the bargain they'd made, she had promised him the freedom to pursue any women he wanted.

She looked up from that disagreeable fact to find him watching her, a slight smile on his face. 'If I can't discourage them from flirting with a snub,' he murmured, that heated, caressing tone in his voice again, 'then I shall just have to play the besotted bridegroom.'

Her mouth dried and panic jockeyed with attraction in the pit of her stomach. She stared at him, unable to tear her eyes from the intensity of his gaze, feeling the looming presence of the wide bed in the room behind them as if it were branded upon her shoulders.

The moment of surrender or resistance was imminent, the knowledge of its nearness pulsing a warning in her blood.

Her body craved surrender with every rapid heartbeat. Her mind, grimly conscious of the danger of the Curse, screamed at her to resist.

Sure she would go mad, pulled between two such diametrically opposing demands, a sudden, frantic desire to put off the decision filled her. She opened her lips, but her brain had gone blank and she could think of nothing else to delay the moment any further.

Would he take her now? In the next few minutes, she would finally find out.

Chapter Seventeen

Torn between wanting him to bed her and dreading that he would, when Max took Caro's hand again, she jumped.

Instead of tightening his grip and leading her into the bedchamber, Max released her. 'Caro, Caro,' he murmured. 'I'm sure you know all about encounters between a stallion and a mare, which don't appear very pleasant.'

She felt her face heat, but better to address the matter head-on, as it were. 'Not for the mare, at any rate.'

'I'm not so sure she doesn't enjoy it, but I'll bow to your superior knowledge of the equine species. I don't suppose you have any experience about mating of the human kind?'

'None,' she admitted. 'I thought gentlemen didn't want brides who had such experience.'

'That may be true, but it does create a drawback. You have nothing but my assurance that coupling between a man and a woman is nothing like what you've observed. It can be gentle, tender, cherishing.'

She nodded, every image his words conjured up stringing her already taut nerves tighter. Oh, how she wanted to experience it! If only she dared let him touch her, boldly and unafraid of the consequences. Still torn in opposing directions, she wished desperately he would make the decision for her and get on with it.

Distracted by those chaotic thoughts, when he touched a thumb to her cheek and stroked it, again she flinched.

He shook his head and chuckled. 'That's what I thought. Relax, sweeting. I promise I will never hurt you. You believe that, don't you, Caro?'

To her dismay, a tear pooled at the corner of her eye, then ran down to wet his thumb. She was acting as dithering and missish as the sheltered *ton* maidens she despised, she thought, disgusted with herself, the battle between his powerful attraction and her need to resist it making her uncharacteristically indecisive.

Before now, she'd always made up her mind quickly and acted upon it. But until now, she'd never imagined there could be something that appealed to her so powerfully that she was tempted to risk the Curse.

He'd just given her a perfect opportunity to tell

him about it, she realised. Why not reveal the true reason for her fear and reluctance?

She was about to confess it...until she remembered Lady Denby's advice. Even the stepmother devoted to her well-being discounted the seriousness of the Curse. Max, who had no experience at all with childbirth, would probably dismiss her concern as laughable.

Or, even worse, pity her cowardice.

Lady Denby was doubtless right about the other, too. Max might not have yet expressed a desire for a son, but, eventually, he would want one. They both knew the promise she'd extracted from him not to consummate their marriage was unenforceable. The best she could hope for would be to delay that consummation long enough to achieve for the stud what her father had dreamed, before Max's desire for a son led to its probable result.

'Caro!' he called softly, telling her that she'd been silent too long, debating how best to answer his question. 'You can't truly believe I would hurt you!'

'No, no, of course not.'

'Good,' he said, relief in his tone. 'Then believe this, too. I respect you and care for you. Yes, I also desire you, as a lovely woman who is much more attractive than she knows. But regardless of my rights as your husband, I will never force intimacy upon you. Never take from you anything you are not willing to give, that you do not hunger for as fiercely as I do.'

Oh, if only she did not hunger for it so fiercely, she thought, suppressing a sigh. 'I understand. And thank you.'

'A kiss to seal the bargain, then?'

Caro eyed Max uncertainly. Was a kiss simply a kiss, or a prelude to more? But he'd just said he wouldn't force her. And surely she was sensible enough to resist letting a simple kiss turn into something else.

Besides, she had burned to kiss him since that interrupted moment in the solicitor's office. Why not stop worrying about what might happen next and simply enjoy claiming what she'd been denied?

Giddy anticipation thrumming through her, she gave in to the force that, since their first meeting in the conservatory at Barton Abbey, had impelled her towards him. 'A kiss,' she agreed.

She angled her chin up and closed her eyes, waiting, a breathless excitement feathering through her veins. Through closed lids, she could sense his face descending toward hers, feel the warmth of his breath on her cheek. Anticipation coiled tighter and tighter within her, impatience mounting to at last feel the brush of his mouth against hers.

But after a moment, when he had moved no further, she opened her eyes and looked up at him, puzzled.

He was gazing at her intently, the energy emanating from the molten blue of his eyes like the crackle in the air before a lightning strike. 'I promised never to take from you, Caro,' he murmured. 'To give you only what you desire. So... show me what you want.'

Somewhat dismayed, she stared back at him. She'd never kissed a man in her life besides Harry and that hardly counted. They'd both been twelve when he surprised her by bussing her on the lips. She'd punched him afterwards.

Max had probably kissed dozens of women. Maybe hundreds.

Struggling with that daunting observation, her cheeks heating with embarrassment and thwarted desire, she said, 'I don't know...what to do.'

She feared he'd laugh at that humiliating confession, but instead he smiled. 'Don't think, just feel. Do what you want.'

What did she want? To touch him. The thick, wavy dark hair that always brushed his forehead. The smooth skin of his forehead and cheeks, the chin that in the late evening showed a dark shadow of stubble.

Uncertain, tentative, she reached up and ran her hand through his hair, to find it thick, luxurious, silky-coarse. Its soft slide against her fingers was arousing, making her want more. Emboldened, she traced the faint lines of his forehead, brushed a fingertip across his eyebrows, drew her nails lightly across the stubble of his chin. Traced her thumb across the surface of his lips, the skin firm, but softer than she expected.

He'd watched her expectantly as she explored

his face, but as she traced her finger across his lips, his eyes drifted shut. 'Yes,' he murmured against her finger. 'Yes.'

Suddenly, she wanted to know if the stubble that clicked against her nails would sound the same, brushed against her teeth. Urging his head down, she leaned up and opened her lips, raking her teeth across his chin, catching the taste of him on her tongue.

Heat and pleasure jolted through her. She added tongue to teeth, her finger twining in his hair as she licked and nibbled the short, wiry stubble that carried the taste and scent of male and shaving soap.

A sharp imperative began thrumming in her blood. Though she'd not yet had her fill of his chin and the strong underside of his jaw begged to be explored, she simply had to taste his mouth.

Rather than joining her lips to his, at first she licked them, tracing them from corner to crest to corner. A deep groan sounded, echoing in her chest—his or hers, she wasn't certain.

Fevered impatience building tighter within her, she licked his lips again, then pressed hers against their wet surface. But that didn't seem to be close enough, deep enough. Her tongue teased at the corners of his mouth and, before she could realise what she wanted, he opened for her.

She slid her tongue inside to discover a new world of wonder. Another wave of shocked, fevered excitement swept through her as her tongue collided with his.

And then his hands came up to cradle her face, gentle but urgent, and he was kissing her back. The rasp of his hot, wet tongue as he stroked it back and forth, back and forth against hers sent a heated excitement pulsing to the very core of her.

Her whole body seemed to be throbbing, melting. Her breasts felt heavy, turgid, the nipples tingling, while warmth and wetness pooled between her thighs.

He teased her with his tongue, tracing the edge of hers, then withdrawing, while, frantic, she pursued his. When he suddenly clamped his lips around her tongue, sucking it deep into his mouth, the pleasure crested until she thought she might faint.

Her breath came in short, fevered pants and she couldn't seem to draw in enough air. A sharp need built in her, driving her towards something she didn't recognize, but wanted desperately. Her nails biting into his back, she clung to him, kissing him urgently, suckling his tongue and lips, trying to get closer, deeper, as if she might penetrate to the very core of him.

And then he broke the kiss, pushing her away before tucking her under his chin and holding her close. Against her ear, she could feel the hammering of his heart, the rapid rise and fall of his chest as he drew in breaths as ragged as hers.

'Well,' he said unsteadily a few moments later, 'that was certainly worth the bargain.'

Her mind was still so fuzzy, she could barely understand his words, much less produce a reply. While she fumbled, trying to recover, he pushed away and slid to the far side of the sofa.

Was that his hardness she saw, straining against his trouser front? A sudden desire filled her to touch him.

Before she could act upon the urge, he said, 'With all you've had to do these last few weeks, you must be exhausted. If we're to leave for Denby Lodge early tomorrow, you must rest. Take the bed; I'll be quite comfortable on the couch here in the sitting room.'

Bringing her hands to his lips, he kissed each fingertip, stirring the fire still not banked within her. 'Rest well, dear wife. I shall see you in the morning.'

So…he didn't mean to claim her. An incoherent protest formed in her still-foggy brain. Suppressing it, her aroused nerves sparking and sizzling with frustrated need, she nodded blankly, struggled to her feet and stumbled into the bedchamber.

Only to return to the sitting room a moment later. 'I'm sorry, but since it was our wedding night, I…I told Dulcie I wouldn't be needing her. I can't unfasten the bodice of this gown without assistance. If you wouldn't mind…?'

'Of course.'

She turned her back to him, still in that half-aroused state where relief that he would not be bedding her battled with frustration.

Her sensitised nerves felt every small tug and touch of his fingers as he loosened the ties of her gown, then the laces of her stays. There were too many layers of clothing, she thought, yearning for just one touch of his hands against her bare skin.

Then, when she thought he'd complete the process without it, he smoothed his hands from the nape of her neck to the edge of her bodice, loosened the material of gown, stays and shift, and pulled it away from her skin. As if he, too, could not end the night without making a small beginning on exploring her body, he slipped his fingers under the loosened garments and slowly stroked the flesh beneath.

She froze, closing her eyes, every bit of awareness focused upon the delicious friction between the slightly rough pads of his fingers and her bare skin. Oh, that he might continue stroking her, working from the back of her gown to the front, where his questing fingers might explore the swell of her breasts, discover the nipples peaked and aching!

For a few thrilling moments, it seemed he might, as he caressed his fingers slowly from the back of the gown around to her shoulders. But he halted there, thumbs resting on her bared collarbones as he pulled her against him and nestled his chin in her hair.

After cradling her a moment, he released her

and stepped away. 'I'd better stop now,' he said, his voice sounding strained. 'Can you manage from here?'

'Y-yes, I think so,' she stuttered.

'Goodnight, then. Sleep well.'

He gave her a little push towards the bedchamber, then closed the door behind her.

In a gradually fading sensual haze, she removed her gown, shift and stays, drew on the night rail and climbed into the mammoth bed. The chill of the linens against her body finally extinguished the last of her fevered tension.

'Sleep well,' Max had advised. As Caro pondered the power of her response to him this night, she wasn't sure she'd be able to sleep at all.

Even now, thinking about kissing him brought her senses simmering back to life. When she reviewed her behaviour since arriving at the hotel, she had to suppress an hysterical laugh. After dithering in a missish quandary between desire and dismay, she'd fallen into his hands like a ripe fruit after one simple kiss.

She'd been right to fear the potent effect he had on her. They'd been wed barely half a day, and if he'd made any move to join her in the big bed she'd not have repulsed him. Indeed, before stumbling into the room, she'd come very close to inviting him.

It didn't do any good to remind herself that though he liked her, he wasn't in love with her; that she'd given him full freedom to pursue other women, a freedom he would almost certainly exercise at some point.

She still wanted him and burned for his touch.

Even reminding herself that giving in to the craving he elicited so easily would surely lead to her conceiving a child and testing the power of the Curse didn't lessen his hold over her—at least, not while he was touching her.

And he was so clever, drat him. If he'd cajoled or tried to coerce her, it would have been much easier to resist him. Instead, he'd promised never to hurt her...and let her desires set the pace of their intimacy.

She remembered the thrill of exploring his face, his lips, the wicked taste of his mouth, and groaned. At this rate, she was going to be dragging him to bed within a week of their return to Denby.

The danger was not just his physical appeal, devastating though that was. Their outings together this week as they prepared for the wedding had shown him to be not just kind and thoughtful, but clever, insightful and amusing. She *liked* being with him and could all too easily imagine coming to depend on his presence. Missing him when he went away, as he surely must.

She didn't want to end up like her cousin Elizabeth, pining away for the husband who'd beguiled and then abandoned her. Not that Max would treat her so shabbily, but it would never do to let herself grow too fond of a man who would probably never see her as more than a pleasant companion.

Sighing, she punched the pillow and turned over. There was still so much work left to achieve the dreams she and her father had had for the stud. War had put a temporary end to negotiations with the Italian owners from whom they had purchased Arabians in the past, but with matters on the Continent stabilising after the final defeat and exile of Napoleon, she could renew the correspondence. Visit Ireland to choose the necessary mares, then begin the complicated and delicate process of breeding the right dams to the correct sires and cross-breeding the offspring into the bloodlines they'd already established.

By that point, the stud would be established enough to turn over to another manager, if necessary. Her father had estimated it would take several years to reach that stage.

How was she going to resist Max long enough?

Despite her need to resolve that dilemma, the exhaustion of the last few weeks began to gather her in its grip. But before sleep pulled her under, she concluded her best hope was to allow Max to escort her to Denby Lodge and introduce him to the neighbourhood, as he seemed to want. Then, before her senses triumphed over good sense, she must persuade him to leave.

Chapter Eighteen

Three weeks later, Max stood at the rails of a paddock at Denby Lodge, watching Caro work with a young gelding. Though he came here every day, he didn't think he'd ever tire of observing the expertise and finesse with which she coaxed, enticed and commanded the young animal to do as she bid.

As soon as she had finished working the gelding, they were to take their daily ride, during which she showed him around the estate and he encouraged her to talk about her horses. Having spent most of his boyhood away at school, he was discovering he genuinely enjoyed the simple routines of country life and learning how she had helped Sir Martin establish the stud.

She stretched a hand out, coaxing the horse—a movement that pulled the fabric of her jacket taut enough to outline her breasts. His breath hitched and his body tightened.

He'd always thought her lovely, even in the breeches and boots, which, with a semi-defiant glance at him, she'd resumed wearing after arriving home. But here on her own land, among the horses she loved, she positively glowed with determination and purpose.

She was driving him crazy. A lithe, unconsciously sensual grace filled her every move. The enthusiasm and passion with which she attacked every aspect of her work, which brought a becoming flush to her face and a dynamic energy to her actions, kept him continually aroused. So far, he hadn't broken his promise to take only what she was willing to give, but keeping it was about to kill him.

Just thinking about that kiss on their wedding night made his pulse jump and his member harden. He'd suspected from the first that she possessed a highly passionate nature; he'd been looking forward to awakening it. But all the passion he could wish for had been present in her very first kiss which, making up in ingenuity and enthusiasm what it lacked in expertise, had nearly brought him to his knees with frustrated desire.

After closing the door to her bedchamber on their wedding night, he'd damn near had to warn her to lock it, fearing he might lose the battle to keep himself from slipping in later. Caressing her, while she was compliant and drowsy with sleep, into the acquiescence he sensed waited just below the surface.

With so promising a beginning, he'd hoped that after returning home to her beloved stables and familiar routine, she might come to him within a day or so. But though he believed she no longer feared him, he still hadn't managed to beguile her into crossing that final barrier and inviting him to her bed.

And so, although he had initially intended to remain at Denby Lodge only long enough to see her settled and meet her friends and neighbours, he found himself lingering, hoping each day might bring the moment when she finally gave herself up to the passion that always simmered between them. How he longed to show her the richness and joy physical union could add to the growing friendship they already shared!

She seemed more relaxed and approachable on their daily rides, sometimes giving him kisses or permitting touches she shied away from at the manor. Innocent that she was, perhaps she believed the possibility of being discovered by some farmer or woodsman and the lack of a proper bed kept her safer from seduction.

His lips curved in a grin. He'd love to demonstrate what could be accomplished with the aid of a saddle blanket under the concealing canopy of an accommodating stand of oak.

Maybe today?

At that moment, a groom trotted over to her.

After turning the gelding's reins over to him, Caro walked to the fence.

'I'm sorry to have kept you waiting,' she said with an apologetic smile as she climbed over the rails to join him. 'I'm making such rapid progress now with Sherehadeen, I'm afraid I lose track of time.'

'I enjoy watching you. It's a true gift, the knack you have for working with horses.'

She shrugged. 'It's more experience than gift,' she replied modestly—which Max didn't believe for an instant. 'Anyone could do so, with the proper training.'

'Maybe you could show me, then.'

Surprise widened her eyes. 'It's such a slow process, I didn't think you would be interested. But if you'd like to learn, I'd be happy to show you.'

'I would like it,' he said, catching up her hand and kissing her fingers. *How I wish I might learn the right touch to use with you*, he thought, watching her eyelashes flicker briefly, as if savouring the contact. How he burned to make her feel more intensely, so intensely she'd be propelled beyond caution into a passion that would not be denied.

'Where are we to ride today?' he asked as he gave her a leg up, letting his hands linger as long as he dared.

'Another place that's very special to me. I used to visit there almost daily, but I...I haven't been back for a while.'

'Then it shall be special to me, too.'

She raised her eyebrows, as if she didn't trust his words. But though he'd never been above making pretty speeches to gratify a lady, he found he didn't even attempt to flatter Caro. She was so straightforward herself, it seemed…dishonest, somehow, to offer her Spanish coin. Somewhat to his own surprise, he found that whatever avowals of interest, support or affection he offered were absolutely sincere.

As they walked the horses side by side, Caro said, 'I did appreciate your treating me as "special" at Squire Johnson's dinner party last night. In fact, I must commend you for playing "the devoted husband" on all our neighbourhood visits with the same perfection you bring to the role of "haughty earl's son".' She chuckled. 'Thereby astounding several matrons who were certain you could never have seen anything appealing about Caro Denby beyond her enormous dowry.'

He found himself irritated with her. 'That's not true, Caro, and you know it. Why do you so underrate your many excellent qualities?'

'Oh, I don't underrate my talents. But you must allow even Stepmama despaired of me and she holds me in great affection! The skills I do have are not those generally possessed by females or esteemed by such arbiters of behaviour as Lady Winston and Mrs Johnson. Who were both astounded, I'm sure, when you repulsed Lady Millicent's attempts to partner you at cards.'

'With my bride garbed in a gown as lovely as that golden dress you wore last night, why would I wish to look at anyone else?'

'Perhaps because she was so intent on trying to seduce you?'

Max groaned, feeling almost…guilty that Caro had noticed the widow's none-too-subtle efforts. He'd been saddled with Lady Millicent, the highest-ranking female in the neighbourhood, as a dinner partner, and she'd taken every opportunity during the meal to brush his elbow, touch his hand or bend low over the table to give him a good view of her assets.

'Was it that obvious?'

'Probably. To me, anyway.'

'In my younger days, I might have found her attentions flattering.' *And in his frustration right after Waterloo, he might have taken her up on her offer.* 'But though she's handsome enough, I thought her casting out lures right under the nose of my wife to be quite distasteful. I didn't wish to cause ill feeling in the neighbourhood, but I had a difficult time rebuffing her advances with even a show of courtesy.'

Caro looked down at her hands on the reins. 'I'm glad you rebuffed her,' she said gruffly, 'even though I have no right to ask it.'

'You have every right, Caro. You're my wife. It would be shockingly bad conduct for me to embarrass you in front of your neighbours by loping off like a hound on a scent after a woman whose pedigree is far more elevated than her morals.' He grinned. 'I far prefer loping off after you.'

She looked back up, her eyes mischievous. 'Should I interpret that as a challenge?'

'Do you want it to be?'

'Very well, race you to the fence at the end of the meadow.'

Before the last of her words reached his ear, she'd kicked her mount to a gallop. He set off after her, loving the rush of wind in his face, the thrill of the chase surging in his blood.

It had been like this since their wedding night, she leading him, he pursuing. Like every day and night since, she reached the end of meadow just ahead of him. But soon, they would reach it together, he vowed.

He was about to applaud her victory, but as they rounded the crest of a small hill near a stone-walled enclosure, she suddenly dismounted, her face solemn. Above the wall, its edges draped by the forlorn, still-leafless branches of a rambling rose, he saw the tops of several gravestones.

Her gaze already focused on the graveyard, she paced slowly forwards. Unwilling to break the silence, Max reined in and jumped down, walking beside her to the gate, where they turned the horses free to graze. He followed her to a pair of marble tombstones whose carvings read Sir Martin Denby, dead the previous year, and Lady Denby, beloved wife, deceased some twenty-five years previous.

When Caro knelt by her father's gravestone, he went to his knees beside her. To his surprise, she reached over to take his hand. He wrapped it tightly in his own.

'I used to come here often when I was a girl,' she said softly. 'Mama died giving birth to me, so I always wondered what she'd been like. A portrait of her hung in Papa's room, but he never visited her here. Not until after his death did I understand why. Riding the farm, working with the horses, sometimes it seems like he's just away on a trip, maybe in Ireland looking at breeding stock. But coming here, seeing the date on that stone, I can't escape the fact that he is really gone.'

Tears tracked down her cheeks. Knowing how rarely she wept, sadness filled him for her grief. 'I'm so sorry, Caro. Lady Denby told me how close you were. Losing him must have been so difficult.'

'Stepmama is wonderful, but we're as different as…as these old boots and a pair of satin slippers. Papa and I understood each other, knew what the other was thinking and feeling without a need for words. He was…everything to me. Father. Teacher. Adviser. Friend.'

She looked over at him. 'This is the first time I've been able to bring myself to visit since…since he joined Mama here. Thank you for coming with me.'

He raised the hand she'd given him and kissed

it. 'You're not alone any more, Caro. You have me now.'

Two new tears welled up, sheening her eyes. 'Do I?'

She did, he thought, suddenly recognising that truth. He'd pledged his faith to her the day they had exchanged their wedding vows, but after sharing her life every day for almost a month, he felt that commitment to her on some deeper level. Before he could assure her of that, she rose and turned to walk out.

As he followed, she asked, 'Were you ever close to your father? Even if you were not, it must have been difficult to face his disapproval.'

Mention of his father called up that familiar acid blend of anger, bitterness, pain and regret. 'Yes, it's hard to accept he considers me a disappointment when, my whole life it seems, I wanted only to earn his attention and approval. I was the second son, not the heir, not the one who received whatever interest he could spare from his public life.'

Remembering, Max smiled faintly. 'I used to wait for his occasional visits at home or school with as much fear and anticipation as if he were the king himself. When I left the army, I was thrilled and honoured that my contribution in the diplomatic corps might assist his work in the Lords. But after Vienna, when I became the subject of rumour and speculation he considered damaging to his efforts, I was banished.'

'What…what did happen in Vienna?' When he looked up sharply, she said, 'I don't mean to pry! But I cannot believe you would do anything dishonourable.'

Warmth filled him at her avowal. 'Thank you. Even without knowing the circumstances, you've shown more faith in me than my father.'

She smiled. 'We've already established his conduct left much to be desired. But you needn't tell me if you don't wish to.'

'I don't mind.' Somewhat to his surprise, he realised that was the truth. He'd fobbed off the curious who'd enquired after he'd been sent home, sharing the facts only with Alastair and his aunt, but he knew Caro would listen carefully and return an honest opinion, rather than mouth useless platitudes.

Leaning against the stone wall, watching their mounts grazing in the distance, he said, 'Going to Vienna as aide-de-camp to Lord Wellington was a great opportunity. Even beyond the chance to assist a great man and do some small bit for my country, it was fascinating to be part of such a brilliant assembly of statesmen and diplomats.'

'I can well imagine!'

'Shortly after we arrived, I made the acquaintance of Madame Lefevre, widowed cousin of one of the French diplomats, whom she served as a sort of housekeeper and hostess. Many of the delegates, after Napoleon's devastation of Europe, despised the French and would have nothing to do with them. But I had to sympathise with the difficult task faced by Prince Talleyrand and his staff, trying to keep the country they loved from being dismembered and punished after all those years of war.'

She nodded. 'As we would wish to safeguard our beloved land.'

'Exactly. At any rate, unlike most of the females present, Madame preferred not to call attention to herself. At the many social events, she kept apart, observing rather than participating. It was that aloofness, as much as her beauty, that first caught my eye and, on a whim, I asked her to dance. Impressed by the keenness of her observations, I sought her out at other functions and we struck up a friendship. Unlike nearly every other woman I'd been associated with—until you—she demanded very little from me.'

Caro made a rueful grimace. 'No, *I* only demanded that you marry me.'

A demand to which he was daily becoming more reconciled, he thought, smiling at her. 'Like you, she never sought compliments or presents or commanded my slavish attention. Quite the contrary—she always appreciated even the most trifling assistance. I soon noticed, however, that she often had bruises on her wrists, sometimes even on her face. When she finally admitted her cousin abused her, I was outraged, but there was nothing I could do about it; despite the rumours later, she was never my mistress, nor had I any legal pretext to intervene on her behalf. Frustrated that I could not improve her circumstances, I did what little I could. She never asked more of me.'

Max laughed bitterly. 'Or so I thought. In the months since Vienna, I've gone over every action and conversation. I truly cannot recall her ever expressing any political opinions. Perhaps she was no more than an unwilling pawn, forced by her cousin's threats of violence to participate in the plot. But the plan worked masterfully; in using her as bait, someone must have known I might resist seduction, but I would never refuse to assist a lady in distress.'

He sighed, gazing sightlessly into the distance as he continued, 'The night of the incident, she sent an urgent note summoning me from the room where I waited to accompany Lord Wellington to an important meeting. After asking my help on a small matter, she deliberately delayed my return; meanwhile, a hired gunman burst into the room where Wellington awaited me and fired at him. Thank the Lord, he escaped unharmed. Madame Lefevre and her cousin disappeared from Vienna that same night.'

'I've combed my memory, trying to find some sign, some indication I'd missed, that a plot was afoot...' He shook his head. 'I just don't recall any. But if I had not allowed myself to be lured into assisting her, the conspirators could not have found such an ideal opportunity to attack England's most skilful general.'

'You can't know that for sure,' Caro objected. 'Had that opportunity not occurred, Wellington's enemies would have searched out others. No one of sense could fault you for responding with chivalry and compassion to what appeared to be a lady's unfortunate circumstances! Did the authorities not pursue Madame and her cousin?'

'I'm not sure. My relationship with her was well known enough that I was…detained that same night, while an inquiry was launched into my involvement. Otherwise, I would have set off to look for her immediately.'

She must have noticed the constraint in his voice. 'You were…confined?' she asked.

He grimaced. 'Not in prison. Just transferred to rooms far from Lord Wellington's and forced to remain there. Under guard. Watched over,' he added, feeling his face flush at the words, 'by soldiers of the unit I'd lately led in battle.'

'How awful for you,' Caro said softly, compassion in her eyes. 'But surely no one believed *you* would have had anything to do with an attack on your commander!'

'Before any official determination could be made, Napoleon escaped from Elba. The Congress quickly adjourned and the principals scurried home to their respective capitals. Then came Waterloo and here we are now.'

'Is there nothing else you can do to finally clear your name?'

'The Foreign Office implied that, with the

whole matter having been overcome by events, it wasn't worth attempting. However, Colonel Brandon, my former commander who's now searching for a new post for me, believes that if I could locate Madame Lefevre and obtain testimony corroborating my behaviour during the affair, it would be quite helpful.'

'Then you must go to Vienna,' Caro said. 'Surely the truth will absolve you.'

'Thank you,' he said quietly, glad to have had his intuition confirmed. Somehow, he'd known she would believe in him and urge him to seek vindication. 'I'm inclined to go to Vienna after leaving Denby, while Colonel Brandon explores his connections. Though I'm not certain, even if I can find Madame and compel her to testify, that it will change my father's opinion.'

'Oh, Max, I'm so sorry,' she said, reaching over to run a finger down his cheek.

He caught her hand and held it there, thrilling to her touch.

'The earl may be a great man in the affairs of the nation,' she continued, 'but he isn't half the father Sir Martin, simple country squire, was to me. Though I shall *try* to keep my disapproval to myself when I meet your father again, I cannot help feeling he is a selfish, foolish man to carelessly throw away his son's affection.'

Once again, the idea of Caro Denby utterly unimpressed with the man whose voice still rang in the halls of Parliament and whose approval was sought by most of his peers made Max smile. 'You did make your opinion rather clear at the wedding. I was quaking in my boots, waiting for him to deliver one of his famous set-downs. As one who's received quite a few, I assure you, he can deliver a jobation that will rattle the teeth in your head.'

Caroline merely sniffed. 'He could try. I shouldn't have chastised him, I know. Since I certainly don't wish to make matters worse between you, I shall attempt to be more conciliating in future.'

'My sweet defender,' he murmured, squeezing her fingers.

'Your defender, yes. You have me, too, now, you know.'

Max felt an odd little pang in his chest at that avowal. She would stand by him, care about him, support him…as none but his fellow Rogues ever had.

It seemed that she didn't find him valuable only as Max-the-earl's-son or Max-the-rising-diplomat or even Max-the-soldier. Simply being Max was enough. A strong surge of tenderness and gratitude tightened his chest.

Uncomfortable with the intensity of the emotion, he pushed it away and turned his mind instead to enticing sensual connotation of her words.

Oh, how he wanted to have her! Under his intense gaze, she blushed and looked away, telling him she'd just realised the double meaning of her words. But in this instance, her protective assumptions about the countryside were correct; he could hardly seduce her with the shades of her parents looking on.

At that moment, a sudden gust of wind nearly sailed the hat off his head and a large cold drop of rain lashed his cheek.

'The weather is looking to turn,' he said, gazing up at the scudding dark clouds. 'We'd better head back.'

'Thank you for coming with me. I knew I must return some time, but I'd been dreading it. Having you here made it…better. Not so lonely.'

To his surprise, he realised that for much of his life, despite the accolades of the sycophants and admirers who'd always wanted something from him, except when in the company of the Rogues, he'd been lonely, too. Until now.

'I'm glad,' he said and led her back to the horses.

He had returned to the house, while, despite the rain that began to fall steadily, Caro headed back to the paddock to work, telling him she'd see him at dinner. Max wandered to the library, thinking to choose a book. Instead, he found himself staring out of the window, thinking about Caro.

He recalled their conversation at the graveyard today. He'd never shared with anyone the conflicting feelings he felt for his father. He'd never before realised how alone he'd often felt in the midst of his own family. Perhaps it was because being with Caro felt so different. Where she was, he felt a sense of warmth, affection and serenity, as if he…belonged.

A stab of unease rose at that conclusion. It would be vastly deflating for Magnificent Max to fall in love with a female who, thus far, gave little evidence that his hopes of fascinating *her* would ever be realised.

Maybe he ought to give up both that and his attempts at seduction—for the present, at least— and head to Vienna. The longer he waited, the less likely he'd find any trace of Madame Lefevre.

He'd not yet decided what he meant to do when Caro burst into the library, excitement shining in her dark eyes. 'I've just received a letter from Mr Wentworth! It seems the breeder in Italy to whom Papa wrote long ago, hoping to obtain another of his excellent Arabians, actually received his offer! Even better, he accepted Papa's terms.'

'That's wonderful news,' Max said, pleased for her. She'd just been telling him of her father's plans to introduce new Arabians into the stud's bloodlines. 'How soon will you be able to get the horse?'

'Almost immediately, it turns out. Signor Aliante had to wait for cessation of hostilities on the Continent to transport the animal, but, Mr Wentworth writes, the stallion has just arrived in London. Mr Wentworth is having him sent down to Denby; he should arrive in a few days. Papa would be so proud! This is the first step toward achieving everything he wanted the stud to become!'

Max smiled, charmed by her enthusiasm and the look of pure happiness on her face. 'We should celebrate, then.'

'We should! I'll have Manners see if there is any champagne in the cellar.'

Max stepped over to give her a hug, but she waved him off. 'Don't; I'm all over mud. I shall see you soon at dinner!'

When they met later in the dining room, the vision Caro presented was worthy of celebration. Her auburn hair was arranged in a delightful tumble of curls and the flattering gown she wore showed her magnificent bosom to full advantage.

She was unusually animated throughout dinner, plying him with questions about the army, everyday life on campaign and his impressions of Spain and Portugal. Normally as soon as they finished eating, she left the table, giving him a hurried excuse for a kiss before going—alas, alone—to bed so she might rise at dawn to begin her workday in the stables.

But this night, she stayed at the table, as if as reluctant as he to end the splendid camaraderie of the evening. She laughed as he told her about the night of pouring rain when he'd bivouacked in a Portuguese stable, wrapped up in his cloak on a thick layer of hay. And been awakened repeatedly through the night by the cows attempting to eat his mattress.

Eyes glowing, she touched his hand, let her fingers linger on his arm. She seemed more relaxed—and less guarded—than at any time since the kiss on their wedding night. All his instincts telling him capitulation was near, Max exerted himself to be at his most charming, teasing her, trying everything he knew to beguile and entice her.

Finally, noticing the long-suffering look on the face of the footmen standing at his post by the sideboard, Max said, 'Shall we withdraw and let Joseph clear the table?'

Caro glanced at the mantel clock and straightened with a start. 'Heavens, it's much later than I realised! Excuse me, Joseph, for keeping you well past the time you should be putting your feet up.'

'Thank you, mistress,' the footman responded. 'Shall I have Mr Manners bring the tea tray to the study?'

'No, it's too late for tea. Tell the kitchen staff to bank the fires and go to bed.'

As the footman bowed himself out, Max claimed the decanter and led her to the study. 'Shall we finish the last of the wine? It will help you sleep.'

'It's been such a marvellous day!' With a slow grin as she sank on to the sofa, she gave him a naughty look that sent heat all the way down to his toes. 'Maybe I don't want to sleep.'

Max tried to tell himself not to read too much into that statement. But a wild hope blazed through him, like lightning in advance of a storm.

Seating himself close beside her, breathing in her enticing scent, a sharp desire filled him to bend down and cover with kisses that delectable swathe of bare skin from her throat to the tops of her breasts. He ought to put up his glass and take himself off to bed before he lost control and broke his promise, but he couldn't bring himself to end this enchanted spell of an evening.

'We should go to bed now, I suppose,' Caro said as she drained her glass. From beneath her lashes, she gave him a look that was part enticement, part hesitation.

Beguiled by her loveliness, hard and nearly mad with repressed desire, Max found it increasingly difficult to hear the little voice urging caution. 'Let me escort you up.'

His heart leapt and his member stiffened further when she replied, 'That would be…lovely.'

She offered her arm. Trying to restrain the excitement racing through him, he took it and walked her out, thinking she must surely be able to hear the thundering beat of his heart.

A few moments later, they reached her room. After he opened the door and walked her inside, his heart seemed to stop altogether.

Would she invite him to stay…or bid him goodnight?

Chapter Nineteen

Standing inside her bedchamber door, Caro smiled back at Max. It *had* been an excellent day, the best she could remember since Papa's death.

She had all the horses for this year's sale, including the gelding she'd been working today, nearly ready. With Max's steady presence beside her, she'd finally had the courage to visit the graveyard and acknowledge that Papa was truly gone. She'd never stop grieving for him, but today, she'd finally allowed herself to lay him to rest.

Best of all, the Arabian stallion, the animal her father had considered the key to bringing the stud's bloodstock to a new level of quality, would be arriving any day.

Max had been the perfect companion, seeming to understand how much the achievement of Papa's goals meant to her. In truth, he'd encouraged her almost since their first meeting to talk about her horses and her plans for stud. And he'd even finally told her something of his own life, his difficulties with his father, his hopes of clearing his name.

Tonight, she would put out of mind the truth that the partnership that buoyed her today could only be temporary, for Max must soon leave, either to Vienna, or back to his life in London.

'Thank you for a wonderful day. A wonderful evening.'

'I'm so glad you'll soon begin realising your father's dream, Caro.'

Wishing she dared ask him to stay, she waited for him to bid her goodnight. Instead, his intent gaze locked on her face, he lingered.

She wanted him to linger. To admit the truth, she burned for another kiss like the one they'd shared on their wedding night.

There would be very few more nights when he would be near enough to kiss. If she were careful, maybe she could chance allowing herself something more intimate than the quick peck on the cheek that had been all she'd dared offer him since they returned to Denby.

Her heart commencing to beat a rapid tattoo against her ribs, she said, 'Won't you kiss me goodnight before you go?'

'With pleasure, my lovely wife,' he said, his deep voice sending a thrill of anticipation through her.

The kiss was delightful—a long, unhurried

brush of his lips against hers, ending with a sweep of his tongue across their sensitive surface.

Excitement shot to every nerve, tingling in her nipples, pulsing between her thighs. Without quite intending to, she found herself kissing him back, deepening the pressure of her lips on his. She wasn't sure whether she opened to him or he to her, but suddenly their tongues were tangling, twining, licking, sucking.

She pulled his head down, wrapped her arms around him, plumbed his mouth with her tongue until she was breathless and dizzy. Until her breasts felt swollen and aching for his touch. As she arched her neck, he trailed tiny kisses from her mouth over her chin, down her neck, to the top of her low-cut bodice, then licked the skin beneath the gown's edge.

Suddenly, more than she'd ever wanted anything, she wanted to have the gown and stays removed and feel his mouth against her bared skin.

Papa was gone; she'd never get him back. But the man who'd helped her accept that loss was vital and alive beside her. Before he left her, too, fiercely grateful and pulsing with need, she simply must have a touch and taste of him.

Ignoring the little voice shouting of danger, she caught his chin and tipped it up to face her.

'I want you to unlace me.'

'Whatever my lady wishes,' he replied, the hard glitter of desire in his eyes making her pulse leap.

Don't think, he'd told her on their wedding night. *Do what you feel.*

Insistent, driven, shutting her mind to everything but the sensations he aroused in her, she directed his hands to the tapes of her gown, the ribbons of her stays. Kissing him still, she let him loosen and pull them away, then guided his head down to her bared breasts.

She cried out at the first touch of his tongue on their sensitive surface, marvellous, exquisite, beyond anything she could have imagined. She threw her head back, gasping, as with fingers and tongue, he explored each breast, from the plump fullness beneath around to the top and finally, thrillingly, suckling the hardened nipples.

Heat and need consumed her. She pulled at his shirt, clawing at the cravat as he unwound it and tossed it aside. Jerking the shirt open, she slid her hands inside, her fingers seeking his nipples as his mouth laved, caressed and pleasured hers.

Emboldened by an urgent imperative that would not be denied, she slid her hands down his chest to his trouser flap and plucked open the straining buttons. His manhood sprang forth and she filled her hands with it, wrenching a cry from him.

While he suckled her, gasping, she fingered his length, from the hot, velvety tip to the coarse sacs beneath. Without realising how she'd got there, she felt the edge of the bed behind her. Her wobbly knees gave way and she sank back upon it.

Max tugged off her skirts while she kicked at

them to help him, until she was clad only in the thin linen chemise. His eyes were a fierce blue in the candlelight that played over his powerful shoulders, his chest rising and falling rapidly in time to his ragged breathing. She leaned forwards to yank down his breeches, then paused to admire him, jutting proudly erect before her. He groaned and shuddered when she grasped him again and traced his length, then laid her cheek against it. 'Beautiful,' she murmured, 'Beautiful.'

With a growl, he kicked off his breeches and pulled her up against the pillows. Kissing her, he smoothed his hands down the thin fabric still covering her belly, then dragged the linen upwards and parted her legs to his view, his fingers tracing the most intimate part of her as he gazed at her. 'Beautiful,' he murmured in return.

When he touched the small nub at her centre, intense sensation rocketed outwards, making her cry out and leap beneath his hand. Murmuring, caressing her again and again while she thrashed her head against the pillows and the intensity built and built and built. His fingers dipped within her wet passage, massaging her in a maddening, delectable, slow liquid slide, in and then out again.

Suddenly she simply had to have him there, the firm hard length of him filling the place his fingers were stroking. With an incoherent murmur, she urged him above her, widened her legs and guided him to that pulsing, aching, spot.

She let out a sob of relief as he entered her,

then stiffened with a little gasp at the stretching, tearing pain. Immediately he stilled, soothing her with kisses until her body relaxed and the pulsing within her began again, impelling her to thrust her hips and pull him deeper.

But holding himself above her, his elbows locked and arms corded with effort, only slowly did he increase the penetration. Wanting him deeper, wanting *something* she craved desperately, but which seemed to dance just beyond reach, she thrust up to meet him as he drove downwards, until she felt him fully encased within her.

He began to increase the rhythm now, faster and faster, seeming as driven as she. Suddenly she reached the precipice and sailed over, while starbursts of delicious sensation exploded within her.

Gasping, spent, she sagged back against the pillows, head whirling from wine and sensation. Murmuring her name, Max cried out. Moments later, he collapsed beside her and drew her close, cradling her against his chest.

Smiling, sated, satisfied, Caro fell asleep.

The warm tickle of a sunbeam on his face woke Max the following morning. As his mind rose slowly to consciousness, he reflected that he must have drunk more wine than he'd thought to have slept so late, when memories of the previous night came flooding back.

Grinning, he stretched languorously, an expansive feeling of contentment filling him. He'd al-

ways suspected Caro would be deeply passionate.
The reality had proved better than his imaginings.

He couldn't wait to test that fact again. Though
judging by the sun, the morning was rather far ad-
vanced, maybe he could do so even now.

But as he prepared to rise, he realised he was
not in the bedchamber he'd occupied since coming to Denby Lodge, but in hers. The linens on the
bed beside him were cold. Where had she gone?

Knowing his Caro, she'd probably tiptoed out
at dawn, leaving him to sleep while she went off
to work with her horses. With only a few weeks
remaining before her sale, he advised his disappointed body, he'd probably not be able to lure her
back to bed again this morning.

Would she meet him boldly this morning or
blush to face him in the light of day, after giving
herself wholly and urgently into his hands? Handling him in return. A hot flush of desire rushed
through him as he recalled how she'd stroked him,
fitted him to her, linked her legs behind his back
to urge him deeper.

Despite her midnight display of passion, by
daylight she'd probably be shy, he predicted. Suddenly he couldn't wait to discover which Caro
he'd meet today, the practical, pragmatic horse-
woman in her breeches and boots, or the wicked
siren who'd stroked him in her bed.

Pulling on enough clothing to be decent, he
jogged back to his chamber, changed into fresh attire and headed downstairs. Stopping in the break-

fast room for some nourishment, he learned from Manners that the mistress had eaten early and gone to the stables. Tossing down his last sip of ale, he gave the butler a broad wink that had the servant hastily biting his lip to keep from smiling as Max walked out.

Max chuckled. The fact that the mistress had slept with her husband last night would be all over the manor by now.

As he neared the barns, Max picked up his pace. From a distance, he could just make out Caro standing by the fence of the first paddock, where she'd been working the gelding on a lunge line yesterday.

Joy, effervescent as the bubbles in last night's champagne, rose in his chest. He couldn't wait to see her, kiss her again. Though he'd been forced to enter this marriage, the reality of it was turning out to be better than he'd ever dared hope. With the passionate relationship he'd needed to seal his satisfaction with the bargain finally developing, he couldn't help but congratulate himself.

After spending every day with Caro for nearly a month, he found her as interesting, intelligent and amusing as he had the day she'd propositioned him for the first time in the greenhouse at Barton Abbey. He'd come to admire her expertise with horses and appreciate the firm grasp of business affairs that allowed her to run the stud with such efficiency. The scope of her interests and depth of her knowledge of the world, on display each evening as they talked over dinner and tea, continued to surprise and delight him.

To have ended up wedding a lady who combined the straightforward demeanor of a man with the passionate response of a vixen was a stroke of good fortune. To have found all that in a lovely woman who was also a substantial heiress made him the luckiest man in England.

All that remained to make his life complete would be to find Madame Lefevre and have her testimony clear his name.

Her back to him as she spoke with the head trainer, Caro didn't see him approach. After pausing until the conversation had concluded and the groom turned away, Max seized her by the shoulders, twirled her around and pulled her into his arms, then leaned down to place a kiss on her forehead.

'How is my lovely wife this morning?'

'Max!' she protested, her face colouring.

Shy, just as he'd predicted, Max thought, grinning.

'Walk with me?' he asked, his hands resting on her shoulders. 'I wish you'd awakened me before you left. I would have liked to demonstrate my appreciation for last night in a most *tangible* way.'

His fingertips first warned him that something was wrong, as he felt her shoulders stiffen under his touch. But his giddy mind still hadn't quite accepted the fact as she pulled free.

'I'm glad you were...satisfied.'

Her cool tone and averted face were so shockingly different from the joyous, passionate woman he'd made love to just a few hours ago, he felt her withdrawal as sharply as a slap. His delight and anticipation swiftly faded.

As he searched her averted face, trying to figure out what had happened, the happiness he'd felt upon waking this morning leached away, as water held in the hand seeps through clenched fingers.

'What is it, Caro? What's happened?'

'There's nothing wrong,' she said quickly, even as she took another step back, as if she couldn't tolerate his nearness. Avoiding his gaze, she added, 'I'm just…tense, with the sale so close upon us and so much left to do.'

He wouldn't let her retreat. Catching her chin, he forced it up, so she had to look him in the eye. 'Don't go all missish on me! Where's the straightforward woman I married? *Something* is distressing you. Why not just tell me what it is?'

To his dismay, her forehead creased and her lips began to tremble, while tears gathered at the corners of her eyes.

'Come on, Caro,' he coaxed, her reaction sparking real concern in him now. 'You know I don't bite.' Trying to distract her, he put a bit of wickedness in his smile as he added, 'At least, not so that it hurts.'

'It may hurt more than you can possibly imagine.'

Before he could ask her what she meant, she

gave him a short nod. 'You're right; I have to tell you. Let's walk.'

A shock of alarmed disbelief ripped through him when he went to take her elbow—and she brushed his hand away.

Crossing her arms protectively in front of her chest, she said, 'You know how strongly I resisted getting married. Though it's true that I never wanted to wed anyone but Harry, there was another reason for my resistance. An even more serious one.'

While he listened in disbelief, she briefly told him about a condition which had afflicted nearly every female of her mother's family, a condition that had resulted in those women dying in childbed with their first child.

'Obviously, I know nothing of childbirth other than that it can be dangerous for the mother. But… you are saying there is some sort of—of flaw of the body that afflicts all women of your blood?'

She smiled without humour. 'I call it "the Curse".'

He shook his head. 'You truly believe in this? Isn't it more probable it is just unhappy coincidence?'

She hugged herself more tightly. 'Lady Denby said you'd probably think that. She doesn't believe it either. But I do. I've seen it. Not in my own mother's case, of course, but with my cousins. Four of them, dying as young women in birthing their first child.'

While he struggled to wrap his mind around those facts, she finally looked up at him. 'So you see, I haven't been trying to tease or bedevil you. As drawn as I am to you—and you cannot help but have noticed how much—I was…afraid,' she finished, two tears tracking down her cheeks. 'Afraid of what might happen, if I let you make love to me.'

Knowing how difficult it must have been for his strong, fierce Caro to admit that, appalled by what he'd just heard, Max could think of nothing to say.

'I thought, since you could have any woman you fancied, maybe you wouldn't desire me. I thought I could resist you. But last night…I wanted you more than my next breath. And it was wonderful beyond anything I could have imagined! But this morning, all I could see in the dull orange of the rising sun was the face of my cousin Anne as she died at dawn, holding my hand. And blood, everywhere blood.'

'Oh, Caro,' he murmured, and pulled her into his arms. This time, she did not resist.

For a long moment, he simply held her, her muffled sobs resonating against his chest, while disbelief, horror and concern for her chased each other around his head.

Finally, she calmed and pushed away. He let her go.

'Why didn't you tell me this before we were wed?' he asked, anger beginning to merge into his tangle of emotions. 'Don't you think I had a right to know that ours could never be a normal marriage, without—without putting your life at risk?'

'I did tell you I wanted a marriage in name only,' she reminded him. 'And you did agree... though we both knew such a condition was not enforceable.' She shrugged. 'I didn't wish to show myself to be the coward I am. Besides, it is *my* risk.'

'Devil take it, Caro, I'm not such a monster as to heedlessly put your life in danger to satisfy my own lust!'

'What's done is done,' Caro said. 'I'm afraid you are saddled with me now. After last night, I shall just have to accept the risk. There are compensations, after all.' She gave him a wan smile. 'I shall no longer have to try to resist you.'

Even knowing the danger he placed her in, having to resist her would be difficult for *him* as well. A few moments ago, despite being shocked and appalled by what she'd revealed, just the feel of her breasts pressed against his chest, her flat belly rubbing against him, had been enough to make his member stir. Knowing the power of passion, he realised how insidiously his body could lure him into ignoring the risk.

Like standing near a burning building as fire consumed it, he felt falling around him the charred bits of this morning's illusion that with Caro, the marriage he hadn't wanted could turn into a close, fulfilling union.

Once again, not her fault. She *had* asked for a

marriage of convenience. One like his parents'. Only he, arrogant bastard that he was, had thought to turn it into something more.

'Maybe it would be best if I made sure we both resisted temptation,' he said at last. 'I'm not sure I really believe in this "Curse" of yours, but it's enough that you do. Damn it, Caro, I don't want you risking your life. And frankly, I have even less desire to be a father than I did to be a husband. Heaven help me, with the example I had, what would I know about fathering?'

She flinched and he realised his reminder about his reluctance to wed must have hurt. But right now, hurting too, he couldn't make himself utter words of comfort.

'Why don't I leave for Vienna, as I've long planned? You've got your horses to train and the sale coming up; I'm sure you don't need me here complicating your work.'

'Distracting me,' she amended, making him feel a tad better. But then, taking an unsteady breath, she nodded her assent. 'Yes, that would probably be best. I've a thousand things to do and you will want to get on with your life.'

On with his life…leaving behind the inconvenience of a wife who cringed at his touch. How easily, Max thought, sorrow twisting like a knife in his gut, Caro seemed able to dismiss him.

Whereas, after their month together, *he* was now linked by affection as well as law to a wife he could not bed. Anger flared hotter. Once again, he was trapped in an impossible situation.

Maybe he could at least right the one in Vienna.

'Very well. I'll make arrangements to leave immediately. Today, if possible.'

She nodded vigorously. 'That would be best. As I shall be very busy all day, I may not be able to see you off, so I'll bid you farewell now. Good luck, Max. I hope you find the evidence you need.'

She stepped towards him, kissed his cheek briefly and stepped back. He made no attempt this time to pull her into his arms.

'Goodbye, Max. May you have a safe and successful journey.'

At that, she turned away and set off at a near-run towards the barn, as if she couldn't escape his presence quickly enough.

Max stood and watched her retreat, the idyll of their country life retreating with her. Joy had already drained away; now even his anger dissolved, leaving in its place a sense of loss that wounded him more sorely than he could have ever anticipated.

If his being gone was what she wanted, he'd oblige. He had a deal of experience in being sent away, too.

Turning on his heel, wildly contradictory emotions churning in his chest, Max set off for the house.

* * *

From the safety of the barn, Caro watched Max walk away. She pressed her lips together, her nails biting into the stable rail as she resisted the temptation to run after him, ask at least for a parting kiss to remember him by.

Ask him to stay.

But he'd been angry as well as appalled when he walked off. Would he ever kiss her again? Would she even see him again?

A throb of emotion made up of strong relief and a deep agony pulsed through her. The tears she'd been suppressing began to drip down her cheeks as she gave in to the memories warring within her.

She'd awakened in his arms, filled with a bone-deep peace and sense of wicked delight as she remembered each delicious kiss, touch and caress from the night before. She'd snuggled closer, trying to decide whether to awaken his quiescent member with strokes and kisses, or begin at his toes and explore every inch of his strong, perfect body.

Until her muzzy, sleep-dulled brain had cleared enough for her to realise the full implications of what she'd permitted—nay, *encouraged*—Max to do. Dismay and horror rushed through her, bringing her fully awake in an instant.

He'd only spilled his seed within her once. Perhaps she hadn't conceived…yet.

But despite her dismay, merely thinking about him buried deep inside her body, moving within her, setting off such exquisite and powerful sensations, sent a rush of arousal through her.

Loving him had been quite simply the most marvellous, incredible, amazingly powerful experience of her life. Even knowing the danger, thinking about it reignited within her the desire to entice him to love her again and again and again. Aware now of its potential for delight, her body hungered for his caress, eager to repeat the journey towards that precipice, wanting to reach it with him and soar over together into ecstasy.

Watching him disappear around the bend leading to the house, fighting to keep herself from trying to recall him, she now understood why her mother and aunt and cousins had been willing to risk the Curse. It had little to do with a wife's duty to bear a son and everything to do with the euphoria of completion and the sense of union with another human soul that forged a bond even deeper than the one she'd shared with her father.

Could she let him go?

After her father's years of preparation, with the arrival of the Arabian, the dream of having the stud fulfil its full promise was within reach. The horse would be here within days. All that remained then would be to visit the breeders in Ireland for suitable mares and the last step of the cross-breeding process could begin.

Papa had estimated several years would be required to evaluate the foals and determine the final, best mix. But if she had at least one full year, she might get the process far enough under way that, if necessary, she could turn it over to someone else. With the stud books kept carefully and with continuous consultation, Newman might be able to carry on the programme without her.

If she worked diligently all that time, perhaps, when all was in place, she could seek out her husband. Ask to start over. Accept the risk of the Curse in exchange for the joy of being fully his wife.

If he would take her back. She tried to put out of her mind all the legions of beautiful, talented, enticing women waiting to amuse, seduce and pleasure a man like Max Ransleigh. Women she'd promised him complete freedom to enjoy.

What a fool she'd been, giving her blessing to that! Doubly foolish, for she'd let herself become attached to Max Ransleigh.

He didn't belong to her. Since it was inevitable that he return to his world, better for her that he leave now.

That bitter truth burning in her gut, she turned away from the door and forced her mind back to the horses. She'd work here until late tonight, hoping he completed his preparations and left today. She wasn't sure she could stand another scene like the one they'd just played.

Another painful stab of emotion seared her chest, shaking loose a few more tears. Angrily she swiped them from her cheeks. She'd felt bereft when Harry first left to go to university, too. But eventually the rhythm of life on the farm, bearing her along its stream of endlessly repeated tasks, had soothed the ache.

It would again.

But somehow, the prospect of accomplishing Papa's dream no longer filled her with the same thrill as before.

Chapter Twenty

Nearly two months later, Max waited impatiently in an anteroom of the British Ambassador's suite in Vienna. After a month of travelling by horse, carriage and mail coach from one inn or boarding house or manor to another, he was tired, gritty and not happy to be kept waiting by the men whose subtle condemnation had propelled him into the position he was in today.

As the door swung open, Max looked up to see Lord Bannerman, the undersecretary to the ambassador, walking in. Immediately Max's spirits rose; Bannerman was a gifted and discerning diplomat whose talents he had come to appreciate during his days on Wellington's staff. Thank heavens this time the embassy had seen fit to send in someone of authority, rather than the clerk who'd met him when he arrived in Vienna six weeks ago.

'Ransleigh, good to see you again,' Lord Bannerman said, shaking Max's hand. 'I understand congratulations are in order? You're recently married, I hear, and to a considerable heiress.'

'I am and thank you,' Max replied, an ache tightening his chest. Long, weary days of travel and fruitless searching had helped him avoid pondering the unresolved matter of what to do about Caro and their marriage...most of the time. But it remained ever just outside his thoughts, a lingering wound that refused to heal.

'Jennings told me he'd given you as much information as we had on Madame Lefevre. Were you able to turn up anything more?'

'No,' Max said, a month of frustration in his voice. 'What Jennings gave me was damned little. If I may be frank, my lord, I don't think the Foreign Office has much interest in my turning up anything.'

Bannerman smiled. 'You have to admit, Ransleigh, the whole situation was awkward. An attempt on Wellington's life, you claiming one of Prince Talleyrand's own aides was involved, Bonaparte's escape from Elba, every delegation in turmoil. Talleyrand insisting he had no knowledge of any plot and offended by the accusation that someone on his staff would stoop to assassination, neither one of the principals available for questioning... I'm afraid no one is very interested in dredging up that old problem.'

'Except me, whose reputation and career were tarnished.'

'Which was most unfortunate,' Bannerman said, genuine regret in his voice. 'You're a man of great talent, Ransleigh. You would have made a fine diplomat.'

A shock ran through Max. Through all the weeks of tiresome and ultimately futile investigation, he'd stubbornly kept alive the hope that he might somehow find vindication. But in the finality of Lord Bannerman's tones, he realised the trail had gone cold and the only authority with the reach to rake up the ashes had no intention of doing so.

He might truly never be able to clear his name.

Before he accepted that, he'd make Bannerman spell it out completely. 'So, as far as the Foreign Office is concerned, that's an end to it? That's why I was fobbed off with a mere clerk when I arrived and sent tromping through half the posting towns of Austria and Italy?'

Bannerman shrugged…and suddenly Max understood why the highly ranked Bannerman had been dispatched to interview him this time. 'Ah, now I see. The ambassador wanted you to find out if I *had* uncovered new evidence, then evaluate anything I might have discovered, so it could be suppressed if the Foreign Office deemed that prudent.'

'Yes,' Bannerman replied without apology. 'Very astute, Ransleigh. You truly would have made a superior diplomat.'

'No chance of that now, when I'm being officially prevented from clearing my name,' Max retorted bitterly.

Bannerman shrugged. 'Which means you must be destined to play some other role. I do understand your eagerness to wipe that blemish from your record. But, speaking as friend now, I strongly advise you to proceed no further with this. Prince Talleyrand has proved himself very helpful in restoring King Louis to his throne in France. The Foreign Office would find it most indelicate for someone to try to prove evidence of Bonapartist plotting amongst the prince's staff, perhaps upsetting the new balance we are trying to achieve.'

'So my good name is to be sacrificed in the cause of maintaining that balance.'

'Talleyrand holds the key to delivering France. We'll not do anything to undermine him. While you were fighting at Waterloo, would you not have sacrificed your life to keep Hougoumont from falling to the French, perhaps giving Napoleon the victory and unleashing a whole new wave of conquest upon the Continent? Of course you would have,' Bannerman answered for him. 'What is happening now in France may not involve cannons firing, but the outcome is no less important.'

Swallowing hard, Max nodded. 'You are right; one man's reputation is not more valuable than the peace of Europe. So I'm wasting my time here.'

'A visit to a city as lovely as Vienna could

never be considered a waste,' Bannerman returned blandly.

For a year, Max had been driven by the burning need for vindication. Pain and despair twisted in his chest as that hope died.

He'd never be seen as redeemed by his father. Never regain the trust of Wellington.

'I assure you, the Foreign Office does appreciate what you are sacrificing. I understand Colonel Brandon is looking for a War Department posting for you? We'll certainly assist in whatever way we can.'

'Thank you for that. And for your candour.'

'The business of diplomacy sometimes involves compromises we wish we didn't have to make. Good luck, Ransleigh. Best wishes to your bride.'

Max shook the hand Bannerman offered and, his spirits as weary as his body, walked from the room. As he passed the clerk manning the desk just inside the embassy entrance, the functionary called out, 'Mr Ransleigh! I have a letter for you.'

Only a few people knew he'd gone to Vienna. Since Alastair, the former poet, now seldom put pen to paper, the missive was most likely from his mother or aunt, Max thought. Thanking the clerk, Max took the letter.

With a shock of surprise, he noted the address was written in a feminine hand he didn't recognise. Might it be from Caro?

The unhappy terms upon which they'd parted had remained a hard, indigestible lump in his gut since that morning by the paddock at Denby Lodge.

After his departure, he'd deliberately thrust the problem from his mind, so that over the intervening weeks, he'd resolved none of those emotions. But now he found himself hoping it *was* Caro who had written—and was eager to see what she might have to say.

Restraining his impatience until he reached the privacy of his hotel suite several streets away, he unsealed the letter and rapidly scanned the lines.

My dear Max, I've directed this letter to the embassy, knowing they most likely will be able to pass it along to you. The sale at Denby went quite well, all the horses being placed with suitable owners and a number of new clients leaving preliminary orders for next year.

Immediately after the sale, she continued, her tone friendly, conversational, as if they'd never parted so bitter and abruptly, *I departed for Ireland, where I'm now visiting breeders with whom my father always worked. There are several very promising mares; after making my final choices tomorrow, I'll be travelling back to Denby.'*

He turned the note over. The words that met his eyes there sent such a shock through him, he sat upright in his chair.

I must apologize for the abrupt and hasty manner in which we parted. I hope, in time, you will forgive me for not revealing everything about my

condition before we were wed, and we can start
anew. I remain your affectionate wife, Caro.

Max re-read the last paragraph three times, the
phrase 'I hope…we can start anew' resonating
deep within him. He shook his head and sighed.
The truth was, despite his anger and frustration
the day they'd parted, he'd missed her. After
barely a month of marriage, she'd inveigled her
way into his consciousness and his everyday life
so quietly but effectively that for these two months
apart, he felt some vital element was missing, even
as he tried to convince himself there wasn't.

With Caro around, almost every day had
brought some new insight, some perspective he'd
never envisioned, born out of a life experience so
different from his own. Some new bit of knowledge about horses or breeding, or a clever flash
of humour that delighted him.

She was different from any woman he'd ever
spent time with. He found her at once maddening, intriguing, impossible…and enchanting. As
he read the letter one more time, the hard lump of
anger began to soften and melt away. In its place
grew an eagerness to see her again and heal the
breach between them.

He let her image, which had been dancing at
the edges of his mind the whole time they'd been
apart, play again on the centre stage of his mind.
Caro, in boots and breeches, coaxing the gelding
on a lunge line, or putting one of the sale horses
through his steps. Sitting at the dining table, tick-

ling his mind with her observations while her bared shoulders and handsome bosom tantalised his senses. Caro, in those ridiculous spectacles and hideous dress, the first day he'd met her at Barton Abbey.

An expansive sense of hope rose in him, filling in the cold despair left by the wreckage of his quest to find Madame Lefevre. Lord Bannerman was correct; if vindication was not to be had in Vienna, his future must lie elsewhere. And his wife would play a part in it.

He was re-reading the letter when a knock sounded on the door. The hotel servant delegated to serve as his valet appeared, announcing, 'A lady calling on you, sir.' He held out an engraved card.

Max didn't need the raised eyebrows of the servant to know a 'lady' would never visit a gentleman at his hotel. Glancing at the card, he noted the caller was Juliana von Stenhoff, a very expensive courtesan with whom he'd had an on-again, off-again liaison throughout the months of Congress last year.

'Did the lady give her direction?'

'She's waiting in the lobby, sir, and asked if it would be convenient for you to receive her now.'

Whatever did Juliana want with him? Curious, he said, 'Send her up, then.'

Though he'd not spent much time in the city itself, he was not surprised that Juliana had discovered he was back; she was impeccably well connected to the upper echelon of official Vienna. Doubtless, she also knew *why* he'd returned.

Perhaps Juliana, like Lord Bannerman, wanted to discover if he'd had any success. Max flattered himself that she'd developed an affection for him during their relationship and had been distressed by the disastrous end of his mission in Vienna.

Too bad he would not be able to tell her he'd found a way to rectify that finale.

A few moments later, Madame von Stenhoff swept into the room in a cloud of expensive perfume.

'Max! It's wonderful to see you again!' she exclaimed, offering him her powdered cheek to kiss before settling in the chair he showed her to. 'I'd heard you'd come back to Vienna. I called earlier, but was told you'd gone off into the countryside.'

'Yes, I've done a good bit of travelling.'

'Trying to find the Lefevre woman?'

'Yes. And frankly, having no luck. Bannerman at the Embassy just advised me to give up the search altogether. It's in the past and all those officially involved want to keep it that way.'

'I'm so sorry! I'd offer to corroborate your story, asserting that, being otherwise occupied by *me*, you couldn't have been bewitched by the French widow. But I'm afraid that wouldn't serve.' She laughed—a tinkling, musical sound that suddenly seemed studied and artificial to Max's ear. 'You men are such awful creatures! None of you would believe that possessing one mistress would stop a man from attempting to entice another.'

Letting that comment pass, Max said, 'I do appreciate your willingness to help.'

'I've always been willing to help…you.' She laid a soft white hand on his arm. 'I'm very fond of you, Max. I've missed you. Perhaps, now that you're back, we could…rekindle old memories?'

Gently he removed her hand from his sleeve. 'There's a small impediment. I have a wife now.'

She shrugged. 'Back in England—and running a horse farm, of all things, I hear! Quite wealthy, though. A clever match, under the circumstances. One that certainly doesn't create any impediments for me.'

The truth was, the fact that he was now married would not be considered an impediment by most of his peers. Nor had he entered marriage promising fidelity. Indeed, the wife in question had already given him permission to indulge himself.

As he knew well, Juliana von Stenhoff was quite a delicious indulgence.

But the fact that Caro had stood by him, believing in him to the point of confronting his father, made taking advantage of that permission smack too much of a betrayal he couldn't stomach. Despite the fact that, unless he was willing to put her at dire risk, they could never again be intimate. No matter how much his frustrated body clamoured for release and his mind whispered there was no harm in it, as Caro would never even know.

But *he* would. Nonsensical or not, tempted though he was by Juliana's sophisticated loveliness, he just couldn't do it.

'I'm afraid this business of having a wife does make a difference to me,' he said, catching up her fingers and giving them a brief kiss before releasing them. 'I appreciate your visit. But you should probably leave now.'

She stared at him for a moment in disbelief. 'Then everything we shared meant nothing to you?'

'Like the Congress itself, momentous and exciting as it was, now it's…over.'

Juliana made a moue of distaste. 'Well, if that's how you wish to look at it… I've never had to beg and don't intend to start now. Enjoy your time in Vienna, Max…alone.'

She rose in a swish of skirts. He could tell she was angry, not really understanding his reluctance to play the game as it had always been played in their world. As he himself had once played it.

Max couldn't blame her. He didn't fully understand what had changed in him either.

As she reached the doorway, she paused to look back over her shoulder. 'She must be special…this wife who runs a horse farm.'

A vision of Caro filled his mind: dark eyes glowing with concentration, auburn hair copper in the sun, as she soothed and gentled and guided a new foal. Spangled by candlelight, stroking and caressing and arousing him.

'She is,' he murmured.

'May she lead you a merry chase!'

Max laughed ruefully. 'She already has.'

Watching the slender, impeccably groomed, seductively dressed figure of the courtesan retreating through his doorway, Max thought that she could hardly be more different from his wife in dress, appearance, background and manner. Yet both women possessed a deep sensuality, cultivated and calculated in Julianna, natural, genuine, unstudied in Caro.

He felt a wave of longing for his wife, her presence, her conversation, her touch. He wanted her back in his life.

Besides, even if full intimacy was denied them, there were any number of other ways to pleasure her—and for her to pleasure him—that would bring them satisfaction without any risk of her conceiving a child.

Suddenly, he couldn't wait to teach her.

Nothing further could be done in Vienna, hard as it still was to concede that fact. Time to accept that and move on.

He probably ought to travel by way of London and call on Colonel Brandon. But then, as soon as possible, he would go back to Denby Lodge.

Caro was a challenge he'd yet to master. But if in spite of her permission, he was giving up all other women—and it appeared he was—he'd better go home and figure her out.

Chapter Twenty-One

Back at Denby Lodge, Caro stood by the barn door, supervising the installing of the new mares brought back from Ireland. The horses had made the transit in very good condition; she could begin working with them tomorrow.

She sighed, fighting fatigue and a vague depression. The day Max left, she'd felt relief that she'd no longer have to struggle with the impossible task of trying to resist him. But once he was gone, she'd missed him terribly. Missed his stimulating conversation over dinner, the interest he showed in the stud and his encouragement to realise her goals; missed their rides around the estate, during which she'd been acquainting him with the fields and woods she loved so deeply.

With her newly awakened senses clamouring for satisfaction, she drove herself hard each day so she might fall into bed too exhausted to yearn for his touch.

And there was something more. At first, she tried to tell herself her abrupt swings of mood and sudden desire to burst into tears were simply nervousness about the sale, even though, under her father's supervision, she'd conducted such sales many times. But by the time she finished her travels in Ireland, she could no longer deny that something more had changed than simply the loss of Max's presence.

For the last month, she'd awakened every morning with her stomach in turmoil, frequently finding herself forced to cast up her accounts before even rising from her bed. The smell and taste of food remained vaguely nauseating; she tired far too easily and her breasts had grown swollen and tender.

Then, for the second consecutive month, she'd missed her courses that were usually regular enough to set a clock by. Much as she tried to resist the conclusion, she knew she must be with child.

After the first flurry of panic, she'd come to a calm acceptance. Unfair as it seemed to have succumbed after only one interlude, if she had conceived, no amount of wishing otherwise could undo the condition. Instead, knowing the time she had left to work the stud might be even more limited than she'd imagined, she'd pledged to devote all her flagging energy and effort towards training horses for next year's sale and beginning the breeding process with her new acquisitions.

She'd written to Max from Ireland, once she'd been fairly sure about her condition. She'd debated telling him her suspicions, but ended by not doing so. If he chose to come back to Denby, she'd tell him then, but she didn't want the fact that she might be carrying his heir to force his hand, if he preferred not to return.

Sadness whispered through her. She could hardly blame him if he didn't come back. She'd already given him her blessing to conduct a life apart from her, in the London that was as dear and familiar to him as the barns and fields of Denby Lodge were to her.

Why should he visit a horse farm, when he had important work in the city…and his cares could be eased by some beautiful Cyprian skilled in the arts of pleasing a man?

She'd thought surely when she returned from Ireland, she would be able to shake off her melancholy, that beginning to work the new horses would revive her energy and enthusiasm.

But for the first time in memory, returning to Denby Lodge hadn't filled her with excitement and unmuted joy. Instead, as she rode about the estate today, she'd found herself thinking about Max.

The wide sweep of meadow by the river reminded her of the day they'd picnicked there, him regaling her with stories about incidents from the

Congress of Vienna. Reining in near the dense wood across from the manor brought back the afternoon they'd stopped there, walking the horses while she answered his questions about managing timber. In her desire to show him all her favourite places, she'd somehow managed to imprint his presence all over Denby land.

Now, everywhere she looked, she saw Max.

Perhaps it was because she carried his child. Now that she'd got beyond her initial terror, she was fiercely protective of the baby. Max Ransleigh was like the prince who visits the peasant girl in a fable: fascinating, exciting, larger than life, but a figure who would touch her life only briefly. All-too-ordinary horseman's daughter Caro Denby would never hold him here with her agricultural pursuits, but if she survived the birth of his child, she would have something of him to treasure always.

She put a protective hand over the slight round of her belly. And if he did, for some reason, return?

She couldn't expect him ever to spend much time at Denby, especially since he'd emphatically stated he had no desire to be a father. Sorrow filled her at all he had missed, having so distant a relationship with his own sire. Oh, that he might discover through their child the depth and richness of the love she'd known with her father!

But if he should come back, she'd made up her mind that, for as long as he remained at Denby, she would cast aside all inhibitions and do everything in her power to seduce him as often as possible. She'd revel in exploring the potent desire that drew them together, until he left for London again or her thickening body made her no longer attractive to him.

If he came back... Sighing, she released the rail and walked towards the groom who held out the new mare's lead.

Two weeks later, Caro was schooling one of the new mares in the paddock when she noticed someone at the bend of the lane walking toward the stables from the direction of the manor. Concentrating on her task, at first she paid little attention, until a familiar *something* about the stance and gait of the approaching figure seized her attention.

It couldn't be...yet she was almost certain the man walking down her lane was Max.

Disbelief turned to surprise and then an upsurge of excitement as the gentleman drew nearer and she identified him with certainty.

Why he had returned, she had no idea, but, dropping the mare's lead, she ran to the fence and scrambled through it. 'Max!' she cried, sprinting toward him. 'Is it really you?'

'Did you miss me, then?' he asked, studying her face as he halted before her.

Too happy to dissemble, she said, 'More than I ever believed possible.'

'Good,' he said, grinning. 'Why don't you show me how much?'

Caro threw her arms around his neck and pulled his face down, her lips assaulting his with two months of pent-up hunger. He opened to her, kissing her back just as fervently, until they were both breathless.

Finally, Max broke the kiss. 'Now, that's what I call a welcome! But I'm all-over dirt from riding; let me get back to the house and make myself presentable. Perhaps we could have tea? There's so much we have to discuss.'

'I should like that. Just give me some time to turn over the rest of today's training to Newman.'

'Shall I meet you in the salon in an hour?'

'Yes, an hour.'

He kissed the tip of her nose. 'I'll see you again soon, then.'

Her heart thudding in her chest with anticipation, Caro watched him walk with long, confident strides back down the lane to the manor, unwilling to let go of the sight of him until the curve of the lane took him from view. Joy filled her heart and mind to overflowing, washing away, at least for the present, all the fears, disappointments and worries that had plagued her.

He had come back. Whatever happened after, she would have him for tea and dinner and through the night.

Recognising the immensity of the joy and gratitude suffusing her at seeing him again, she finally had to admit another truth she'd long suspected, but had avoided acknowledging. Despite her counsel and caution and knowledge of the dire consequences, she'd fallen in love with her husband.

Just as it was too late to avoid the power of the Curse, there was little she could do now to protect her heart. Though she knew he was fond of her, he would probably never return the intensity of the affection she felt for him. But though he might not love her, she was certain she could seduce him into making love to her.

For however long he remained at Denby, she intended to fully enjoy his presence…and his touch.

Calling out for Newman, she hurried into the barn.

After reviewing the training schedule in record time, Caro raced back to her chamber and had Dulcie help her into her most attractive gown, scandalising the maid by leaving off her undergarments. One good thing about increasing, she thought as she regarded her reflection critically in the glass—her breasts looked even more voluptuous than usual.

She hoped he wouldn't be able to take his eyes off them.

When the maid finally finished, she nearly ran down the stairs to the parlour. She slipped quietly in, feasting her eyes upon Max, who stood facing the hearth. 'Hello again, Max,' she said, walking toward him. 'Welcome home.'

'Hello, Caro,' he said, and pivoted to face her. To her satisfaction, after greeting her, his eyes dropped immediately to her neckline. The thought of his eyes—and soon, his lips—lingering there made her nipples tighten and sent a spiral of desire through her. *My dear Max*, she thought, excited anticipation filling her, *you're about to get a welcome I hope you will never forget.*

Caro was even lovelier than he remembered, Max thought as his wife poured tea. She wore that gown of soft green he liked so much—not the least because it showed off her figure to perfection. Indeed, that taunting glimpse of her full breasts in that scandalously low-cut gown—he must remember to have her order a dozen more just like it—had his mouth watering and his whole body throbbing with desire.

He tried to summon enough wit to ask her about the sale and her trip to Ireland, and to respond to her questions about Vienna. But having not availed himself of the delights offered there, all he could think of was how long he would have to wait before he could coax Caro up to bed and begin leading her down all the many paths to delight.

'How goes Colonel Brandon's quest to find you a post?' she asked as she handed him a cup. 'I imagine you talked with him in London before returning here.'

'Actually, I didn't stop in London,' he replied,

seating himself beside her on the sofa. *After two months away, he'd been too impatient to see Caro again.* 'Now that the sale has concluded, I thought perhaps I could wait for news here.'

'Of course you can, as long as you like.' She looked down at her teacup, her cheeks colouring. 'I'm…so sorry about what happened before you left. As I told you in my letter—'

'Apology accepted, Caro. You don't need to explain. I would have preferred knowing the whole truth at the beginning, but there was no deception; you made your preferences plain from the first. I was the one who wilfully misunderstood.'

She looked up, a film of tears in her eyes. 'I should have made myself tell you the whole. After I had not I…I wasn't sure you'd ever forgive me enough to come back.'

'I had to come back. I missed my wife.'

She smiled tremulously. 'You did?'

'Yes. You did say you missed me, too, didn't you?'

Nodding, she put down her cup. 'And promised to show you how much. Shall I do so again?' she asked, a hot glow in her eyes that sent an answering blaze of heat through him.

'By all means,' he replied, setting aside his own cup, his fingers trembling with eagerness.

She put her hands on his shoulders and kissed him again, then placed little nibbling bites over his chin and lips.

He responded avidly, opening his mouth to her.

Another blast of desire roared through him when he felt her hands under his coat, tugging at the buttons of his waistcoat, scratching aside the linen of his shirt to find bare skin beneath. With her fingertips, she kneaded and massaged the muscles of his chest, all the while licking his lips, sucking and nipping at his tongue.

Dizzy, his pulse hammering in his temples, Max could scarcely catch his breath. Though he finally broke the kiss, he clamped his hands over hers to trap them under his shirt, craving the feel of them against his bare skin. 'I love the way you welcome me, dear wife,' he said unsteadily, 'but if you don't stop, I won't be able to wait until dinner, much less tonight, without trying to woo you into bed.'

'I don't want to wait, either,' she said, taking his hands and moving them down to her breasts. 'Touch me, please. Oh, I've burned for your touch!'

'And I've burned to touch you,' he murmured. With Caro so eager—and himself beyond eager— the idea of waiting hours, through dinner and conversation and the tea tray, was simply unacceptable. But he didn't wish to ruin what was promising to be a spectacular reunion by having some footman or housemaid stumble into the parlour and discover her sitting on his lap with her bosom bared and her skirts about her waist.

Mind made up, he leapt up from the couch.

'Where are you going?' Caro gasped, dismay on her face.

'Nowhere, sweeting,' he said, smiling at her distress. 'And neither are you.' Striding over to the hearth, he snatched the key from its place on the mantel, swiftly locked the door and returned to the sofa. Dropping the key beside his cup, he said, 'And where were we, wife?'

'Ah, my clever husband,' she said, raising her smoky gaze to his. 'We were right—' she placed his hands over her breasts *'—here.'*

'I love *here*,' he murmured before leaning to take her mouth hungrily while he cupped her breasts and rubbed his thumbs over the prominent nipples. With a little cry, she yanked down her bodice and suddenly his hands were filled with warm, bare flesh. She must have left off both chemise and stays, he realised, before turning his attention to laving and sucking first one nipple, then the other.

While he suckled her, she moved her hands in a sensuous slide down his bare chest. When the constriction at his trouser front suddenly eased, he realised she was unbuttoning the flap. He felt cool air as she freed him; an instant later, the coolness was replaced by the warmth of her hand. His member leapt and he cried out as she gripped him lightly, stroked him, rubbed her thumb over the tip.

'Not yet, or I'll never last,' he gasped. Gently

plucking her hands away, he said, 'First, let me show you how much I like being back.'

'I give myself into your hands,' she said, angling her head back upon the sofa cushions and arching her back, displaying her bare breasts to him. 'What of these, my lord?' She guided his hands under their ripe fullness. 'Do you like these?'

'I love them.'

'Then show me…with a kiss.'

Eagerly Max leaned forwards, cupping and caressing one breast, his thumb working the nipple, while he sucked the other into his mouth.

He felt her nails bite into the skin of his back, through his shirt. 'Ah, I like that, too,' she panted.

His mouth still at her breasts, he reached down with one hand, tugged up her skirts and slid his fingers beneath them. Grasping her leg, while he suckled her, he smoothed and caressed the back of her knee, the satin expanse of one thigh.

Moaning, she let her legs fall apart, giving him the access he needed. While he lightly nipped first one nipple, then the other, he slowly moved his hand higher, to the velvety inside of her thighs. Teasing the tight curls apart, finding her moist and ready, he rubbed the nub at their centre.

She gasped and bucked against his hand. Soothing her with a murmur, he pressed her back against the cushions and stroked her again, matching the rhythm of his fingers to that of his tongue against her nipple. Her breath sobbing in and out, she began moving her hips against his ministering hand.

He followed her frantic motions, increasing the pace. Her breathing turned to short panting gasps, her nails cutting into the flesh of his neck. He slid one finger, then another, into her slick depths while massaging the tender nub above with his thumb. Seconds later, she reached her peak and came apart in his hands.

For a few moments, she lay limp against the cushions. Then she opened dazed eyes and smiled at him.

'That was amazing.'

He felt like a strutting peacock, full of self-satisfied masculine pride at the compliment. 'Thank you. I found it rather amazing, too.'

'Did you? But I do think it was unfair of me to find pleasure, while you had none.'

'Watching you is a pleasure.'

'I should like to return the favour…if you will let me. Though I'm not perfectly sure just what to do, I expect you can guide me.' She reached to slide a finger down his still-rigid length.

Gasping as pleasure pulsed through him, he caught her hand. 'I think you have a natural talent.'

'And does that…not please you?' she asked, her tone anxious.

He wondered if she'd been told that wives were to lie still during their husbands' efforts, enduring with silent decorum. 'It pleases me immensely.'

'Good. I was never brought up to behave like a decorous lady. And with you, I fear I can't make myself behave like a lady at all. So won't you let me please you…more?' Extracting her fingers from his restraining hand, once again she traced his length.

His manhood leapt beneath her stroking fingers and he gasped for breath. He'd wanted only to give her a taste of passion, intending to wait for the privacy of a bedchamber and the lazy uninterrupted hours of the night to show her more.

But the exquisite feel of her stroking him, the idea of her exploring his body not in the dimness of a candle's faint glow, but boldly, in the full light of day where he could see her every expression, was so enormously arousing he couldn't make himself tell her to stop.

'Do you like that?' she asked softly.

'Yes,' he said on a groan.

'Good,' she said and kissed him. And as he had done for her, in rhythm to the stroking of her tongue within his mouth, she slid her hand up and down his length, fondling the taut sides and creamy tip, until he shattered in her hands as she had shattered in his.

After a few moments, when strength returned to his boneless arms, he gathered her close. For a long quiet moment, they simply held each other.

With her head cradled on his chest, listening to the sigh of her breathing as it steadied, Max felt a surge of new hope for the success of their union.

Finally, he moved her back to arm's length. 'I'm afraid we must now tidy ourselves and prepare for dinner before the household is scandalised.'

'Why should they be? We're respectably married, and you've been gone a long time. A *very* long time.'

Max thought of the many occasions when his father had been gone for months. But he couldn't imagine his reserved mother or the rigidly formal earl enacting a scene at Swynford Court such as the one they'd just played out in this parlour, no matter how long his father had been absent.

While he smiled at the very notion, Caro said, 'I suppose we must tidy up. I'm afraid I've quite ruined your neckcloth.'

'To say nothing of the silk of your bodice and skirts.'

'I'll order a tub. Will you come and help me bathe?'

Despite their recent activity and his fatigue, desire stirred in him again. Was she inviting him to what he thought she was inviting him? Even if just to watch, he was ready.

'I wouldn't miss it.'

With a sigh, she levered away from him. She gave his spent member a loving stroke before doing up his trouser flap. While he in turn tried to restore her ruined bodice, she helped him tuck in his shirt and button his waistcoat.

'There. We're not quite respectable,' she said, 'but at least we are clothed.' She linked her hand in his. 'Walk with me, won't you? It's shameless of me, I suppose, but I can't get enough of touching you. Does that displease you?'

'Not a bit. I can't get enough of touching you.'

They had repaired to their separate chambers while water was fetched. A few minutes later, she responded to his knock, bidding him to enter. He found her wrapped in a dressing gown, standing beside a steaming tub.

'I was waiting for you to help me in.' She surveyed his coat and breeches with a frown. 'But you're not ready.'

'Did you plan to wash me, too?'

'If you like.'

He imagined warm, wet silky skin, with her touching him all over. Hardening immediately, he said, 'I should like it very much.'

'Let me act as your valet, then.'

And so she did…nearly driving him mad in the process. After peeling off his coat and waistcoat she took her time removing the remaining clothing, rubbing and stroking each new area of skin uncovered. His wrists and forearms, biceps and shoulders, chest and flat nipples that puckered under her touch as she removed his shirt. She pulled his breeches down over his bottom, opened her dressing gown and wrapped it around the two of them, hugging him close, rubbing her belly against his erection and the soft rounds of her breasts against his chest.

After pulling his head down for an urgent kiss, she said, 'We must climb in before the water gets too cold.'

He helped her in and followed, sinking into the blessed heat. But before she could turn to face him, he lifted her to sit on his lap, facing away from him. Pulling her against him, he kissed and licked her neck, cupping her breasts to hold her against him in the gentle ebb and flow of the water.

He found it delicious, exciting, and soon they were both panting with arousal. He lifted her, guided himself between her legs and anchored her against him with one hand cupping her mound, the other parting her curls to caress the little nub.

'Please,' she gasped. 'This time, I want to feel you inside me.'

'No, sweeting, we don't need to take the risk. I can show you other ways to pleasure that will not endanger you.'

In one swift motion, she levered herself off his lap, turned to straddle him and, before he realised what she was doing, thrust down hard, taking him deep within. He cried out as a wave of heated sensation engulfed him—the warmth of her body, her scent, the hot sweet tightness of her passage embracing him, rocking against him in the semi-weightlessness of the water. Taking his hand, she touched it to where their bodies joined.

'See,' she gasped. 'Is this not…better still?'

In the tiny part of his brain not overwhelmed

with sensation, he knew he should push away and
withdraw. But then she kissed him, her tongue
ravishing his mouth as she wrapped her legs
around his back and thrust against him again and
again, rocking into him with the ebb and flow of
the heated water.

And then there was nothing but wetness and
heat and ever-higher waves of sensation as the
tension built and built until all he could do was
kiss her back and clutch her to him and ride out
the pleasure. Finally, she cried out and writhed
against him while he pulsed and emptied himself
deep within her.

She sank back against him limply. Cradling her
to his chest, he leaned back against the side of the
tub, resting his head on the edge, his soul filled
with a deep sense of peace.

He *had* come home, he realised. There was nowhere else he'd rather be than right here, a wonderfully passionate Caro naked in his arms, his
member sheathed in her.

But no...he should not be sheathed in her!
Conscious thought returning in a rush, he sat up
straight. 'Caro, sweeting, we mustn't do this. I
didn't come back to place you at risk, but to—'

'Hush,' she said, putting a finger to his lips.
'You don't have to worry about that any more.'

His nascent guilt subsiding, he relaxed back
into the tub. 'You've discovered the Curse is an
illusion?'

'No, I still believe it. But there's no longer any

reason for me to fear intimacy because…because I'm already with child.'

His sleepy languor dispelling as effectively as if the bathwater had suddenly turned to ice, he cried, 'With child! Caro, are you sure?'

'Almost positive. I have all the signs and I've twice missed my courses.'

Consternation displaced the sense of peace and well-being. 'Devil take it, Caro, what are we to do?'

'Nothing. There's nothing that can be done now. Except, I hope, more of this.' She rocked against him.

Despite his dismay, a pulse of sensation throbbed through him, stiffening his member. Before he could form some response, she pressed a long soft kiss on his lips.

'My dear Max, what happens now is in God's hands. But if something untoward should transpire—'

'Don't even think it!' he interrupted.

'—then I should like to know that I had tasted all the sweetness life can offer. And nothing I have ever tasted is sweeter than this. Did you not find it wonderful, too?'

'Yes,' he affirmed. 'It is indeed wonderful. But, Caro, shouldn't you see a doctor? Let me take you to London with me when I go to meet with Colonel Brandon. Surely there's a specialist there who could examine you and determine—'

'No, Max. My cousin Anne consulted the best

physician in London. He checked her carefully, laughed at her fears and told her there was absolutely nothing wrong with her. But there is some good news in all this; those few who do not succumb to the Curse seem to have no difficulty with subsequent births.'

A *frisson* of hope lightened the weight of guilt and apprehension. 'That is good news. We shall just assume that you will fall in that group.' *And so he would maintain, to ease her fears, if nothing else.*

She nodded. 'I'm not going to spend the next few months looking over my shoulder for the Grim Reaper, but savouring every bit of enjoyment life has to offer. Won't you help me?'

What else could he do, but try to make these next months happy for her? Though he would never have knowingly put her at risk, if he had not called up every charm and trick he knew to seduce her that long-ago night at Denby, she might have resisted him…and not now be facing this test. 'Of course.'

'And, Max…I know you have no desire to be a father. I'll try to make sure that the child isn't a burden to you.'

Another little shock zinged him. In his concern for Caro's health, it hadn't really registered that, at the end of it all, he would be a father. He could hardly think of anyone less suited, he thought, his dismay and apprehension deepening.

Those emotions must have been writ clear on

his face, for Caro laughed softly. 'It won't be as bad as all that. The farm is a wonderful place for a child to grow up. Don't worry; on your visits, he will only be presented to you when he's on his best behaviour, his face freshly washed and his nankeens clean.'

Her eyes glowed as she spoke about the child… his *son*. 'You are happy about the prospect?'

'I love it,' she said simply.

He wished he could avow some excitement of his own…but his tongue seemed stuck to his teeth. He realised it probably hurt Caro that he was unable to respond with enthusiasm about the child she now seemed eager to bear, but he'd never dissembled to her.

He'd concentrate on handling one challenge at a time. While he tried to dredge up some anticipation for being a father, he'd work to keep Caro's spirits cheerful…and try to persuade her to see that London physician.

Suddenly he was conscious of how cold the bathwater had become. 'Come, we'd better get you out before you catch a chill.'

She let him help her out. After they'd both wrapped up in thick robes, she said, her tone wistful, 'Could I ask a favour?'

Ignoring a stab of alarm, he said, 'What would my lady have of me?'

'Sleep in my bed tonight. Let me touch you, taste you…everywhere.'

Max blew out a relieved breath. 'Willingly. Though I suppose we must dress and dine first.'

'I'll order a tray. I want to dine with you clad only in your dressing gown, knowing there is nothing beneath it but skin, every inch of which you are going to allow me to explore.'

Amazingly, he felt desire rising again at the thought of Caro touching him, tasting him.

'Then I am at your service.'

So, wrapped in dressing gowns—he imagining as eagerly as Caro her dining with nothing but bare skin beneath the soft covering of her robe— they huddled together on the sofa in her sitting room. Once the food arrived, Max discovered he was starving and fell upon the cold ham, cheese, biscuits and ale with enthusiasm.

They talked of the investigation in Vienna, the success of Caro's sale at Denby Lodge, the pedigrees of the new mares she'd just purchased and the prospects for the foaling season to come.

Finally, replete, he took Caro's hand and kissed the fingertips. 'Now, my dear wife, to bed.'

'Finished at last, my lord glutton?' she teased. 'I hope your appetite for other pleasures is equally robust.'

'I shall be delighted to demonstrate just how insatiable I can be,' he promised.

'Good.' Taking his hand, she led him through the door into the bedchamber. Slipping beside him on the bed, she guided him back against the pillows and tugged his robe open. 'Now, it is *my* turn to gorge myself.'

And she did, beginning at his toes, stroking, nipping, suckling and tasting, in a long slow assault that had him breathing hard by the time she reached his ankles and gasping by the time she reached his knees. His fingers clutched the linens as she worked his thighs, parting them, stroking, kneading them with her fingers. His aching member jutted up proudly when she reached it, his body already dewed in perspiration at the thought of what she might do there.

She rubbed her face against him, wrapped his hardness in the silk of her hair up to the smooth tip, then traced the tiny opening with her fingertip and her tongue, caressing the sacs beneath with a silken brush of strands, before taking him in her mouth.

His hands splayed on the bed, his back arched, he moaned and cried out as she explored him, tasted him, devoured him. Just when he felt he couldn't hold on another second, she climbed up and straddled him, thrust him deep inside and rode him, her beautiful full breasts jutting above him.

Afterward, he pulled up the bed linens and wrapped her in his arms, too full of awe to speak. What a wonder she was, shy yet brazen, calm and patient with her horses, yet sensual and demanding. Intelligent, inquisitive, thoughtful, an expert in her realm, though she focused on pursuits unlike those of any woman he'd ever known.

Uniquely Caro. *His* Caro.

Max woke several times in the night, to find Caro touching him—her lips to his, or her hands tracing the muscles of his chest, or her fingers exploring the contours of his manhood, nuzzling his chest as it swelled at her caress. He showed her how he could pleasure her as she lay on her side with him behind her, stroking into her while her tender nub and breasts lay open to his touch. In the dark of early morning, he kissed her from sleep and cradled her beneath him, her legs wrapped around his back as he thrust deep and hard, driving her into the softness of the mattress.

Finally, one last time as dawn began to light the sky, he insisted it was his turn to taste and explore her. He began at her temples, licking and sampling, moving down to her chin, the hollow of her throat, the tender skin beneath her ears. While he kissed her, he slid his hand down to cup her mound, parted her moist folds to caress the plump nub within, slipped a finger inside and back out, massaging mound and nub and passage. Continuing his gentle efforts there, while she gasped and murmured, he moved lower to lick her shoulders, her collarbone, her elbows, her wrists. After tasting her breasts again, he proceeded to her belly, nibbling on her hip bones, licking the deep recess of her belly button until she shattered against his fingers.

Giving her a few moments for her ragged breath to steady, he set off again, this time to the silk of her inner thigh. He revelled in the warmth and scent of her, his goal almost within reach. Finally finding what he craved, he circled her nub with his tongue, suckled it, raked his teeth over it.

By now, she was gasping and straining against him, but he refused to hurry. Wanting to inflame her by gradual degrees, he slowed the rhythm as he licked and stroked her passage, intoxicated by the taste of her, almost painfully aroused by the thought of being embraced within her heat as she reached her climax.

But before he could tease her over the edge, she pushed at his shoulders, urging him back. 'Go with me,' she pleaded.

Drawing himself up, he entered her as she wrapped her legs around him to hold him deep. For sweet exquisite moments, they moved together, one flesh, one purpose, one goal. At last, she cried out, her hands gripping his shoulders, as his seed burst within her.

Exhausted now, they lay spent in each other's arms and slept.

It was nearly noon when they finally woke. Looking out of the window at the full daylight, Caro groaned. 'I must do some work, I fear. Though with you here, I wish never to leave my bed!'

'It will still be here later...and so will I,' he assured her.

To his delight, she asked him shyly if he'd like to accompany her to the stables. He quickly agreed, marvelling how she could be so reticent about that when she seemed not at all embarrassed to descend the stairs with him at nearly noon and demand a plate of bread and cheese from servants who must know what they'd been doing abed all those hours.

Content to stand at the rail and observe Caro's expertise, he found the routine of training as fascinating as ever. When he complimented her on her skill in soothing the skittish young mare she'd been working, she said, 'It's easy, really. You just have to observe what she's telling you with her neck and ears and haunches, and move at her pace. Would you like to try?'

'I'm a rank novice,' he replied. 'I don't want to make a mistake and set back her training.'

'You won't. Horses are very forgiving, if they sense you mean them well. I'll show you what to do.'

And so he proceeded to the centre of the paddock, where she taught him how to hold the lead rein, how much pressure to apply from it to the mare's halter, what verbal commands to use.

Then she had him stand behind her, his hands on the reins along with hers, while he tested and mastered the touch. After several circuits around the ring, she removed her hands, letting him do it on his own.

The mare continued to circle on command, just as she had for Caro.

'Excellent,' she told him. 'See, you do have the touch.'

He felt a glow of pride at her praise, even though, with her standing before him, her warm round bottom rubbing against his legs, he was finding it increasingly difficult to concentrate on technique.

Finally he abandoned the attempt altogether, dropping the reins and wrapping her in his arms. Murmuring, she leaned into him and pulled one of his hands down to cup her breeches.

Amused and tantalised by her boldness, he caressed her, his member leaping when she shivered under his touch. Whirling her around, he gave her an open-mouthed kiss, his heart exulting.

Who could have imagined he would find Venus in an old pair of breeches and her father's worn riding boots? The angle of her cheekbones, the contour of her lips, the sleek curve of her hips and roundness of bosom; the scent of her hair and skin, the taste of her mouth; everything about her intoxicated him. He wanted to inhale and devour and savour.

Breaking free with a mischievous glance, she snatched up the lead rein. 'We'll set her free in the meadow and take the tack back to the barn.'

After turning the mare loose, they walked inside to hang up the reins, leads and halter. Caro looked up at him, her eyes heavy-lidded.

'What are you thinking about?' she asked.

'Bed,' he answered promptly. 'Or tea, like yesterday's.'

'Beds are very nice,' she agreed. 'But I've always loved the scent of the barn...all that sweet, fresh hay, forked into mounds as soft as a feather mattress.' Slowly she wet her lower lip with the tip of her tongue.

His body responded instantly. He couldn't banish the threat of what might happen in seven months. But he would willingly give her all the pleasure she wished for now.

'Soft as a feather mattress?' he repeated, pulling her into the nearest box stall, empty now that all the horses had been loosed in the pastures. Turning to face him, she plucked open the buttons of jacket and blouse and bared her breasts. 'Are you thinking of these?' she murmured.

With an incoherent growl, he bent and drew one taut nipple into his mouth, raking it with his teeth, while she arched her neck, gasping. Her fingers fumbled for the buttons of his trouser flap, wrenched them open, found him hard and eager.

His breathing grew ragged and his pulse accelerated as she stroked him while he suckled her. Finally, lifting his head to kiss her lips urgently, he half-walked, half-stumbled with her to the mound of hay in the corner of the box. After pulling off her boots, he settled himself into the fragrant cushion. With hands now trembling with eagerness, he pulled down her breeches while she unbuttoned his trouser flap, then lifted her to straddle him and guided her on to his lap. They both gasped as his hot, hard member touched her moist folds. Seizing his shoulders, she kissed him and thrust down hard, taking him deep.

His breath coming fast and hard, he cradled her soft bottom, pulling her tightly against him as he moved slowly within her. Whimpering, she tried to speed the pace, but he wouldn't let her, maintaining instead a steady, barely quickening rhythm that soon had her crying out with every thrust, until she spasmed around him and he followed her over the brink.

For a few moments, Max lay back, lazy and replete, twining her braids around the fingers of one hand while he trailed the fingers of the other over her breasts, admiring their voluptuous fullness, the nipples cherry-red from his teeth and tongue.

'You continue to amaze me,' he murmured.

'I can't seem to help myself. It's no wonder full knowledge of lovemaking is kept from maidens. If they knew it could be like this, there would never be another virgin bride.'

'It isn't always like this.'

'Isn't it?'

'Well, it's always good. But not…amazing, wonderful. You make it so, Caro.'

She smiled, her expression tender. 'No, I'm quite sure it is you who make it so. Thank you,

Max. I never expected to know such happiness. I...thank you.' She kissed him gently.

Just then, Max heard the murmur of voices and the sharp strike of hoofs on the stone floor. 'We'd better get presentable, lest we scandalise the grooms as we have the household staff.'

Grinning, he pulled her up. Kissing and touching delaying their efforts, she managed to button his trouser flap and tuck in his shirt while he retrieved her boots and helped her into her breeches. Hand in hand, nodding to the grooms as they passed them, they walked out of barn.

Max stood in the sunlight, breathing deeply of the soft country air, his senses replete, his mind filled with a sense of peace more profound than he could ever remember experiencing in London or back at Swynford Court.

Here there was no autocratic father to please, no hunting for a suitable position. Only his deeply sensual, straightforward Caro and days filled with the rhythm of challenging work. He had the odd thought that he could almost believe he would be content to stay here for ever, pleasuring and watching over Caro and her horses.

'What next, my fair taskmaster?' he asked, pulling a stray bit of straw from her hair.

Smiling, Caro had opened her kiss-swollen lips to answer, when suddenly her eyes widened at something she must have seen behind him. A look of incredulous delight lifting her face, she cried, 'Harry!'

By the time Max recalled the identity of the person with that name, his wife had run over to throw herself into the arms of the man she'd told him she'd always intended to marry.

Chapter Twenty-Two

A jolt going through him, Max watched as a tall blond man in the uniform of the 33rd Foot caught his wife and swung her around before setting her back on the ground. 'Caro! It's so good to see you again!'

'When did you get back?' she demanded. 'Why didn't you write you were coming?'

Dropping a kiss on her hands before releasing them, the officer stepped back. His smile fading to a frown, he gave Max a hostile glance.

'There wasn't time,' he replied, turning his attention back to Caro. 'When I got your letter, I talked the colonel into letting me come back to take care of some battalion business he was going to entrust to another officer.'

'My letter?' she echoed, looking puzzled.

'The one you wrote telling me that Woodbury had convinced the other trustees to sell the stud.

You sounded so desperate, I thought I'd best get back here with all speed. I feared I'd find you distraught, maybe with the horses already gone. Instead,' he said, his tone turning frosty as he inspected her, 'you look like you've just been trysting in the barn. With him?' He transferred his disapproving gaze to Max.

Caro's cheeks flamed a guilty red, turning the lieutenant's expression even grimmer. But before Max could intervene to tell the man a thing or two, Caro said, 'I have a lot to explain. But first, let me introduce you. Max, as I imagine you have guessed, this is Lieutenant Harry Tremaine, my oldest and dearest friend. Harry, this is Max Ransleigh.'

After the two exchanged stiff bows, Harry said, 'Earl of Swynford's son, aren't you? On a buying trip for him, I expect? Let me wish you well before you depart.'

'Please, Harry…' Caro protested. 'With your permission, Max, I'd like to tell Harry what… has happened since I first discovered Woodbury meant to sell the stud. We'll rejoin you in the house a bit later.'

'Why do you ask for *his* leave?' Tremaine demanded.

'Because he's my husband, Harry,' she said quietly. 'Did you not know?'

The stunned shock on Tremaine's face announced quite clearly that he had not. 'Husband!'

he echoed. 'No, I hadn't any idea. What the deuce has been going on?'

'It's…complicated,' she allowed, giving him a strained smile. 'With your leave, Max?'

He would have preferred to order the man off the property. Everything about Lieutenant Harry Tremaine made him bristle with outrage, from the proprietary manner in which he looked at Caro to the way he strutted about the paddock with an unconscious air of authority, as if he had every right to be at Denby Lodge, monopolising its mistress.

Still, though he'd much rather challenge Tremaine to a bout of fisticuffs, Max bowed to Caro's wishes. He supposed her 'oldest friend' did deserve to receive an explanation of the radical change in Caro's life—without an outsider listening in. 'I shall see you later,' he said grudgingly. 'Not much later, though,' he added in a warning tone.

'Thank you,' she said simply. 'Come along to the paddock, Harry. While we talk, you can see the new mares I have just purchased.'

Max walked back towards the manor as his wife led the interloper into the paddock, trying to master the anger, resentment and, yes, jealousy nipping at him.

So this was the man she loved, the one she'd always thought to marry. He hadn't much worried about Lieutenant Harry Tremaine while the soldier was halfway around the world.

Now that he was back in England, was Max

playing the fool, letting his wife speak to her old lover in private?

After the last two days, Caro ought to be sated. But she'd shown herself to possess an incredibly sensual appetite.

Might she try satisfying it with Tremaine?

Stop it, he ordered himself. This way lay madness. Caro had made him a solemn promise before God and he knew down to his bones she meant to keep it. He'd talk to her about Tremaine when she came back to the manor, but he'd not insult her honour by going back to fetch her.

He reached the house, went to the library and poured himself a large glass of wine. He only hoped their talk would be of short duration.

Meanwhile, at the paddock, Caro distracted Harry for a short time as, with a true horseman's interest, he inspected the new mares. Soon enough, though, he completed his appraisal and turned back to her.

'Married!' he exclaimed. 'How is that possible?'

'I think I'm offended. It's not *impossible* someone would want to marry me,' she said, trying to lighten Harry's thundercloud expression.

'You know what I meant,' he said impatiently. 'The marriage is final, then? You can't get out of it?'

'No. We wed in church, before God and witnesses. It's fully binding.'

'Why Ransleigh? I didn't even know you were acquainted with the man.'

Omitting that she'd originally requested Max to ruin her, Caro briefly summarised what had happened at Barton Abbey, her refusal of Max's first offer, then the desperation over the sale of the stud that led her to reconsider. Harry listened in grim silence.

'I'm sorry, Harry, if you feel…betrayed,' she said when she'd finished the account, 'but truly, it was the only alternative—'

'I understand,' he interrupted. 'I don't like it, but I understand. As soon slay you where you stand as take away the stud. Damn Woodbury! I just wish I had been here, so you could have turned to me. Or that India wasn't so damned far away, that I could have returned here before it was too late.'

'I wish you'd been here, too. But you weren't. And that's an end to it.'

'An end…to us?' He shook his head disbelievingly. 'I can hardly imagine such a thing. I've never even considered marrying anyone else.'

Caro felt tears welling in her eyes. From the moment she'd decided to marry Max, she'd dreaded having to eventually face Harry and explain why she'd all but jilted him. She'd thought then that he would write her before returning from India, so she'd have time to prepare for the difficult reunion.

Groping to find the right words, she said, 'I

never had either, until circumstances forced me into it. But if I had to marry someone else, I'm glad it was Max. You'll like him, Harry; he's a good man—kind, intelligent, sympathetic.' *Whose touch drives me wild*, but she didn't need to tell Harry that. 'Most importantly, he understands how I feel about my horses and supports my continuing to work with them, much as Papa did.'

'You must give me leave not to like him...now that he possesses all I've ever wanted.'

Caro felt another jolt of sadness and stiffened, fighting it. She couldn't weaken; she owed Max more than that. 'No. But some day you'll find someone else worthy of you. Probably a lady better suited than me to be your wife.'

'Forgive me if, at the moment, I don't find your prediction very comforting,' Harry said bitterly.

The pain and sadness of her best and oldest friend slicing her to the quick, Caro wished she could find something more soothing to say. But even in her distress, a subtle awareness distanced her from his pain.

Deep within her glowed the memory of Max's kiss, his fierce possession, the shared passion that bound her to him and made them one. Much as she might regret Harry's heartache and the fact that there could never be a future between them, she belonged to Max now.

'I expect not. I had weeks to reconcile myself; being hit with the news all in an instant, it will take time for you to accept it.'

'Or to persuade you to run away with me.'

She smiled. 'I couldn't and you know it, or you'd never have said such a thing. Well, that's the whole of it. We'd best go back now.'

'I suppose. I wouldn't want your *husband* to get jealous.'

Caro laughed. 'I sincerely doubt he would. But staying out here tête-à-tête is bound to cause gossip. And—' the sudden realisation sent a pang of regret through her '—now that I'm married, I suppose you mustn't run tame here any more.'

She looked up to find Harry watching her, his face bleak. 'On the voyage back, I thought of all the changes I might find when I arrived. The stud sold, the horses scattered. You sunk into despair and depression. Never once did I dream I might have to give up the dearest friendship of my life.'

Not until this moment had it struck her that marrying Max inevitably meant the death of her closeness with Harry. Max could become an even better friend, a little voice said. She pushed aside that probably vain hope.

'I'd never thought it, either. But there's no use repining over facts that cannot be changed. We can only face the situation with honour, and go forwards.'

As she turned to walk towards the manor, Harry grabbed her shoulder. 'Just once more, I want to hold you like you were still to be mine,' he said. Before she could think to resist, he pulled her roughly into his arms and kissed her.

At the shock of his lips brushing hers, she slammed her hands into his chest, shoving him away.

'Last time you tried that, I planted you a facer!' she cried angrily. 'I ought to do so again.'

'I'd deserve it, I suppose. But despite that lapse, I am a man of honour. I'll not cross the line again.'

Reading the sincerity in his eyes, Caro knew he meant it. 'Let us try to salvage something of friendship, then. Come in with me. I'd like you to become better acquainted with Max.'

Harry shook his head. 'I couldn't greet Ransleigh now with any appearance of courtesy. Perhaps later, before I return to India. I'll send a note first…so you can ask your *husband* for permission to receive me.'

She nodded. 'That would be helpful.'

'Helpful. Devil take it!' He closed his eyes, obviously trying to take in the enormous implications of her marriage. 'Goodbye for now, then,' he said when he opened them, his face now shuttered. 'My sincerest wishes for your continued health and happiness.'

'Goodbye, Harry. Give my best to your family.'

He bowed, then walked back to the stable to retrieve his mount. A moment later, she watched him ride by on the trail through the woods leading back to his father's manor. A chapter in her life now closed for ever.

Sighing, she trudged towards the house. She must get back and reassure Max. Not that she thought he would truly be jealous, but it must be disconcerting to watch one's wife fling herself into the arms of the man she'd once proclaimed she meant to marry. Even though said wife had vowed she'd given up all ties to her former lover and pledged her loyalty to him.

She wondered how long Max would stay…if she could entice him to linger. Sighing, she shook her head at her own idiocy. Two nights and days of delicious lovemaking and she was falling further than ever under the spell of her dynamic, sensual, compelling husband.

She probably ought to urge him to return to London…before she grew to long for his company even more keenly.

The thought struck her then, and unconsciously her hand strayed to her lips. She'd been shocked by Harry's unexpected kiss, filled by an immediate sense, on a level deeper than reason or honour, that having him touch her was *wrong*. Beyond that sensation, though, she'd felt…nothing. No stirrings of desire, no immediate tingle of sensual arousal like that which suffused her whenever Max touched her.

Apparently she now belonged to Max even more completely than she'd known.

Despite that truth, forcing her oldest friend to ride away from the wreckage of their friendship left an aching pain in her breast, as decades of fond memories clashed with honour and commitment, splintering into sabre-sharp shards within her heart.

Her emotions in turmoil, slowly she walked back to the manor.

Where her husband waited.

Chapter Twenty-Three

Max paused in pacing the library to pour himself another glass of brandy. He glanced up at the steadily ticking mantel clock, then out the window again. How long could a simple talk take?

He had to clutch the glass and take another gulp, trying to resist the almost overwhelming urge to pace back to the stables and put his hands in a stranglehold grip around the neck about which his wife had recently clasped her arms. A furious, irrational rage boiled in him at the mere thought of the possessive look Tremaine had cast at Caro, a rage made even more inexplicable since, if he considered the situation rationally, he didn't really doubt that his wife would do nothing more than explain to her childhood friend the tangled trail of events leading to their marriage.

Tremaine had been genuinely shocked to discover Caro wed. Max tried to force himself to dredge up some sympathy for the unhappiness and chagrin her old friend must be feeling.

He wasn't having any luck.

The intensity of his instinctive response to Tremaine and his inability to reason it away disturbed Max. He'd vied for female attention before, and though admittedly he'd seldom had to yield a woman he wanted to another, he'd never experienced anything like this fierce, primal sense of ownership, this desire to maim and destroy any man who dared touch *his* lady. This must be what jealousy felt like and he didn't much enjoy the emotion.

But then he'd never been married before, nor entered into any relationship with a woman meant to last longer than an affair.

For the first time, he began to understand the ferocity of the pain and rage that had driven his cousin Alastair after he'd lost the woman he'd loved.

Not, of course, that he loved Caro like that, he assured himself. He'd told her from the very beginning that he expected fidelity in a wife, though at the time he hadn't dreamt how strongly even a hint of attention from another man would affect him.

He was still wrestling with this unprecedented tangle of emotions when a knock sounded at the door. His spirits leapt, but instead of Caro, the butler stood at the threshold, offering him a letter newly arrived from the post.

Recognising Colonel Brandon's hand, he broke the seal and scanned it. The colonel wrote that he'd found a promising post in the War Department and wished Max to return to London and consult with him about it.

An honourable position where he might do some good, the Colonel described it. What he'd sought ever since returning from Waterloo appeared now within his grasp.

He should leave immediately. But pleased as he was at the prospect of employment, he felt a curious reluctance to leave Denby Lodge. Max didn't want to look too closely at how much Lieutenant Harry Tremaine's unexpected return played in that hesitation.

Before he could examine the matter further, the door opened again and this time Caro herself walked in.

She gave him a tentative smile. Immensely happy to see her in a way he could not explain, Max walked over to kiss her forehead. 'Lieutenant Tremaine is not joining us?'

'No. He's not yet been back to see his family.'

Guiltily aware of how delighted he was she'd returned alone, Max said, 'I hope the interview wasn't too painful.'

'I hope you're not angry I wished to see him alone. But I did feel I owed Harry an explanation.'

'No, I'm not angry.' As long as explanations were all she gave Tremaine, he was satisfied.

'Being totally unprepared to see him, I'm afraid

I greeted him with…rather too much enthusiasm, for which I apologise. I'd completely forgotten that I'd written to him the night I returned from the solicitor's office, before I thought of coming to you. Elizabeth's father still franks her letters; one of the servants must have put it into the post.'

'How did he take the explanation?'

'He…wasn't happy, but he's a man of honour, as you are. In any event, I made you a promise of loyalty and fidelity before we were married. I fully intend to keep it. That and my…affection belong to you now.'

He'd known as much, but having her reaffirm it eased the turmoil of emotions churning within him. Reassured on that front, he recalled the colonel's letter.

Holding it up, he said, 'I've just heard from Colonel Brandon. I must return to London to consult with him. Why not come with me? You could see a physician, buy whatever you need…'

Smiling, she shook her head. 'I've already told you there is nothing a physician can do for me. And I have everything I need. It's sweet of you to be concerned, but with the new mares just arrived and the stallion to work, plus all the training to supervise, I must stay here, where I belong. Doing the work that marrying you, dear Max, allowed me to continue.'

A brief shadow flitted across her face. 'With luck, work I can bring to completion before time runs out. But enough of that.'

Max frowned, her words reviving his worry over her health. He still wasn't sure he really accepted the reality of the Curse, but he didn't want to take any chances with Caro's life. 'Are you sure you should continue working the stud?'

'I'm feeling quite well…except for first thing in the morning. And though I suppose after several more months, I may have to give up riding, for the moment I am fine.'

'Can I not coax you to at least consult a physician here, if you will not travel to London? It would make me feel easier.'

Giving him a look of resignation that said she was just humouring him, she replied, 'I suppose I could, if it would ease your mind.'

'It would. Being responsible for your condition, I want to take every possible precaution.'

With a little sigh, she looked away. 'Yes, you would feel responsible, I suppose. Though you shouldn't.'

He caught her hand and kissed it. 'There will really be a child? I confess, I find it hard to accept the truth of that.'

'Sometimes I have trouble believing it, too, even as I feel my body changing.'

An unprecedented sense of awe and tenderness filling him, he gathered her into his arms. She came willingly, laying her head against his chest. For a long moment he held her there, her cheek against the steady beat of his heart while he nestled his chin into the sweet fragrance of her hair. He found he didn't want to let her go.

He wished she'd agree to accompany him to London, but it was only reasonable that she'd want to stay at Denby, training her horses and working with the new breeding stock.

'Do you…think you will return to Denby before the birth?' she asked.

'Of course! In fact, I'll probably return here immediately after I consult with the colonel. I'm going to try to convince you to come to London for your lying-in, where there will be physicians and midwives to attend you.'

'We have those in the country, too, you know,' she said with a chuckle. 'After all the horses I've helped birth, I probably know as much about the process as any midwife. When the time arrives, Lady Denby will come to assist me. I hope to give you a healthy son.'

'Right now, I'm more concerned with having a healthy wife. You are…' He hesitated, his tongue trying to form other words before he made it say, 'Very dear to me, Caro.'

She leaned up to kiss him. It started as a soft slow brush of her mouth against his, but then, as if she just couldn't resist the temptation, suddenly she teased his lips apart and slid her tongue into his mouth.

A rush of desire flooding him, he kissed her back with equal hunger, moving his hands down to cup her bottom and fit her against his arousal.

After a moment, with a sigh, she pulled away. 'Would that we could "take tea" again now, my naughty husband! But there are tasks I must finish before nightfall.'

Stepping away from him, she licked one finger and painted the moisture over his lips. 'Until later, my dear Max,' she promised, chuckling as she danced away from the hand he tried to snag her with before she could exit the room.

Max smiled as he watched her go. He hoped she never stopped surprising him. His disappointment with the outcome of the investigation in Vienna and this afternoon's jealousy of Harry Tremaine faded as an effervescent feeling of hope and well-being buoyed his spirits.

He'd have new, fulfilling work, a tantalising, amorous Caro for his wife…and, with any luck, a healthy child. With Caro's help, he might even work out how to be a better father than his own.

In London ten days later, Max sat once more in Colonel Brandon's study as his mentor poured some refreshment. He couldn't help recalling that the last time he'd shared a brandy with the colonel here, he'd returned to his rooms to find a frantic Caro, imploring him with a new proposition he hadn't been able to refuse.

Thank heavens he hadn't! He smiled, recalling their last night together before he set out for London. She'd certainly proven her affection, in so many delectable ways that he'd been doubly reluctant to leave for London without her. Indeed, he told her outright that she was spoiling him; he simply couldn't get enough of her.

With a naughty smile, she'd replied that she couldn't get enough of him and tilted her hips to take him deeper.

She'd thought he was teasing, but the words had held more truth even than he wanted to admit. He'd had affairs with women much more practised than Caro; it was her utter lack of artifice that so mesmerised him. He found her uninhibited joy and considerable inventiveness endlessly arousing.

'Here's a brandy to toast the business,' the Colonel said, pulling him from sensual reverie. 'First, congratulations on marrying your heiress. Your wedding, and the earl's blessing on it, helped speed the business of finding a suitable post.'

'What does this posting involve?'

'Logistics and procurement. Requires a man with a talent for organisation, a good head for figures and the ability to, shall we say, persuade sometimes recalcitrant suppliers to deliver contracted goods on time and as specified.'

'I'd work out of London?'

'For the most part, though you would need to visit the suppliers and army units upon occasion. If you accept it, would your bride join you here?'

'Probably not. She's a country girl at heart and very devoted to her farm and her horses.'

'Aye, I'd heard as much.'

Recalling the pains Caro had taken to present

an unflattering picture of herself to the *ton*, Max could only imagine what the Colonel had heard. 'You should probably discount anything that's been said about her. She's clever, intelligent... and utterly bewitching.'

'All April-and-May with you, is it?' The colonel chuckled, slapping him on the back. 'I'd heard 'twas a match of convenience, so I'm happy to learn 'tis more than that.'

At the colonel's words, Max suddenly realised that, some time between his first visit to the colonel's lodgings several months ago and tonight, their relationship *had* become more. Just how much more, he wasn't quite sure. 'How soon would you need my answer?'

'Take your time. There's no one else of your ability and lineage who'd be better for the job, so I can persuade the head of department to wait on your answer.'

'I would like to talk it over with my wife. She's increasing, and I don't like leaving her alone.'

'That's wonderful news! Here's to the safe delivery of an heir!'

That being a toast to which Max could drink with enthusiasm, he raised his glass to the colonel. Though he remained for a time longer, chatting with his former commander about the activities of other acquaintances from their regiment, with the business concluded, he found himself eager to be off.

It hadn't been mere politeness when he'd told

the colonel he was impatient to return to Caro. Even if the Curse were an illusion, he wanted to be there, so she wouldn't have to carry alone the burden of worrying over it.

If he did accept the colonel's post—and it seemed so ideal, there was no reason he shouldn't—he probably would have to assume it before Caro reached her time. All the more reason to try to persuade her to come to London to deliver the child.

Maybe he could also talk her into having some competent female stay with her at Denby Lodge after his departure. Lady Denby would be occupied with her daughter's Season until summer, but perhaps her cousin Elizabeth might agree?

He didn't intend for the person holding her hand in his absence to be Lieutenant Harry Tremaine. Surely the man would need to return to India before Max had to take up his posting in London.

Perhaps, before he returned to Kent, he'd pay a quick visit to Caro's cousin Elizabeth. And while he was there, he could ask her about the Curse.

Chapter Twenty-Four

Half an hour later, Max knocked on the door of Lady Elizabeth Russell's town house in Laura Place. Learning from the butler who admitted him that his mistress was at home, Max told him to tell her he wished to consult with her about her cousin, Caroline Denby.

After showing him to a parlour and pouring him wine, the servant departed to fetch his mistress. A short time later, Lady Elizabeth entered the room.

'Good evening, Mr Ransleigh. What a pleasure to see you again! Did Caro accompany you to London?'

'No, I'm afraid I couldn't persuade her to leave Denby Lodge. She's just taken delivery of a new Arabian stallion and several mares from Ireland.'

Elizabeth laughed. 'Then I doubt you'll get her

to budge from the stables before next spring. All is…well with her, I trust?'

'She is in excellent health at present. I'd like to ensure that she stays that way. Which is why, although I have not yet consulted her about this, I wished to speak with you.'

Elizabeth's smile faded. 'Is something wrong?' Her eyes widening with alarm, she cried, 'Sweet Heaven, please tell me that she's not with child!'

Until that moment, Max hadn't been sure he really credited the existence of the Curse. But as he watched the colour drain from Lady Elizabeth's face, the anxiety that he'd been suppressing since Caro had first told him about her pregnancy boiled to the surface.

Consternation drying his mouth and speeding his pulse, he said, 'She believes she is. So maybe you'd better tell me everything you know about the Curse. How can I help her through it?'

Elizabeth shook her head, tears welling in her eyes. 'I don't know that there is anything you can do.'

Frustration sharpening his tone, he snapped, 'So she seems to believe, but there must be *something*. Does it spring from some weakness of the body? Will she lose the child before term?

'No, it's not until after the birth that the difficulties begin. Bleeding. Fever. Death. It happened that way with her mother, aunt, cousins—nearly every female on her mother's side for the last two generations. When we were little, we used to joke about it…until it claimed cousin after cousin.'

Max had wanted to believe the deaths were coincidence, illusion, tales told to frighten young brides. But this much loss seemed far more than random coincidence.

'The physicians can do nothing to prevent it?'

'Apparently not. Our cousin Anne consulted every prominent practitioner. She was examined several times and each doctor pronounced her perfectly normal. But when her term came, she died anyway, just like the others. Whatever flaw causes this, it must be deep within the body.'

Max's mind raced while he tried to think of something else that might be done to counter the threat. But if physicians could do nothing…

'Is she…in good spirits?' Elizabeth asked.

'She was distressed when she first told me about it, before I went to Vienna.' After what Elizabeth had just revealed, Max wished even more fervently that she'd first told him about it before he'd seduced her, rather than after. 'Since my return, she's seemed quite unconcerned.'

Elizabeth shook her head. 'That's so like Caro. Knowing that if she is with child and nothing can be done, there is no point worrying about it. No wonder, with new horses arrived, she won't leave Denby! She must be desperate to push the training along as quickly as possible in case—' She broke, flushing. 'What can I do to help?'

'I've been offered a posting in the War Department. If I accept it, I may have to leave Denby Lodge before Caro reaches her time. I'll return for the birth, of course, but I shouldn't wish to leave her alone in the interim and Lady Denby will be occupied with her daughter until the end of the Season.'

Elizabeth nodded. 'I'm expecting my grandmother from Ireland for a visit, but I could bring her with me. Just let me know when you'd like me to come to Denby.'

'Thank you.' He grinned ruefully. 'Caro will probably have my head for washing for finding her a companion without consulting her wishes first, but I would feel better if she were not alone these next few months.'

'Of course. You…care about her, don't you?'

'Very much.'

Elizabeth smiled. 'Then go back to her. And tell her I'll be praying for you both.'

Little more than a day later, Caro was about to hand over to the head trainer the lead line of a young horse she was breaking to saddle when the familiar gait of a tall man approaching the paddock made her heart skip a beat.

'Max?' she cried, tossing the reins to Newman and pacing over to the fence. 'I didn't expect you back so soon!'

Delight lightening her spirits and a smoky sexual awareness firing her blood, she reached for the top rail, hungry for the first touch of him.

'Hello, Caro,' he called as he approached.

He looked dusty and tired, as if he'd been travelling swiftly and hard, she thought as she climbed the rails. He held out his hands to steady her as she clambered down the other side.

Then gathered her into his arms. 'I missed you, sweeting.'

Pulling his head down, she kissed him fiercely. With a groan, he wrapped her in his arms and kissed her back just as fiercely.

Some time later, regretfully, she broke the kiss. 'Shall I walk you to the manor? You can tell me everything Colonel Brandon said.'

'Do you have time now? I don't want to interrupt your training.'

Normally, she would be annoyed to have her routine disturbed...but this was Max and she'd missed him acutely. 'Yes, I'm ready to take a break...to see you.'

Linking her arm in his, she said, 'What did you learn about the posting? Do you think you'll accept it?'

'It involves the purchase and shipment of supplies to army units. And I'm inclined to take it. Are you sure you couldn't consider coming to London with me? I'd feel much easier knowing you were nearby, with all the superior resources of the city—the best physicians, midwives, aides, close at hand.'

She shook her head. 'As I told you before, we

have doctors here. And I have my work, as you will have yours.'

Much as she hated to ask it, best that she know straight away how much time she had left with him. Trying to keep her tone casual, she said, 'When must you return to London?'

'No particular time. The colonel said he would hold the position until I'm ready to take it. I thought to stay at Denby with you for a while, perhaps until your stepsister finishes her Season and Lady Denby returns.'

'But 'tis only January and she probably won't return until May or June at the earliest.'

'I happened to speak with your cousin. Lady Elizabeth. If I must leave earlier than that, she mentioned she might be able to come for a visit. I don't like to think of you here alone.' He shook his head and sighed. 'I wish there were something more I could do to protect you.'

'There's nothing,' she said, reaching up to stroke his face. 'But as I told you earlier, the handful of Mama's female relations who didn't perish after birthing their first child seemed to go on to bear others without problem. So don't be burying me yet.'

He snaked out a hand to still her lips. 'Don't even joke about that! Perhaps I'll stay until May or June, then. If you'll have me.'

'Then let us enjoy each other to the fullest until May or June…or until I'm too large and cumbersome to be desirable.'

'You will always be desirable to me.'

'That sounds most promising,' she said, a thrill going through her at the welcome news that she might be able to seduce him again and again, right up to the end.

But even as she rejoiced in the news, a little voice warned that the longer he stayed, the more impossible it would be to keep her heart from shattering when he left. But she couldn't make herself lie and tell him she'd prefer him not to remain.

Instead, she said, 'If you will stay for a while, could I ask you a favour?'

'Of course.'

'Would you mind having me show you the stud books and operating records for the farm? Acquaint you with the horses we have and which stage of training they are in, introduce you to the trainers? So if…anything should happen to me, you'd be more knowledgeable about the stud and better able to decide whether you would want to keep it or sell it off.'

He stopped abruptly and turned to cup her face in his hands. 'I would love to learn more about the Denby operations. But not for that reason. You are going to survive and thrive, Caro, and so is our child. I won't accept anything else.'

Once again her heart did that little flip, and for a moment, she considered confessing her love for him. Might he have come to love her in return?

If fondness was all he could muster in response, such a declaration would likely just make him feel uncomfortable, especially since it seemed he felt guilty about getting her with child. Unwilling to spoil the warm intimacy of the moment, she pushed the question from her mind.

'My sweet Max,' she said instead, 'the outcome isn't in your hands, you know. But I do like having you here. I was so lonely after Papa died, some of my joy in being at Denby was lost. You've restored it to me.'

'I'm glad. Strange as it seems, you've made me feel more at home at Denby in the short time I've spent here than I ever did growing up at Swynford Court or in Papa's vast house on Grosvenor Square. Thank you for that.'

He leaned down to kiss her, softly and gently this time. She closed her eyes, savouring his touch. She would savour every moment with him, she thought fiercely. Since she could not know how many—or how few—there might be.

Chapter Twenty-Five

Approaching six months later, Max leaned against the paddock rail, watching Caro work with the young colt on the lead line, coaxing him to follow. Though heavy with child, she still moved gracefully, he thought with affection, watching her smooth, economical gestures.

'The colt looks better today.'

'Yes, he's getting used to my touch. It also helps that he's finally decided the leaves blowing in the trees and the grasses tapping against the railings aren't a danger to him.'

'I wish I could convince you to stop working the lead line.'

'Really, Max, you worry too much. I've already agreed not to ride any more and train only the smallest colts.'

'Even colts are large and powerful enough to do you an injury,' he countered, concern for her sharpening his tone. 'They may be smaller than two-year-olds, but like Balthazaar here, more skittish and less predictable.'

'Skittish, yes, but none of my horses are unpredictable, if one is alert to their signals. It's my own fault if I fail to heed what he means when he stretches his neck or pricks up his ears.'

Concerned about the danger or not, after months of watching Caro with her horses, he still marvelled at her deft touch and the almost mystical way she seemed able to communicate with the steeds, from foals to four-year-olds fully trained and ready for sale.

'If you don't like my working with Balthazaar, why don't you take him?' she said, breaking in on his thoughts.

'Gladly, if it will get you on the rail and me in the ring.'

As she'd taught him, he walked slowly to the centre where she was working the colt, careful to let the horse see him and accept his presence, not taking over the reins until the animal continued his circuit at a steady pace.

For the next half-hour, while Caro watched, Max eased the horse through a series of patterns, exerting more and more pressure as he taught the animal to accept his commands to advance, stand, move right and left. So absorbed had he become in this slow but exacting process, he was surprised when Newman, the head trainer, appeared at the rail.

'I'll take him in now, Mr Ransleigh. Well done, by the way. You're looking to become almost as good a trainer as Miss Caro.'

'Thank you, Newman,' Max replied, a swell of pride and satisfaction lifting his spirits at the man's rare words of praise. 'Still, it seems to take me so long.'

'As long as is necessary, sir. You heed that old horseman's motto: "If you think things are going too slow, go slower." But you've got a real touch; the beasties respond to you.'

'You do have a deft touch,' Caro said, joining him at the rail as Newman led away the colt.

Max's pleasure deepened. Caro was as sparing with her praise as Newman. Growing up an earl's privileged son, for much of his life he'd had fulsome praises heaped upon him, whether or not his performance merited it. He prized Caro's honesty; one never had to question whether her compliments were genuine.

'If I earn your approval, I'm doubly pleased.'

'It's all trust and patience, Max. This isn't a battlefield,' she said, gesturing towards the training paddock, 'with a winner and a loser. Either both win, or both lose.'

'Like in a marriage?'

'Exactly,' she said, then made a face at him as he snagged her elbow, pulling her down before she could clamber up the rails. 'We'll go through the gate, if you please.'

'Honestly, you're fussier than a brood hen with its chicks,' she protested.

'If I were truly fussy, I'd order you to stay in the house.'

'Where I'd go mad within a week, cooped up with nothing useful to do. Besides, if you *ordered* me to remain, I'd feel nearly honour-bound to climb out of a window.'

'Perhaps I'd just order you to stay in my bed.'

Her eyes danced. 'Now, that's a command I might feel inclined to obey.'

Leaning down, he gave her another kiss, his hands cradling the heavy round of her belly. He'd thought, living with her day after day, their passion would mute, or that as her body grew bigger with child, her appetite for the sensual would decline.

But neither had happened. As her expanding belly limited certain romantic encounters, she thought of new and unexpected ways to pleasure him. He found her body, ripe with his growing child, irresistibly erotic.

'You've made great strides as a trainer,' she told him as he walked her out of the gate. 'Not that I should be surprised, since you apply to that endeavour the same intensity of concentration you employed when memorising the blood lines of the stud and the system used to keep the estate books.

Though I must admit, I never really expected you to stay long enough to learn it so well.'

'Why should I not stay?'

'After spending your life at court, in the halls of Parliament, and engaged in great battles, I thought you would find living on a small farm deep in the countryside far too boring.'

'I admit, I once thought that might be true. I've come to enjoy being a part of the rhythm of life on a great agricultural property, involving myself in activities I barely noticed when I lived at Swynford Court. There's a deep satisfaction in coaxing horses to follow my lead, as I used to coax men. I think I've come to love it at Denby almost as much as you do.'

'I'm rather surprised, though, that Colonel Brandon hasn't been urging you to take up your position.'

'I've stayed this long, I might as well remain until after the child comes.'

'Truly?' she asked, surprised.

'Truly.'

'I admit, I will feel…easier, knowing you won't be leaving.'

He would too, Max thought. After months with the potential of the Curse simmering at the back of his mind, he was too concerned for her welfare to tolerate the chance of being away when her time came, only if all he could do to help was encourage her. And he truly had found a measure of peace and contentment, working the stud with her, as profound as it was unexpected.

In fact, he was beginning to wonder if he really wanted to accept Colonel Brandon's post at all... particularly as it meant he would have to leave Caro and his child for months at a time.

Suddenly Caro gasped, jerking him from his thoughts. 'Oh, that was a sharp one!' she said, putting a hand to her belly.

'What is it?' Max asked, immediately concerned.

'A contraction, that's all. Mrs Drewry, the housekeeper, says it's quite common to have these pains off and on as I near my time.'

'Are you sure? Maybe we ought to summon the midwife.'

'Just like a brood hen—' she teased before stopping in mid-sentence. Pain contorting her face, she began breathing rapidly.

'Let me carry you to the house,' Max said, his concern deepening.

'I don't need to be carried,' she said fretfully.

'Take my arm, then. We're sending for the midwife.'

Before she could reply, another pain hit her. She latched on to Max's arm, her fingers biting into his flesh. To his further alarm, she made no further protest about calling the midwife.

Ten hours later, the contractions had not abated. Rather, they had grown steadily stronger and more frequent. The midwife had arrived to assist; Dulcie and the housekeeper scurried in and out with hot water, candles, spiced possets and lavender-scented cloths to mop Caro's sweat-drenched face.

Max alternately paced the room and sat by her side, wishing there was more he could do than rub her back and hold her hands through the worst of the contractions. Looking down at his wrists ruefully, he realised he was going to have bruises.

But as the night wore on towards morning, her suffering intensifying without the labour seeming to progress, the midwife began to exchange worried glances with the housekeeper. The relatively trouble-free months of Caro's pregnancy had lulled Max into an increasing confidence that the uproar over the Curse was just a myth, but at the growing concern on the midwife's face and the deep groans of misery Caro was not able to suppress, he was beginning to lose faith in that theory.

After one particularly painful bout, when Caro lost the struggle to keep herself from screaming, the midwife examined her, then removed her hands, shaking her head.

'What's wrong?' Max demanded.

'The babe's turned. Most come head first, which is easiest, but I can feel the babe's feet. It's much harder to birth one backwards.'

'Whatever is keeping the damned doctor?' Max barked, looking over at Dulcie, whom he'd charged to dispatch one of the grooms to bring back the local physician.

'I'll check again, master,' Dulcie said, hurrying out.

Caro's eyes, which she'd closed to rest between pains, flickered open. 'Baby…is turned?'

'Yes, missus, I fear so,' the midwife said.

She nodded absently, her face pale, her hair damp with sweat, dark circles of fatigue beneath her eyes. 'Happens…like that sometimes…with horses. Must turn baby.'

'I expect the doctor will try that, when he arrives,' the midwife said.

'Don't wait. Do it now.'

'Mistress, I'm not sure I want to try that.'

'Must. Can't…go on much longer.'

Icy shards of panic sliced through Max's veins. If Caro, who never gave up on anything, felt she couldn't bear much more, things were very bad indeed.

'Do you know what to do?' he asked the midwife.

'Aye, sir, but 'tis difficult. And will be very painful for your lady wife.'

'If you can't get it to turn, the baby is going to kill her,' Max said harshly, putting his worst fear into words for the first time. 'I'll hold her. You turn the child.'

'Oh, sir, I be not sure I want to—'

'Do it,' Caro said again, not opening her eyes. 'Mrs Thorgood, you…know what to do. Do it now.'

The midwife took a deep breath. 'Hold her still as you can, sir.'

Murmuring encouragement, Max slipped his arms around Caro's shoulders, leaning her back against his chest. At his nod, the midwife went to work.

With a wail, Caro bucked in his arms. Ignoring her agony, the midwife pushed and pulled at her belly, while Caro writhed in his arms. Nausea rose in Max's throat, but he choked it down. If Caro could endure this, so could he.

Finally, with a cry of triumph, Mrs Thorgood said, 'Look ye, sir, the babe be turning!'

Max wasn't sure exactly what he was seeing, but the contours of Caro's belly shifted, as if a leviathan inside was flexing and stretching. A few moments later, the midwife said, 'Babe's crowning! Hold on, missis, won't be much longer now!'

The rest of the birth seemed to happen all in a rush. What seemed a very short time later, the midwife had eased the slippery body free, wiped its mouth, given it a slap on the bottom, and as Max heard his child's first cry, wrapped it in soft flannel and handed it to him. 'It's a fine son you've got, Mr Ransleigh.'

Exhausted himself, Max sat back, looking with wonder at the miniature face peering resentfully up at him from within the flannel folds. 'It seems my son isn't any happier about his passage into this world than his mama.'

Despite his light words, Max's heartbeat sped

and a sense of awe and humility filled him as he looked at the miracle in his arms. He reached over to grasp Caro's limp hand.

'We have a son, Caro. It's over now, sweeting.'

'Not quite,' the midwife said. 'There's the afterbirth to come.'

Before Max could ask what that meant, Caro groaned. Suddenly the sheets beneath her turned red, as if a swift crimson tide had flooded the shore.

'What's happening now?' he demanded.

The midwife's face blanched. 'She's bleeding, poor lamb. Oh, if it weren't the same thing what killed her poor mama!'

Max had seen blood on the battlefield, severed limbs, men missing arms, hands, bodies missing heads. But this was *Caro*, and a fear he'd never felt when facing the enemy's guns flooded him as the stain on the linen grew wider and wider.

'Can't you stop it? Stanch it somehow?'

'It comes from within her, sir, where the cord attaches. It'll stop on its own…if it does.'

Before the blood loss kills her, his mind filled in the unspoken words.

'What can we do, then?'

'Pray,' the midwife said.

So, tucking her cold hand in his, Max prayed. Surely she'd not suffered all the agonies of birth to slip from him now. He pleaded, bargained, begged the Almighty, promising to do whatever the Lord directed, if only he would spare Caro's life.

She seemed so still, her pale face waxy. But suddenly he realised the red stain was not getting any larger.

'It's stopped,' he whispered to the midwife. 'Is she safe now?'

'Depends on how much blood she lost. And whether fever sets in.'

Max stifled a curse. Each time he thought all the perils had ended, another presented itself. The midwife and Dulcie tried to talk him into leaving the room, bathing and changing out of his stable-grimed clothing, taking some dinner, but Max couldn't bring himself to leave her side. He felt the wholly illogical but none the less overwhelming conviction that if he left the room, he'd lose her for ever.

So he choked down some soup the housekeeper insisted on bringing him and, as the long hours of the night crept towards morning, he dozed fitfully.

Max came fully awake just before dawn...when he realised the cold hand he'd been holding was now burning hot.

He called for the midwife, who touched her forehead and roused the maid to send for cool water. He was bathing her hands and face with sponges dipped in cool water when at last the doctor arrived.

'Thank heavens you're finally here,' Max cried, overwhelmingly relieved to have someone with medical expertise to buttress his ignorance.

Quickly the midwife related to the doctor what had transpired. After checking the baby and pronouncing him healthy, Dr Sawyer came back to Caro's bed.

'The fever's not breaking,' he observed. 'I should bleed her.'

It was the common medical practice, Max knew. 'But she's already lost so much blood,' he protested.

'Bleeding is the only thing that will remove adverse humours from the body,' the doctor said. 'It may seem harsh, but better harsh remedies than to lose your wife, eh? If you'll move aside, sir, I'll get started.'

Panicked indecision, worsened by fatigue, distress and the horror of having to stand by impotently while Caro suffered, held him motionless, stubbornly clinging to her hand. He was no medical expert…but on some subconscious level, he felt beyond doubt that bleeding Caro now would kill her.

'I can't let you,' he said at last. 'She's too weak.'

'She's too weak to support the contagion in her blood. If I don't remove some of it, I assure you, she *will* die.'

'I can't let you,' he replied desperately.

'You wish to go against my considered medical opinion, Mr Ransleigh?' When Max nodded, the doctor said, 'Then there is nothing else I can do for her. But know this, sir; if the worst happens, her death is on your hands.'

Considerably affronted, the doctor gathered his tools and left the room. Max stared down at Caro, tossing her head restlessly on the pillow.

Had he just condemned her to die? Would she die anyway, no matter what anyone did?

Max had commanded men in battle, ordered troops into positions that had resulted in the death and maiming of many men. But never had he given an order that might have more dire consequences than this one.

His back ached, the stubble on his cheeks itched and he was tired beyond comprehension. But as dawn moved into daylight, he waved away again any suggestion that he leave Caro to the midwife's care and sleep.

He would see her face when she woke…or watch her breathe her last.

He'd thought he'd felt helpless after Vienna, when control over his future had been wrenched from his hands. He'd thought he'd reached the depths of despair after his father had repudiated him and Wellington had refused to have anything further to do with him. But never had he felt as despairing and helpless as he did sitting by Caro's bed, his numb hands bathing her face as Mrs Drewry and Dulcie changed tepid water for fresh.

Unable to bear the thought that he might never talk with her again, he said, 'Newman told Dulcie that Sultan is pacing his stall. It seems he knows you are ill and is concerned for you. He wants his favourite rider back again. The grooms are putting the two-year-olds on lunge lines today and half the four-year-olds began dressage; you should see Scheherazade high-stepping, as if he were born to the knack! But I'll need your help with the colts who aren't yet saddle-broken; I still don't know how to do that. Your son is waiting to become acquainted, too. You do know you have a son, don't you?'

She lay still and silent now. His vision blurring with unshed tears, Max continued, 'He'll need you to sit him on his first pony, teach him to train his horse and read its moods, as his mother can. Caro, you can't l-leave me yet. There's too much left for us to share.'

On and on he talked, as if he could hold her to life by the power of his voice. That slight figure on the bed, now shivering with fever, now burning his fingers with her heat, had been the sole focus of his life for nearly six months now. Every day, she'd come to fascinate him more than she had the first time he'd met her, in that preposterous gown and those ridiculous glasses.

She'd touched his soul as profoundly as she'd pleasured his body. He couldn't envision a future without her. As soon as she was out of danger, he'd write to Colonel Brandon, turning down the post. What need had he to puff himself off with a high government position, trying to persuade his father or anyone else he was important?

He belonged at Denby Lodge with Caro…

whose opinion of him was the only one that mattered.

Why had he not realised until this day, when he might lose her for ever, how much he'd come to love her?

Finally, some time after noon, exhaustion claimed him. Slumped over her bed, he fell asleep, his head resting beside hers on the pillow.

It was dark when he woke, the room illumined by a single lamp. He sat up with a start, rubbing sleep from his bleary eyes. Then he clasped Caro's hand.

Which was clammy—cold now, where it had been hot before. His gaze shot to her pale face and colourless lips, the eyelashes collapsed limply against her waxen cheeks.

Alarmed, he squeezed the hand he still held. Then, while he looked on with a relief so deep he thought he might pass out from the force of it, she stirred and opened her eyes.

'Max,' she whispered, a tiny bit of colour returning to her face. 'You stayed.'

'Every minute.'

'I was so tired and I hurt so badly. It felt like I was wandering in a fog, uncertain which way to go. Your voice brought me back.'

Gently, as if she might shatter at a touch, he wrapped his arms around her. 'I was so afraid I was going to lose you.'

She gave him a glimmer of a smile. 'I thought if

I died, you could have my money and still marry the woman you wanted. You may be stuck with me now.'

He put his fingers over her lips. 'I don't want any other woman. I don't want any other wife. Only you, Caro. Only the outrageous, passionate, unconventional woman who's turned my whole life upside down.'

Weakly she squeezed his fingers. 'I'm so glad. In fact, over the last few weeks I decided that, if all went well, I didn't want to live the rest of my life apart from you. I've already turned much of the work of the stud over to Newman. I could turn over the rest and go with you to London. If…if you want me.'

Max sucked in a breath, shocked by the enormity of what she was offering him. 'You would give up the stud?'

'Since Papa's death, all I wanted was to realise his dream. But now I have a dream I want even more. To be your wife.'

Humbled, Max kissed her limp hands. 'I love you, Caro Ransleigh. But you needn't make such a sacrifice. I'd like to stay here and run the farm with you, building the stud's bloodlines…and watching our son grow.'

'What of Colonel Brandon's post?'

'I suppose I've known it for some time, but after last night, the truth became perfectly clear. Someone else can have Brandon's post. You and Denby and our new babe are my world now. I don't ever want to leave it again. Do you think you could teach me how to be a proper father, as you've taught me so much else? Could you love me and share Denby with me?'

'Foolish Max,' she murmured. 'Couldn't you tell? I've loved you almost from the first, though I fought accepting it for months. You won't need me to teach you about fatherhood; from the gentleness and patience you show the horses, I know you'll be a wonderful father to our baby. But I must insist that the terms of our bargain change. I withdraw my permission for you to dally with any lady you fancy. I'm a selfish, greedy woman, who wants to keep all your passion for herself. And if you're ever tempted to stray, I warn you, I'm a crack shot.'

Max grinned. 'I don't doubt it. Shall we begin again?'

He dropped to one knee. 'Caro Denby, will you marry me and be my wife, my one and only love, never to be parted, for the rest of our lives?'

Joy lit her weary eyes. 'Now that, my sweet Max, is a bargain I can accept with my whole heart.'

* * * * *

A sneaky peek at next month...

HISTORICAL

IGNITE YOUR IMAGINATION, STEP INTO THE PAST...

My wish list for next month's titles...

In stores from 5th April 2013:

- ❏ The Dissolute Duke — Sophia James
- ❏ His Unusual Governess — Anne Herries
- ❏ An Ideal Husband? — Michelle Styles
- ❏ At the Highlander's Mercy — Terri Brisbin
- ❏ The Rake to Redeem Her — Julia Justiss
- ❏ A Man for Glory — Carolyn Davidson

Available at WHSmith, Tesco, Asda, Eason, Amazon and Apple

Just can't wait?

 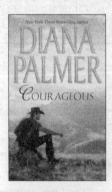 

The World of Mills & Boon®

There's a Mills & Boon® series that's perfect for you. We publish ten series and, with new titles every month, you never have to wait long for your favourite to come along.

Blaze.
Scorching hot, sexy reads
4 new stories every month

By Request
Relive the romance with the best of the best
9 new stories every month

Cherish™
Romance to melt the heart every time
12 new stories every month

Desire™
Passionate and dramatic love stories
8 new stories every month